The Fabian Waltz

The Fabian Waltz

a novel based on the life of
George Bernard Shaw

Kris Hall

For my parents:

Don & June

ACKNOWLEDGEMENTS

The author would like to thank The Society of Authors on the behalf of the Bernard Shaw Estate for permission to reprint some material from the letters of Bernard Shaw. The author also thanks the London School of Economics for permission to reprint material from the letters of Sidney and Beatrice Webb.

"The one duty we owe to history is to rewrite it."

~ Oscar Wilde

ONE

From the unpublished memoir of Bernard Shaw:

Edward McNulty, friend of my Dublin youth, suggested in a letter that I find romance with a woman who shares my political views. Being a reasonable sort of fellow who takes good advice where he can find it, I made just such an attempt and the result has been disaster.

The woman was Bertha Newcombe and a more promising candidate for a romance with a budding socialist, a novice playwright and experienced theatre critic could hardly be imagined. She is a fellow member of the Fabian Society and is therefore my socialist comrade. She also is a gifted painter and has an instinctive artistic sensibility of the kind that I gained only through years of study and application. It must be admitted that she is not a great beauty; she is both short and round of face. But her intelligence and talent do much to atone for these defects and her affection for me seemed to grow with every conversation.

After some weeks of friendship, she proposed to paint a portrait of me. I have the usual vanity of an artist—which is to say about one hundred times the vanity of an ordinary human being—and readily consented to posing on the condition that this would not interfere with my obligations to the Fabian Society and my playwriting duties. For two weeks I posed, Bertha painted and both of us were satisfied. Bertha got to practice her art and I was content to write plays or socialist lectures in my head and would quickly transfer the most important thoughts to paper as soon as the posing was done.

I found her studio to be a pleasant refuge from the demands of my multiple careers. While many might have found it a chaotic jumble of half-finished canvases, stacked cans of paint and sagging easels leaning against the wainscoting, I appreciated the way it was cluttered. I have seen too many pristine studios of amateur artists to have any great respect for neatness. I have often found that a great mess is the sign of a productive mind.

The trouble began when I realized that she had completed the portrait and was pretending to paint in order to avoid the moment when I would see the finished work and pronounce judgement on it. I stopped posing and stepped towards the easel and canvas.

"You promised that I could see it today," I said.

"It's not ready," said Bertha.

"Nonsense. Your brush hasn't touched the canvas for ten minutes."

She rushed to me to hold me back. "Don't look!"

I realize that not every artist has been as hardened to disappointment as I have. I have written five unpublishable novels and am now as indifferent to rejection and criticism as a duck is to the rain. But seeing that Bertha was truly concerned with my good opinion, I unpacked all my Irish charm, took her in my arms and said: "Dear Bertha. Am I such an ogre you need fear me? I must see it sometime."

At last, she silently nodded.

I examined the portrait.

The painting was of me as a platform speaker. My hands were planted on my hips in a confident gesture. My mouth was slightly open as if talking or about to talk and white upper teeth were visible below my jaunty mustache. My face was turned to my right as if responding to some unseen questioner.

"That is not me," I said at last.

Bertha looked stricken.

I continued: "That is the man I must become. It's magnificent. You've captured every essential quality: determination, intelligence and vanity."

"Oh, thank God." Bertha laughed and joined me in front of the easel.

"Have you read *The Picture of Dorian Gray?*"

Bertha nodded. "The man sins and his portrait corrupts."

"You have reversed it. I shall spend the rest of my days attempting to live up to my portrait, Dear Bertha."

I kissed her. She responded with passion and we passed some minutes in a very pleasant way.

But when she began undoing the buttons of my vest, I realized that the entire day would be lost if I did not immediately leave. I grabbed my overcoat from the coatrack.

Bertha stared at me in shock. "But . . . you're not staying?"

"I am a writing machine. There are pages to be filled."

"But we must celebrate."

"I shall rejoice in my heart every step of the way home. Frank Harris is expecting a review of *The Notorious Mrs. Ebbsmith* and I must have it completed tonight or I will miss my deadline. And I have two different lectures to prepare— one for the North London branch of the Socialist League and one for the Woolrich Radical Club."

"Bernard, I love you!"

"Yes. That love has inspired your talent. I have induced you to surpass yourself which is more important than any romantic pleasantries which could pass between us."

Bertha's voice grew cold. "Oh, I see. You've received today's ration of admiration and affection and now you're leaving."

"I'm not running to another lover. I'm returning to pen and paper."

"Pen and paper are your lovers! Time spent with flesh and blood is wasted!"

It was at this point that my innately diplomatic nature deserted me. While I believed then and still believe that I was completely in the right, I realize now that I should have had more patience for the claims of passion. Instead, I let my temper speak and the words it used were less than kind.

"What have I done to deserve this abuse? I have posed for days and let you practice your art. But when I declare that it is time for me to practice mine, you contrive to trap me in your studio. You admire my work and then keep me from it. You paint my genius and then try to rob me of it."

"Rob you? All I've ever done is fawn on you! Henry VIII never received such flattery!"

Her face was now so contorted in fury that I retreated from her rage.

"You . . . Narcissus!"

Bertha grabbed an open tin of paint from her table and flung it in my direction. A spray of red flew through the air. I stepped to the side and managed to avoid being soiled. But the splatters on the naked floorboards looked far too much like blood.

Bertha seized another tin.

"Bertha! Stop!"

She pried the lid off with her fingers and flung the contents at me. This time a splatter of brown stained my coat sleeve.

"Get out!" Bertha screamed. She scrambled to find another open tin.

I rushed out the door and slammed it with a bang.

I walked home. Too many of my unpleasant scenes with women have occurred on freezing nights in distant parts of London after the trains have stopped running for me to be daunted by a stroll in the afternoon sunshine. I had a handful of almonds in one coat pocket and an apple in the other. What need had I for a train or omnibus?

Why do I infuriate so many women? I am always forthright about the importance of my work. If women refuse to believe that I am in earnest when I state that I will never break an engagement with my pen, am I to be blamed? I describe my personality to women in great detail, but I am apparently so unlike the average male creature that women refuse to believe that I will behave in the very way that I have predicted. They are astonished at my bad manners when I remind them that I warned them again and again what to expect from me. In short, I always make them unhappy and with the best of intentions.

I pondered these mysteries for two whole minutes in my room before setting pen to paper and writing my socialist lectures. Once one sentence was written, the engine was engaged, women were forgotten, and the writing machine chugged on at full speed and didn't stop until the job was done.

TWO

Dear Miss Darling,

    I hope you have settled into your new role at the school and that you find Queensland to your liking. I know from my travels with my father in America and Canada when I was a girl that all nations do not look like England. I half-envy your adventure in the wilds of Australia. I can almost picture the vast herds of kangaroos covering the plains near your town and the soaring flocks of emus that block out the sun as they fly north for the winter. I see koalas as big as grizzly bears hanging like ripe fruit in the trees outside your window. If my imagination has caused me to exaggerate any aspect of your new land, pray do not disillusion me. My life lacks romance in every meaning of the word, and I would like to believe that the possibility of adventure exists for you on the other side of the world.

    My life is currently dedicated to social investigation. My father's condition has neither improved nor worsened, but my sisters have decided that it is unfair for all his care to fall on my shoulders despite my unmarried state and they are taking turns looking after Father so that I may have some leisure. But I care little for leisure and my cousin Mary and her husband have started me on work that I believe will be truly useful.

    Mary married Charles Booth who is now famous for his survey of the London poor. The success of that survey and the attention it received only increased his appetite for social investigation and he has recruited several disciples to help him in his work. I am one such disciple. Charles is a strange gaunt man so dedicated to his work that he even forgets to eat. Social investigation has become his mission in life because he sees a vacuum that no one else will take the trouble to fill.

Our politicians make policy for the destitute without knowing the numbers or condition of the poor, or what their real needs are. It never occurs to any of them that their ignorance could be remedied with a little effort. So instead of being based on facts, policy is based on common assumptions and class prejudices. It is this void that Charles Booth is attempting to fill with facts, statistics and first-hand accounts in the hope that government will act with greater compassion and intelligence.

Charles suggested that I start my investigations by exploring conditions at the London docks. The docks were once a source of well-paying jobs for working-class men, but the over-supply of labor has driven wages down until now a majority of dock workers are poor. There are perhaps ten thousand casual laborers looking for work on a given day, but only enough work for three out of every ten. Having so many men idle causes great hardship, but it does make social investigation easier because there are always so many men willing to tell you their stories for a cup of tea and perhaps a cigarette.

I was exceedingly nervous when I first began this work and I wondered if the men would resent an educated woman poking her nose into their business. My fears were groundless. It is a universal aspect of human nature that we all appreciate a fellow creature who takes an interest in our lives and most men were happy to describe their work, their wages and their daily rounds.

After my investigations, I wrote an article for *Nineteenth Century* magazine called "Dock Life" that was published in October and which received many favorable reviews. Some real good has come from this article. Sir James Knowles, the editor, was appreciative and flattering and he has promised to publish any new piece of social investigation that I care to write.

After consultation with Charles Booth, I decided to investigate the sweating system which permeates the East End tailoring trade. This trade is dominated by the Jews, many foreign-born and in the streets of Stepney and Whitechapel where trouser hands search for work one is more likely to hear the languages of Eastern Europe than an Irish or Scottish accent. In certain streets, it is easier to imagine oneself in a Polish town than in a lane only miles from the center of London.

Three nights ago, I arrived at the Devonshire Arms Hotel and was pleasantly surprised by the quality of the lodgings. If he were forced to stay here, Father would find the hotel unbearably shabby with narrow rooms and thin blankets, but the East End has its own standards and I have been in too many filthy buildings not to appreciate simple cleanliness.

Mrs. McArdle, the elderly proprietress, noted my accent and said, "You must be a long way from home, dearie." I did not satisfy her curiosity.

I was strangely apprehensive about this endeavor and it took me some time to analyze my own fears. I had donned disguises before to investigate the working class. My several visits to Bacup in Lancashire were not only successful, but they also were great fun. The simple Midland folk were welcoming to a woman seemingly down on her luck and their hospitality was somehow made even more enjoyable by its lack of sophistication.

But I was doing this new imposture on my own, with no distant relation to vouch for me. I knew I must find employment without help and sew with the speed and skill of a professional seamstress. I feared I might have bitten off more than I could chew. If I could not find employment, I would have to return to Charles Booth and confess that this investigation was beyond my powers to complete.

The next morning, I set out to find work. I stepped into every doorway that looked even remotely like a tailor's shop and asked, "Do you want a plain hand?" The proprietor (who was a woman nearly as often as it was a man) would shake his head or say, "We're suited." And I would be off to the next shop. After an hour or two of this, my disappointment became habitual and did not sting as it did the first few times, but my hopes were ebbing. I was reminded of the London docks where the supply of labor always vastly outweighed the amount of work available and the sight of other women in threadbare dresses going from door to door caused a great feeling of cold discouragement in my chest.

But at last, I came to a shop with a sign in the window that read: "Trouser and vest hands wanted." I hurried in the doorway lest some other woman sees the sign and get the job before me.

A large middle-aged woman with a round, deeply lined face marched toward me with a skeptical expression. Her gray dress was covered with bits of thread and lint.

"I'm looking for work as a trouser hand," I said with a hint of a cockney accent. I somehow feel like a fraud when attempting a full cockney accent, but I can make my Hs a bit shaky without feeling too silly.

"I'm Mrs. Moses," said the woman, looking me up and down. I believe her accent was Polish. "Be here tomorrow at eight o'clock."

Before I could even thank her, she had turned her back to me and returned to her work. I mumbled some thanks in her direction and left without ceremony.

The next morning, I arrived at the shop on time and learned that I was now one of thirty women who were expected to work around two long plank tables in the center of the shop. The women ranged in age from a girl who was probably not yet twenty to a few women who had attained their sixtieth birthdays many years ago. As each woman sat on her wooden stool, she produced a tin box or battered cigarette box which she opened in her lap. My neighbor, a woman of perhaps twenty-five years of age, saw my look of alarm.

"Don't you have your trimmings, love?" she asked me.

I shook my head as I watched her pull needles and thread from her own box.

"You can borrow some of mine to get you started," she said, handing me a needle, a spool and a thimble.

I stammered my thanks.

"I'm Jenny," said my neighbor. "You new to the work?"

"Yes, I was a governess in Cornwall, but I had to leave."

"The man, was it?" Jenny asked. This remark caught the interest of several other women sitting nearby and I could see them waiting for my reply.

"No. The children caught fever and died," I said. " After that, no one in the town would hire me."

Jenny nodded sympathetically, but I could see that her interest had diminished.

I would soon learn that the women spent most of their days talking about their troubles while they sewed and that most of their troubles were caused by men. If I had to form an opinion of the male sex judging only by what I learned from their conversations, I would probably conclude that the world would be a better place if the entire male population were exterminated or exiled to some remote island.

Are the men of the lower classes naturally morally inferior to the men of the upper classes, or is poverty so debilitating to human nature that the conduct of all men would be corrupted and coarsened if they were stripped of class advantages?

Mrs. Moses soon arrived pushing a wheeled bin containing garments. Each woman grabbed a garment as the bin passed her stool and began sewing on buttons. Mrs. Moses took one look at my empty lap and said, "No trimmings?"

"She can use mine," said Jenny. "She's new to the work, but she'll learn fast."

Mrs. Moses grunted and cast a skeptical eye on me but said nothing.

"Thank you," I said to Jenny when Mrs. Moses had pushed the bin away.

I soon learned that the women regarded each other as comrades and often shared thread and small packets of food with each other. A few young men arrived to work the steam presses at the back of the shop, but the women treated them with an air of amused scorn. Any man who dared to attempt to flirt with any of the women was met with such universal abuse that he soon retreated to his machine.

Mrs. Moses worked alongside the women and the only distinction she enjoyed was a stool that was slightly larger than the others. She would periodically check on what the men were up to, but otherwise worked as diligently as any of the other women.

By early afternoon my back ached and my fingers were numb. All afternoon, my distress increased until I wondered if I could continue until the end of the day.

Jenny could see a grimace on my face, and she said: "After the first week or two it'll get easier."

As six o' clock approached, about three quarters of the women packed up their trimmings, said their good-nights and hurried out the front door. But Jenny and several other women remained.

"When do you leave?" I asked.

"Oh, those that need the money stay till ten," she said.

My heart sank at the thought of working from eight o'clock in the morning until ten at night.

Mrs. Moses appeared in front of me. "Six or ten?" she asked.

"I'm leaving now," I answered. As I stood up, a bolt of pain stabbed the muscles of my lower back.

Mrs. Moses took the coat that I was working on from me. She looked it over and then shook the coat with a flick of her arm. Two buttons flew from the coat and bounced on the floor.

"This will not do," she said with a voice that sent my spirits sinking. She looked me in the face and then looked at Jenny and then stared at me again. She pointed at Jenny. "Tomorrow Jenny will show you how to do it right."

"Yes. Thank you, Mrs. Moses."

Mrs. Moses gave a grunt as if disgusted by her own leniency and waddled back to her stool.

Jenny smiled at me as I took my leave.

So, I survived my first day as a trouser hand. I may not be a smashing success, but I believe I can do this work for as long as it takes me to complete my investigations.

When I returned to the hotel, I found Mrs. McArdle waiting for me. She saw my pained expression and said with a smile, "Not so easy, is it, dearie?"

What does she think I have been doing? Why does she derive such satisfaction from my suffering? Does she imagine from my accent that I am a fine lady fallen on hard times? Is that a source of amusement for her? Why should any of us rejoice in the misfortunes of others?

In my room, I found a letter from my father waiting for me on my bed. The envelope contained a letter from Mrs. Clara Ryland that my father had forwarded to me. Mrs. Ryland is the sister of the Great Man that I wrote to you about. Her letter was an invitation to visit the Great Man's estate in Birmingham. Perhaps my life will not be entirely without romance after all.

Sincerely,
Beatrice Potter

THREE

"How did you find Egypt?" asked Oscar. "Have the Pyramids grown taller? Did the Sphinx reveal her secrets to you?"

Bosie sighed with disgust. "I didn't have time for tourist trips. Mother asked the Cromers to introduce me around. They kept me busy meeting the most boring diplomats from countries you never heard of. I believe that whenever a government has an ancient official who is too decrepit to be of use in any normal capacity, they send him to Cairo to be an ambassador to the mummies."

Bosie's look of disgust was so exaggerated that even I had to laugh. Oscar still finds Bosie's jests charming, but lately I've begun to tire of his humor and only when he is at his wittiest does he still amuse me.

We were having a late luncheon at the Cafe´ Royal. Oscar was welcoming Bosie back to England and he wore a china blue velvet jacket that I had never seen before. Surely, he had not bought it just for this occasion?

"Oscar, it's very good of you to buy us dinner," I said, raising my champagne glass to him in a silent toast. I hoped to spark some gratitude in Bosie.

"A gentleman doesn't thank his host in the middle of dinner," Bosie said.

"A gentleman doesn't offer definitions that might seem vaguely insulting to other dinner guests," said Oscar. He looked pointedly at Bosie, but I could see there was no real anger in his eyes. Bosie scowled but decided for once not to make a scene. I suppose it had been too long since he had last dined with Oscar.

A year ago, one would have thought that dining out was their joint profession. It would have been amusing if they could afford it.

But they can't. Or rather Oscar can't. Bosie can afford it because he never pays. We take it for granted that Oscar will pay and I have just become aware of how unfair this assumption is to Constance and the boys.

I had met with Constance earlier that day. She had sent a brief note by post asking me to stop by Tite Street and see her and I sensed that she had a favor to ask. I was not mistaken.

I arrived in late morning. She was as beautiful as ever and Oscar's comment that having children destroyed her looks seems to me absurd. She was as tall, slim and elegant as I remembered her and if the years have added a pound or two to her frame it is all to the good.

The boys greeted me as an old friend. Cyril is growing tall and at ten years old is still far from his final height. Vyvyan follows his brother around like a puppy and always seeks Cyril's approval. I have noticed that both Oscar and Constance treat Cyril as the favorite child, and I have often felt sorry for poor Vyvyan.

Cyril wanted me to observe the war of his toy soldiers and his enthusiasm was so infectious that I was reminded of Oscar romping on the floor with his sons, laughing and inspiring laughter in turn. How long had it been since

Oscar had stretched his great height out on the floor next to his sons?

"Go upstairs and let me talk to Robbie," said Constance.

The boys reluctantly departed.

Constance ushered me into the White Room. The room is of a style that never grows old, perhaps because it was never in style. Everything in the room is white and the delicacy of the furniture contrasts so extremely with the heavy chairs and tables that one finds in most houses that the room seems like the habitation of creatures lighter and more refined than typical Londoners. Constance bade me sit in the chair nearest the window and she sat in the chair beneath the peacock feathers that are impressed into the plaster of the ceiling.

She inquired after my health and we talked of mutual acquaintances for a few minutes. I knew we had reached the true topic of our conversation when her face grew grim and she announced: "Lord Alfred Douglas is back in England."

Of course, I knew that. Bosie had been sent to Egypt by his mother who hoped that a prolonged visit with her friend the Earl of Cromer might kindle some ambition in her indolent son. No one who knew of her agenda expected much success. Oscar had been in favor of Bosie's exile and had actually written to Lady Queensbury to encourage her to send Bosie abroad. But Oscar has never been resolute in matters of the heart and as soon as I heard that Bosie had returned to England, I suspected it would only be a matter of time before he was reunited with Oscar.

"He's gone back to Oscar, of course," said Constance. There was such distress in her voice that I was filled with concern.

"What is it that worries you?" I asked. "Is Oscar missing deadlines?"

"He's not writing reviews anymore," she replied. "We're living on royalties from his plays. And the money from *A Woman of No Importance* is almost gone."

This sent a shiver of apprehension through me. I had never been told exactly how much money Oscar had earned from his plays, but I knew that *A Woman of No Importance* had generated at least one hundred pounds a week in royalties. Any normal man could live in London for years on the small fortune that Oscar had earned from that play and *Lady Windermere's Fan* which also had been a success. Oscar could be overly generous with his money, but his playwriting genius had earned more than enough royalties to keep any average spendthrift afloat. That Oscar had run through his fortune could only be attributable to the profligate tendencies of Bosie Douglas who spent Oscar's money as if it were his own.

In criticizing Bosie I am guilty of hypocrisy; I have benefited from Oscar's generosity many times. But if Bosie and I are guilty of the same sin, his is an epic vice that makes my offenses seem tiny and inconsequential by comparison. I was always happy to eat at whatever restaurant that Oscar suggested and considered that Oscar's friendship was the chief reward of the evening. Bosie constantly urges Oscar to dine at only the most expensive establishments and he orders all the most expensive dishes, and he considers a week wasted unless Oscar lavishes some outrageous present on him. Bosie takes the most extravagant generosity as his due and while he will show some appreciation for the quality of a gift, I cannot remember him ever actually saying "thank you." It is such a small thing and yet such a big thing.

"Can you try to get Oscar to work? Or at least stay away from Bosie?" Constance pleaded with me.

"I will do what I can," I promised her. "But if Oscar won't listen to you, I don't know that he will listen to me."

"You see him more often than I do," she said simply.

I felt a sudden stab of guilt. I believe I was the first one to introduce Oscar to Greek love. I have never regretted doing so even though it soon became clear that I was not to be the love of Oscar's life. I believe that Oscar had to follow his own nature and that his life would have followed much the same course even if he had never met me.

But I was a lodger in their home at Tite Street for some months and I know and appreciate Constance and her sons. Bosie dismisses Constance as a mere inconvenience, a woman who must be given small tokens of time and money so that Oscar can pursue his real life with Bosie and whatever rent boy has caught their fancy this week. But I have dined at her table too many times to condescend to her. Constance has brains and talent and a dutiful nature and of the two I would prefer her to Bosie for all his wit.

She is in an impossible position and I realize that I have played a part in putting her there. It is not clear what she understands or suspects about the nature of her situation. Oscar is absent from their home for weeks at a time and his excuses must by now be quite threadbare.

Does she realize why Oscar spends so much time in male company? I do not know, and I don't believe Oscar himself knows what she truly thinks. He may no longer even be interested and that is another reason I pity her.

"I will try to find a way to talk about money with Oscar," I said to her. "But it will be awkward."

"Thank you, Robbie. You've always been a friend."

She clasped my hand in gratitude and another stab of guilt chilled my soul.

I am neck-deep in hypocrisy. I dine out with Oscar while trying to broach the subject of thrift. I ponder Oscar's duty to his wife while wondering if a lover less profligate than Bosie might lessen Oscar's debts.

"We must be grateful that the stone lips of the Sphinx will never reveal her secrets," Oscar said, pouring the last of the champagne into Bosie's glass.

I realized he had been speaking for some moments while I was considering his dilemma—and my own.

"A secret is a mystery, and all mysteries are romantic," he continued. "But a secret revealed is merely a fact and all facts become banal."

"Oscar, there's your old employer," said Bosie.

We turned and saw a waiter seating the stocky figure of Frank Harris and a man I did not recognize at a table on the far side of the restaurant. Harris still waxes his mustache in a way that has fallen out of fashion of late, but he has the energy of a man in his prime. I could hear his booming voice over the din of the luncheon crowd and the waiter hurried off to fill his drink order.

"Ah, Harris," said Oscar. "He has lived in Ireland, America and England and he embodies the worst qualities of each nation. But he did publish some pieces of mine that no one else would touch so we shall forgive him."

An idea occurred to me: the beginnings of a plan. I would never be able to save Oscar from Bosie on my own. I needed help.

FOUR

Dear Miss Darling,

I have enjoyed your descriptions of your adventures as a teacher. You seem to think me brave for venturing into the poorest parts of London, but I think it takes more courage than I could muster to face a classroom of children from whom I could not flee if their natures proved rebellious. I have adventures on my own terms, but you have committed yourself to a term of employment with several strangers whose natures could prove surprising and distressing in any number of ways. Who is the brave one?

My work in the sweatshops culminated in my writing an article for *Nineteenth Century* magazine titled "Pages from a Working Girl's Diary." You would laugh if you knew how conceited I am about this tiny literary triumph. But this article had an unexpected result: I was called to testify for the House of Lords Select Committee on Sweating. The committee turned out to be a gathering of white-haired gentlemen, each more elderly than his fellows.

The first old man to question me seemed to doubt my veracity. "You expect us to believe that you worked as a trouser hand in the East End? And that your employer did not suspect that you were a lady?"

I replied with my best imitation of a Cockney accent. "Yes, M'Lord. I had to talk a bit differently for a week and dress less fancy, but that was no great hardship." You may be sure that I did not pronounce the "H" in hardship.

The Lords seemed unsettled that a woman dressed in my finery could talk with such an accent.

"You found this work to be hard?" an even older Lord asked me.

"I have no right to complain," I replied. "I worked for a week. The women who worked beside me do it for a lifetime. And for a pittance."

"Who is to blame for the low wages?" asked this second peer. "The shop owners? So many of them are foreign Jews."

"The popular image of the Jew as an exploiter of the poor is a myth," I replied. "The Jewish shop owners work beside the women in the same conditions and for the same hours. Someone must be getting rich off the sweating system, but it isn't the shop owners."

"But the Jews choose to pay these women the lowest wages," my interrogator insisted.

"The shop owner and the women they hire are both at the mercy of competition," I insisted. "There are too many poor women chasing too little work. And any shop owner who wanted to pay more would find himself driven out of business by owners who pay less. Only the hand of government can change conditions that pauperize both shop owner and seamstress."

The oldest of all the committee members bestirred himself. I had truly thought he had been asleep, or perhaps had died in a vertical posture. "Miss Potter, why do you spend so much effort on social investigation? Don't you feel you are meant for something better?"

"How would you know of the details of the sweating system if I had not investigated it?" I said. "The government makes policies for the poor without knowing anything about them. We must have policies based on more than assumptions and class prejudices."

The ancient men scowled at this criticism, so I concluded by stating my personal creed.

"And as a Christian, I believe I must help my fellow man. If I am meant for something better, I do not know what that could be."

I don't know if my testimony will lead to any change in law or policy. A heart hardened to all Christian impulses will not likely be pierced by mere facts. But I am content that I have done my best to contribute to good government.

I have retreated once again to Box House and the care of my father. But the invitation from Clara Ryland to visit the Great Man remains. The letter sits on the table beside my bed, taunting me for my lack of nerve. I have only to write a quick reply and my life could change. Will I have the courage?

Your friend,
Beatrice Potter

FIVE

From the unpublished memoir of Bernard Shaw:

After a few weeks devoted to the socialist cause, my time and attention has been once again unexpectedly claimed by the theatre. Florence Farr, an actress-manager of my acquaintance, summoned me to a meeting at the Avenue Theatre. Miss Farr (legally her name is Mrs. Emery, but her husband has disappeared in the wilds of America to avoid debts and no one expects to ever see him again) has charge of the Avenue Theatre and is producing a series of new plays with money from an anonymous donor. But her first play was such a catastrophe that I should have been expecting her summons.

"*A Comedy of Sighs* will close as soon as we can find a play to replace it," said Miss Farr. "When will your military play be ready?"

"I can have it ready the day after tomorrow," I said. "It is finished, and I only need to add a few historical details to complete its authenticity."

I should note that Miss Farr is one of the most beautiful of the young actresses now attempting to make their living on the stages of the London. Her hair is clipped short in a style that few women would dare to try, but which flatters her face. Her thin crescent-shaped eyebrows emphasize her wide-spaced eyes.

"Is there a part in it for me? I ask only because I need to prepare my schedule for the next few weeks. Todhunter's play has been such a fiasco that I would accept yours even if the entire cast were ugly old men."

I had attended the opening night of *A Comedy of Sighs and* I cannot remember a play that inspired so many catcalls. Florence, playing the female lead, had soldiered through the endless evening and I give her credit for not fleeing the stage, fleeing London and fleeing her chosen profession.

"There is a prime part for you. A saucy servant girl with the pride of the devil. She bewitches a handsome soldier and earns the admiration of everyone in the play and in the audience."

"Get the script to me as soon as possible. We will be lucky to have a week to rehearse."

"Then I'm off. My pen will be fleeter than the winged feet of Mercury."

"Good. I've done a horoscope for you and the stars indicate a success in the near future."

"The only stars that concern me are the ones that will shine down on you when you walk hand-in-hand with me in the moonlight."

I kissed her on the lips. I lingered there until Florence pushed me away.

"Go! I need your play more than your kisses."

"I wish every theatre manager felt that way."

I rushed out the theatre door. As an exit line, this last remark was imperfect—what other theatre manager would want my kisses? But I decided a quick exit would be better than a delay in the hope of coming up with a more inspired piece of wit.

A few hours later, I had an early supper with Sidney Webb at the Wheatsheaf, one of my favorite vegetarian restaurants.

"Sidney, I need a war for my play. A little war, not too much bloodshed. A distant war, not one in which the British public has a stake. Eastern Europe most likely. One in which mercenaries could have played a part because my hero is a Swiss mercenary fighting as an officer for one side. He falls in love with the daughter of a general of the opposing side."

Sidney Webb is my closest Fabian comrade, and he is renowned for his encyclopedic mind. Strangers often stare at him; his accent is Cockney and he sounds like a London dockworker, but he looks like a professor of an obscure foreign language. He is a short man with an overly large head. A mustache and van dyke beard give him a resemblance to Napoleon III, but his pince-nez and shabby black suit hint at an intellectual occupation. In fact, he works at the Foreign Office by day and for the Fabian Society at all other times. A more clear-headed common-sense man cannot be imagined.

"I think the Serbian-Bulgarian war is what you need," said Sidney. "The war wasn't very long, and it has the added advantage that few people in England are likely to know anything about it."

"Splendid! I can find out the details in the library of the British museum. I'll be finished by nightfall."

"What's the hurry?"

"A play is closing at the Avenue Theatre. They need an immediate replacement. Miss Farr insists that it be mine."

"Farr? Is she the actress with the wonderful face?"

"She is indeed. Her eyebrows alone could inspire sonnets. Although to kiss that face one must tolerate a certain amount of astrological nonsense."

"To kiss that face, some men would tolerate severe epilepsy and a wooden leg."

From Sidney's mournful expression I guessed that it had been a long time since anyone had kissed him.

"I appreciate beauty in women as much as the next man, but I will not be bound to it," said I. "I believe it was Thoreau the American who said that a man is free in proportion to the number of things that he can do without. Few men realize that one of the most enslaving possessions a man can have is a mistress with a pretty face."

Sidney shook his head at my perverse views.

"Is a pleasurable captivity a true captivity at all?"

"A pleasurable prison is certainly one of the most inescapable. I will leave it to you to decide if that makes it better or worse. Anyway, keep your nights free at the end of the next week. For your help, you can have a free ticket to *Arms and the Man.*"

And so, I have begun another venture in the theatre. I have high hopes for this play, and I intend to invite the theatrical elite of London to my opening night. A closer friendship with Miss Farr is not the least of the attractions of this adventure and I doubt that she will try to claim me in the way that led Bertha Newcombe to frustration. Florence has already had one bad husband and so is not likely to be in a hurry to have a second. So much the better for me.

SIX

Dear Miss Darling:

My romance with the Great Man has reached a climax of sorts, but only time will tell if I have made the right decision. I am tormented by doubt and at times I feel that I would give everything I own to be able to go back and change my mind. The intensity of my agony is so acute that even work is no longer a consolation. I drag myself through my days out of duty with no hope that any ray of sunlight will break through the clouds of my despair.

Do I seem maudlin? Very well, I am maudlin. I can conceive no wit or irony that would put my situation into humorous perspective and a straightforward recounting of my dilemma is all that I can manage.

I arrived in Birmingham by train two weeks ago and found a carriage waiting to take me to Highbury, the Great Man's house. It is a huge dwelling outside of town and if there is not enough land around it to make a true grand estate, the house itself must impress all visitors with the wealth and station of its owner.

Mrs. Ryland was waiting to greet me; she acts as her brother's hostess since the death of his second wife. Both of the Great Man's wives died in childbirth and all of London has been waiting for him to take a third. My attendance at dinner parties is increasingly rare these days, but when I do, I often hear speculation about who the Great Man will marry.

Mrs. Ryland and I took tea in a large drawing room made memorable by the conspicuous ugliness of the furniture. I would soon see that the entire home was cluttered with an overabundance of pieces of heavy dark furniture and the house—which could have displayed not only the wealth but the good taste of its master—merely showed his poor judgement. He had mistaken solidity and weight for beauty and had assumed if four chairs make a room habitable then twelve must make it worthy of a palace, an error that made navigating across any room of the house akin to threading a maze. There was a small table in front of every window and on every one of these tables was a vase of artificial flowers. It had apparently not occurred to the decorator that come spring these would block the view of the real flowers that would undoubtedly surround the house (I know the Great Man employs at least two gardeners and his buttonhole always demonstrates his love of flowers.)

The house also was overheated to the point of making me uncomfortable and I found I had little appetite for the scalding tea.

Do not let these caustic comments prejudice you against Mrs. Ryland. She has always been a courteous hostess and if I do not consider her a close friend, I at least regard her as an altogether admirable acquaintance. She undoubtedly knew of the Great Man's affection for me and has done all she can to promote a possible romance. Part of the Great Man's appeal for me was the charm and quality of his daughters and sisters. I have enjoyed the company of all these women and although their political views may be conventional, their personalities are all convivial and generous. A man who is surrounded by so many estimable women must have many sterling qualities.

Mrs. Ryland reminisced about my past meetings with the Great Man and I soon realized she was trying to encourage happy memories of our friendship. This led me to wonder as to her purpose, but the continuing conversation made it impossible to wonder for long.

"We will see Joe tonight at the City Hall," explained Mrs. Ryland. "He will be making a short speech. The people love to see him. And he loves them."

I was skeptical that any politician could engender universal affection, but I kept these views to myself.

Mrs. Ryland asked about my work as a social investigator and if she was merely feigning interest in my work, it was impossible for me to detect a false note. Of course, as the sister of a leading member of Parliament, public affairs surround her, it is in the very air and she could converse intelligently on any number of political topics.

As the afternoon waned, other members of the family gathered and at last we set out for town in two carriages. The Great Man's daughter Beatrice rode with me in the carriage and she gave me a humorous report on her experience of the London social season. Perhaps it is because we share a first name that I am especially drawn to her, but her charm and education is a testament to the quality of her father.

The size of the auditorium of the Birmingham City Hall took me by surprise. Like many who have spent their lives in orbit around London, I unconsciously regard London as the city and everywhere else as the country. It sometimes seems as if England has only one city and all other places that we call cities are merely large towns. But the Birmingham City Hall shows how wrong this impression is. The hall could seemingly accommodate half the population of Birmingham and they arrived by the dozens until the room was packed with hundreds of enthusiastic citizens. If you have ever attended a symphony then you know how loud a packed auditorium can be before the music starts. Imagine that noise and then triple it in volume and you may have some idea of how loud that crowded room became.

The good spirits of the crowd also impressed me. It seemed as if many were on holiday and some had brought candy, sandwiches and even beer. Neighbors greeted each other and many shared cigarettes with friends. Children ran in the aisles and acquaintances waved across the hall to each other and shouted greetings.

"Are all these people here only to greet Mr. Chamberlain?" I asked.

Mrs. Ryland nodded. "His speech is the only event of the evening. You must remember he was mayor for some years. To them he's good old Joe."

Presently, a portly local dignitary appeared, and the crowd roared its approval that the evening was finally underway. The dignitary raised his arms for quiet, but it was some moments before he could make himself be heard.

"My friends, I have the great honor to introduce your friend and my friend and the friend of all Birmingham, the honorable Joseph Chamberlain."

As the Great Man entered the hall, a wave of jubilation erupted from the crowd such that I have never heard before. Every person was instantly on his feet, stamping and applauding, whistling and making noise in every way possible. This was the kind of greeting that I imagined only the most popular military heroes would ever receive, but there was no denying the joy in every face. "Joe! Joe!" cried many.

You may have seen photographs of Mr. Chamberlain in the newspapers, but they do not do justice to him. Photographs do not capture his great height or the breadth of his shoulders. He towers over ordinary men and his face has the stern dignity that we seek in our heroes. In short, he looks like an ideal father, handsome, commanding and confident, at ease in his public roles, generous and fair in his private moments. Such is the impression one gets from his face.

Mr. Chamberlain strode to the center of the stage and held his hands up for silence. He smiled as the crowd slowly obliged him.

"My friends," he said in a voice that easily carried to the farthest corner of the room, "How good it is to be back in Birmingham!"

There was such a fresh explosion of applause and rejoicing that I thought I might go deaf. The crowd was clearly looking for any excuse to shout their approval to their hero.

The Great Man had to wait many moments before he could make himself heard again. "Many of you have asked me what is happening in London. I can tell you that what is happening now is what always happens: the rich and powerful are running the nation for their own benefit!"

The crowd began to jeer these far-off enemies of fairness and good government.

The Great Man again held up his hands for quiet. "But do not despair! We are changing the world. In 1870 only four out of every ten Englishmen had the vote. Today the vote has been given to twice as many men. And we will not rest until every Englishman in the land has the vote!"

Mr. Chamberlain shouted the last part of this sentence and his enthusiasm worked to goad the audience to new heights of ecstasy. Waves of sound rebounded from the walls and even I began to succumb to the passion of the moment.

I had to wait a long time before being able to converse with Mr. Chamberlain alone. After his speech, he spent nearly an hour receiving the congratulations of local officials and the best wishes of the citizenry. Then we traveled in crowded carriages back to his estate where a feast awaited us. The food seemed as overly heavy as the furniture and although I ate lightly, I still felt as if I had eaten too much. Beatrice showed a lively interest in my adventures as a social investigator and I tried to make my ordeals into a humorous tale.

After dinner, Mr. Chamberlain offered to show me his greenhouse, an addition to the original house in which he has much pride. If the main house was over-heated, the greenhouse was stifling and humid and I soon found myself longing for a breath of cool air.

A gas lamp near the entrance of the greenhouse and the moonlight shining down through the panes were the only illumination and I could see little of the orchids in their beds. But of course, Mr. Chamberlain had not invited me here to admire his flowers, but for conversation.

"It was good of you to come to Birmingham," he said. "It rejuvenates me to be in the country. I spend far too much time in London. Far too much time with my work. I mention my work because it is my only excuse that I have not attended to our friendship as much as I should like."

"Mr. Chamberlain, you need make no excuses to me," I replied.

"You should know the value in which I hold your friendship. And the reasons I have seen you so seldom."

"I know the demands made of you. I know how little of your time is your own. I follow your career in the newspapers. It has become a game with me; to see how many times I can find your name each day."

"Really?"

As soon as I had said this, I regretted it. And yet it was the truth.

"Miss Potter, my name is likely to appear more often in the newspapers. The demands made on me are likely to increase. I'm afraid our friendship will suffer. In our present circumstances I will find it ever more difficult to see you."

"I understand," I said. I made this statement with no tremor in my voice and yet I suddenly had a sinking feeling in my chest as if my heart had become unmoored.

"And so, I find myself with no alternative but to say good-bye to you and trust to your forgiveness—or to ask you to be my wife."

"Your wife?" I repeated like a fool. It seemed my brain no longer functioned.

The Great Man now got down on one knee. "Miss Potter—will you marry me?"

It took me a very long moment to collect my thoughts. My heart—which seemed to have dropped within my body only moments before—now seemed to rise.

"Yes," I said. "Yes, Mr. Chamberlain. I will."

"Ah. Well. Good."

It took the Great Man a few moments to realize that he should kiss me, and it occurred to me that a man who must have proposed marriage at least twice before should be better at it. But this unkind thought could find no purchase in a mind made giddy by the circumstances and it disappeared as Mr. Chamberlain kissed me.

Mr. Chamberlain held me in his strong arms. "My darling," he said. "Shall we marry soon?"

"Yes," I replied. "I would like it to be soon."

"And would a small wedding suit you? With just a few friends. My entire life is a public function; I should like our wedding to be private."

"Whatever you want," I said.

"I am afraid there will be no honeymoon. I cannot be spared just now."

"I understand," I said, and I meant it. Mr. Chamberlain's politics are my politics and social progress in England may depend on his success and the success of his allies.

"There will be precious few holidays for us. The demands on my time—I never get far from London."

"I know the importance of your work. I understand as few women can because of the strength I find in my own work."

Mr. Chamberlain looked me square in the face. "My darling, I need hardly add, once you are my wife you will discontinue your career as a social investigator."

"But why?" I asked.

"Why? You need ask that? You will have more than enough duties to occupy your time."

"What duties? Your daughters are almost grown women now. They don't need me to look after them and they would probably resent it if I tried. And your servants and cooks have been preparing your dinner parties for so long that my direction would be superfluous."

Mr. Chamberlain sighed with impatience. "It is not merely your duties. It is your position as my wife."

"But my career entirely supports yours. Your work can only be aided by social investigation. The facts that I discover can be weapons that you use to fight for progressive laws and government. Our careers are not opposed but complementary."

Mr. Chamberlain shook his head. "My dear, you don't understand the necessities of politics. Gladstone is over eighty years old. He must retire or die eventually. And there are only two or three men who could replace him."

"And you are one of them, I know."

"The most likely one. I may soon have the opportunity to usher in the most progressive government in England's history. The dreams of every social reformer in London may be made reality—by me. The poor that you investigate—those that are so wretched and ignorant that they don't know where to turn to for relief—will find it. If I become Prime Minister."

"You know that I wish you success with all my heart."

"Then put away your work. A married man makes a more respectable figure than an unmarried one—even a widower. But no Prime Minister can have a wife who dresses in rags and works as a seamstress in the East End."

I felt a growing unease at the impatience in his tone. "Even if it is to gather information on the working conditions of the poor?"

Mr. Chamberlain nodded. "Even then. It is eccentric."

Some of my own impatience now found expression in my voice. "It is honorable work! It is necessary. I do not think it is kind of you to ask me to give it up."

"But you will be married! Social reform is a fine career for those spinsters who have too much ambition to be content as governesses. But a married woman has no need of a career."

"A married woman often needs a career for the same reason as a man: to exercise her talents, give her life purpose and to improve as much of the world as she can."

"It pains me to hear my views contradicted. I require from my wife intelligent sympathy."

Mr. Chamberlain did not shout these words, but he said them with such force as to leave no doubt how strongly he felt them. I felt a great dismay swell inside me and when I could find my voice it was tinged with sadness.

"Surely you don't expect everyone in your household to hold precisely the same opinions as yourself. Your daughters—you don't believe that their ideas are identical to yours in every point?"

"I can't help it if people in my house think differently than me."

"But you don't allow expression of that difference?"

Mr. Chamberlain did not answer at once. He was surely contemplating what the results of each possible answer would be. At last, he paid me the compliment of an honest answer.

"No," he said.

"I see," I said.

Mr. Chamberlain took my hands in his. "My darling, don't be cross with me. I am sure that on most matters our opinions are already so similar that little adjustment will have to be made. We both believe—"

"Mr. Chamberlain, I feel that are differences are irreconcilable. And so, I must respectfully decline your kind offer of marriage."

I said this in a rush as if I instinctively knew it must be said quickly and, in its entirety, before I could change my mind.

"Miss Potter, you are acting from pride. Only pride."

He tried to take my hands again. I turned to conceal my emotions. I feared that if he saw how close to tears I was, he would find a way to use this knowledge against me.

"We love each other," he said. And now there was distress in Mr. Chamberlain's voice.

"I must respectfully decline…"

"Beatrice!"

"This greenhouse is uncomfortably humid. I must get some fresh air." I hurried toward the door.

"My darling! Please, think!"

I fled the stifling atmosphere of the greenhouse.

I have little memory of the details of the rest of the evening, except that it was as painful and awkward as can be imagined. In the morning, Mrs. Ryland accompanied me to the train station. She was disappointed in the outcome of my visit, but there was no reproach in her conversation.

Now I must live with my decision. Did I make the right choice? If Mr. Chamberlain is a true domestic tyrant then I have had a narrow escape.

But is he? I have seen no signs of unhappiness in either his daughters or his sister and it may be that he imagines himself lord of the household without ever knowing how independent his women truly are. Or it may be that he is so consumed by his work that he pays little attention to the domestic sphere and so his absence creates a freedom for those he imagines to be under his command.

I am in an agony of doubt. Often, I am sure that I made the right decision. Just as often I am convinced I am a fool who sacrificed her last chance at love on the altar of independence.

I only know that I must press on with my work. I would be a truly pitiable creature to have forsaken love for work only to be made so unhappy that work becomes impossible. I will wipe away my tears and wear a face of determination. Only you in distant Australia will know my anguish and my doubt.

Your friend,
Beatrice Potter

SEVEN

From Oscar Wilde's secret journal:

"Is it true his first play was a dreadful socialist tract?" asked Bosie.

We were standing in the lobby of the Avenue Theatre waiting to be seated for the opening of Bernard Shaw's new play *Arms and the Man.* I wore my winter coat trimmed with beaver fur that I acquired when lecturing in America. In truth, it was a little too warm for a winter coat, but the American coat is the one item of apparel of which I never tire, and I find a cloudy day a sufficient excuse to wear it. The fur-trimmed cuffs are enormous and extend from my wrist almost to my elbow and these are ostentatious enough to draw admiring glances from friends and strangers alike. Bosie wore a tan linen suit he had acquired in Egypt which emphasized his slim build and standing next to me I daresay he looked like a sapling beside a mountain.

"Yes," I said. "It oozed socialism like a vapor. But it was fascinating, nevertheless. The women, Bosie! Shaw writes women like no one else. They can be as bad-tempered and ill-mannered as the men and with much the same concerns. You will not find a fainting romantic heroine in a Shaw play."

"Is that the playwright?" asked Bosie, gesturing toward a thin, red-bearded figure wending his way through the crowd.

"It is indeed."

We watched as Shaw approached a strange little man in a black suit who was holding a thick book.

Bosie went to talk to an acquaintance. I took the opportunity to step closer to Shaw, but I turned my back to him so that I could eavesdrop without appearing to. This is a minor vice of mine and I cultivate it because I need a few minor vices to balance out my major ones.

"What are you reading?" I heard Mr. Shaw demand in his Irish accent.

"*Principles of Modern Economics* by Alfred Marshall," said another voice in a Cockney accent.

"Yes, I frequently bring my copy to the theatre," said Shaw and I almost laughed out loud at this Irish sarcasm. "Many is the time I've relieved the tedium of Hamlet's swordfight with Laertes with a brisk review of Jevon's critique of Marx's theory of value. I assume you will read it in the pauses between the actor's lines."

"I will read it in the pauses between the acts," said the Cockney voice." I'm sorry, Bernard, but I promised to review the book for the *Star* and I must have it done before tomorrow night."

"Sidney, you're the only man I know who likes work more than I do. Don't read it during the play or you'll miss a couple of very pretty actresses who have had only a week to memorize their lines. Their terror makes them vibrant. Now, you must excuse me. I have to remind my cast that they will be horse-whipped if they misplace one comma of my dialogue."

I had to smile at this amusing conversation. Bernard Shaw is growing ever more interesting. When Shaw first appeared at my mother's at-homes many years ago, he was a witless and beardless youth and I saw nothing interesting in him except his Dublin accent which was musical and attractive. Over the years he has grown in confidence and wit and his theatre criticism has made him a valued member of the London theatre scene. When he began writing plays, I sent a note to him jesting that we two were creating a Hibernian school of drama and the invitation to *Arms and the Man* is undoubtedly his thank-you.

The final lines of the play were spoken, the curtain descended and the applause began.

I was the first to leap to my feet and I shouted "Bravo!" again and again.

Bosie reluctantly got to his feet and his applause was half-hearted. "You're over-doing it, Oscar. It wasn't as clever as one of your plays."

"I'm not sure that's true and even if it is, all the more reason to be generous. To act as if I were jealous would be to admit that Shaw is as fine a writer as myself. Bravo! Author! Author!"

After the cast had taken their bows, the playwright appeared. As he neared the center of the stage, the applause swelled. Shaw nodded his appreciation to the audience.

A single cry of "Boo!" came from the side of the theatre. The applause instantly died.

Shaw's head pivoted toward the sound and he took a step in that direction.

The theatre was silent. It was as if the entire audience were holding its breath.

Shaw gestured in the direction from whence the catcall came. "My dear sir, I quite agree with you. But who are we two against so many?"

Shaw shrugged at his helplessness and the audience roared with laughter. As the laughter faded, it was replaced by a renewed burst of applause.

I stood thunderstruck by what I had heard. Bosie finally noticed and jostled my arm.

"Oscar, what's wrong?"

"That was the perfect thing to say. That was the absolute perfect line for the situation and Shaw found it."

"So, he's clever."

"I thought I was the only man who knew exactly what to say on all occasions. It was my gift. But not my gift alone, apparently. It seems one merely has to be an Irish playwright residing in London to know the exact correct thing to say in every situation."

"That can't be true. Shaw just got lucky."

"I don't think so. I think Mr. Shaw is just beginning to show London what he's made of."

"Well, it can't be every Irish playwright then. What about Yeats? He's Irish, isn't he? And he's a playwright. He wrote that dreadful verse play. You think he's a great wit as well?"

"You're right. Yeats couldn't coin an epigram if it would save him from the gallows. Being Irish and a playwright in London is not enough. There must be a spark of genius. I am relieved. You reassure me, Bosie."

Bosie pulled a cigarette case from a pocket and extracted two cigarettes. "You're welcome. Where are we going to eat?"

We ate at Willis', of course, but my mind kept returning to the play I had just seen and the playwright. I am guilty of more than one of the seven deadly sins, but my heart has seldom been stained with envy. Now, I contemplated my own feelings about Mr. Shaw. His play was funny enough to be a success, although this particular production perhaps did not do full justice to it. It was evident that the actors were not in full command of their lines. But it seemed likely that Mr. Shaw was to be a future rival, challenging me for the position of preeminent playwright of the London theatre.

I decided that I approved of his ambition and his talent. A rival will bring out the best in me. Surely, Shakespeare's ambition had been whetted by Marlowe's success. In a similar fashion, Mr. Shaw's endeavors will spur my own industry. I merely must stop underestimating him. If only he would dress like a successful man and stop wearing those ragged red woolen suits, I would find it easier to take him seriously.

But perhaps his down-at-heels appearance is a warning in itself. A man who will not borrow money to improve his appearance is likely a man of iron discipline. A shabby Shaw is probably an industrious Shaw.

He will bear watching.

EIGHT

From the unpublished memoir of Bernard Shaw:

Another romantic smash-up. I find the increasing frequency of these disasters disheartening. But perhaps this one could not be helped.

The morning after the opening night of *Arms and the Man,* I awoke to find a shaft of sunlight blessing Florence's bed. Florence was nowhere to be seen. I looked around for my clothes. Not every woman appreciates a naked lover in the morning. Besides, the air was chill.

My trousers, shirt and coat were draped over a chair next to the bed.

Florence's flat had the creative clutter of the true artist. A print of a Japanese landscape was side by side on the wall with a watercolor of the cliffs of Dover. Plays by Ibsen were stacked with plays by Shakespeare on the floor. A primitive statue of some god with the head of an elephant squatted near one wall. In a corner was a small writing desk with a thick pile of manuscript upon it.

I pulled on my socks and trousers and stepped to the desk. The manuscript was handwritten in Florence's neat script.

Florence appeared in the doorway, a steaming mug in her hand. She wore a red Japanese robe decorated with white flowers.

"Cocoa," she announced and held out the mug.

"Thank you." One of the things I appreciated about Florence was her attention to detail. I had only once mentioned that I enjoy Van Houten's cocoa and here was a hot cup waiting for me.

"What does a vegetarian have for breakfast?" Florence asked. "I suppose you don't eat eggs."

"No, I don't. Oatmeal porridge is my usual breakfast."

"I'm sorry. I have no porridge. But I do have some apples."

"An apple makes a splendid breakfast."

Florence disappeared into the kitchen. When she reappeared with an apple, I asked her: "What are you writing?"

Florence gathered the manuscript and dropped it in a drawer.

"It's not finished. It would not interest you."

"That was a thick stack of pages. Much labor was expended in the writing of it. What subject matter has earned such effort?"

"If you must know, it is about Egyptian magic."

Florence crossed her arms and glared at me as if expecting an insult.

"Fiction?" I asked. "A story about Egyptian magicians?"

"Not fiction," Florence said with an air of defiance. "A book about uses and channeling of magic."

"Magic? I would have thought the stage produced enough magic for any actress."

"Don't mock what you don't understand. There are a great many people in London interested in the mystic arts."

"There are a great many people in London who hear spirits rapping on tables during séances, but that doesn't prove the existence of ghosts."

"I'm not interested in your skepticism."

Florence took a bite out of the apple. I gently took hold of her upper arms and looked her in the eye.

"I'm interested in your talent. Your true talent. That you displayed so ably last night on the stage. You have beauty and charm and a fearlessness that is rare for one so relatively inexperienced. Now you must hone your natural gifts to a fine edge. With discipline and application you could have all London at your feet."

"With you as my tutor, I suppose."

"Of course. You've read my theatre criticism. Do I understand acting or not?"

Florence slipped from my grasp and sat on the bed.

"There are many talents I may wish to explore. Acting is only one of them."

I pointed at the drawer that contained the manuscript.

"But not this. You have too much sense for playing with magic."

"There are more things in heaven and earth than are dreamt of in your philosophy, Horatio." Florence's voice had gained a playful tone, but I suspected her mood was darker than her tone indicated.

"I was born on July twenty-sixth which means that I am a Leo. And like all my tribe, I am naturally resistant to superstition, occultism, augury and humbuggery in all its forms."

Florence got to her feet. All amusement had vanished from her face.

"I told you not to mock me. I think you had better leave."

I knew I would lose her if I could not make it instantly clear why I valued her.

"Florence, I only wish to help you. To make myself useful to you and to make you useful to the world. If you insist on exploring fairyland, I cannot follow you. This world is far too real to me to go inventing others."

"So, the only new worlds I should be allowed to explore are the ones you create onstage. No, thank you, Mr. Shaw. Your plays are amusing, but they are only plays."

I sat on the bed and put on my shoes. "I seem to have a talent for offending the women I like the most."

"Is that an apology?"

"No. We each have done nothing to apologize for. We are just not the person that the other one needs."

I shrugged on my shirt and then my coat. At the door, I gave Florence a sad smile, but said nothing.

As I walked home under a sky the color of stone, I felt a pain in my chest. But I knew that once I returned home and began to write, the pain would vanish. I wonder: does that make me a strong man or merely a heartless one?

NINE

From the memoir of Robert Ross:

It took me two weeks to speak to Frank Harris alone. He dined at the Cafe´ Royal almost every day, but he was invariably accompanied by journalists or other guests. He was a man who delighted in company and I could often hear his booming laugh even when I was seated alone in some obscure corner of the restaurant. Sometimes his guests would depart only to be replaced by fresh acquaintances who Harris would recognize when they entered the restaurant and who he would then summon to his table with extravagant gestures and loud cries of greeting. There always seemed to be at least one bottle of wine at his table, but more often several and the conversation and laughter would grow louder as the bottles were emptied. His guests were always men, but the subject of conversation was usually women and several times I noticed Harris glancing around to check the nearness of waiters before he lowered his voice to tell a story that I supposed was risqué. These stories would end with an explosion of laughter from his guests and Harris himself would turn bright red as his guffaws reverberated around the room.

I have often found that grown Englishmen are like schoolboys: they will find the most witless joke irresistibly funny if the teller spices it with an element of sex. After several days of observation, I concluded that Harris was a prime example of this type.

One afternoon, Harris's two guests departed early from his table, but he lingered to finish eating the beef that he had neglected while entertaining his friends. I took the opportunity to stroll past his table in such a manner as to suggest that our meeting was pure chance.

"Mr. Harris? Mr. Frank Harris?" I said, as if recognizing a great celebrity.

"That's me," said Harris, wiping food from his waxed mustache with a forefinger. "What can I do for you, young man?"

"My name is Robert Ross. I am a journalist of sorts. I believe we have a mutual friend. He pointed you out to me in this very restaurant. He said: "That is Frank Harris, the editor of the *Saturday Review and* my very good friend. You should make his acquaintance if you want to be a London journalist.""

"Who is this mutual friend who pointed me out?" said Harris with an undercurrent of suspicion in his voice. He probably suspected me of being a talentless hack trying to drum up work with spurious claims of mutual acquaintances.

"My friend is Mr. Oscar Wilde."

Harris's face was transformed. I have often noticed that when Oscar's name is mentioned smiles blossom on every face. His very name summons memories of conviviality, humor, wit and amusing companionship and even those who have only met him on an occasion or two are reminded of some jest or ironic compliment and their eyes brighten with the recollection of distant mirth.

"Mr. Ross, please seat down. Any friend of Wilde is likely a man worth knowing."

"You flatter me, sir," I said while seating myself across from him.

"You must help me finish this bottle," said Harris, indicating the wine. He gestured for the waiter and ordered a clean glass be presented to me. When the glass was set before me and the waiter had filled it with red wine, Harris leaned back in his chair. "How is Wilde? I don't see him nearly as much as I would wish. He has a pretty wife and children, too, if I remember rightly. No more journalism for Oscar. Lost to the theatre, alas."

"Yes, he mostly writes plays now. But he can't turn them out fast enough. I believe he has debts."

"Everyone has debts," said Harris.

"Not like poor Oscar. He has never been disciplined with money and some of his friends are worse. He is far too generous with some young men who are shamelessly extravagant. They spend Oscar's money as if it were their own."

I knew I was treading on thin ice here. I needed to make clear Oscar's financial situation without making Harris suspect that Oscar was the center of a circle of sodomites who could besmirch anyone who knew them.

Harris looked at me in silence. The humor was gone from his face and had been replaced by an evaluating intelligence that made me uncomfortable. I remembered that Oscar had once called Harris "a man of the world," and I now feared that such a man might suspect all the hidden realities behind my hints and equivocations. Harris had doubtless seen Oscar dining with a table of young men at one restaurant or another and I may just have provided him with enough clues for him to reinterpret the nature of the comradeship he had witnessed.

When Harris next spoke, his voice was subdued and had lost all emotional inflection. "Mr. Ross, I have a feeling that this was no chance meeting today. What do you want from me?"

"I don't know exactly. I wish only to save Oscar from himself. He needs to get clear of bad companions and I thought that you might have a writing assignment that might get him out of London."

"If he has given up journalism, why would he accept such an assignment, even if I had one to give?"

"I believe Oscar is of two minds. I know part of him wishes to devote himself to his family and to be a good husband and father. Part of him may be looking for an excuse to repent of his life of extravagance. I am hoping you could provide that excuse."

Harris gave me a grim smile. "I am not often called upon to reform the souls of men. I am more often accused of leading them into temptation."

I said nothing.

"I can see that your concern for Wilde is genuine," said Harris. "I will not mock true friendship, no matter what its nature. There is too little of it in the world. But I have no idea of how to help our friend. If there was an easy solution to this problem, you would have already thought of it. Don't expect much from me. Men chart their own course. If Oscar won't heed his own wife and children, a boisterous editor is not likely to make much difference." Harris wiped his mouth with his napkin and then gave me a smile that was meant to be encouraging. "But if an idea occurs to me, I will act on it. I won't wait for your approval."

"Thank you," I said, pushing back my chair. "I can ask no more."

I left the restaurant feeling lighter of heart. Like Harris, I believed there was little chance of saving Oscar against his will. But I felt better for having tried.

TEN

From the unpublished memoir of Bernard Shaw:

My romantic misadventures have earned me a scolding from Sidney Webb who seldom comments on such matters. He was to give a Fabian lecture at the St. Pancras vestry hall on Saturday last and I caught up with him on the sidewalk on the way to lecture.

Sidney stopped in his tracks when he heard me calling his name. I dashed up to him and thrust a sheaf of papers at his chest.

"Here is your speech. If you follow my modest revisions, the whole thing should go off like a firecracker."

He looked over the first page, then thumbed through the rest of the pages.

"I don't see the point of lecturing on statistics and removing most of the statistics from the lecture."

"To be susceptible to argument, an audience must remain conscious," I said. "Now, I was thinking that we might look for our summer house soon."

"I thought you were staying in London this year. I thought you'd be writing plays for the actress with the wonderful face."

"The actress you're thinking of cares more for the magic of Egypt than the theatres of London. I was not Caesar enough to tame this Cleopatra."

Sidney smiled. "I find it hard to take actresses seriously. At least you have a socialist artist at your command. By

September, I expect to see enough portraits of you to fill a gallery."

"The only way I'll get more portraits of myself is if I commission them. The female artist you're thinking of would rather paint a Calcutta leper than look on my face again."

Sidney stopped walking again and glared at me.

"Oh, not Bertha, too!"

"Why does every woman who admires a man's genius, vitality and independence dream of enticing him to forfeit all three?"

"Bernard, this has got to stop."

I should have guessed the cause of Sidney's displeasure, but in my innocence, I merely spread my hands and looked puzzled.

"These endless love affairs. You may regard them as harmless flirtations, but to lesser souls these things are quite serious. You are causing a great deal of unhappiness and you may be harming the Fabian Society. It's getting harder and harder to find any women who will serve on a committee with you."

"Any woman who would desert socialism to avoid being social isn't worth keeping."

"Then think of your own happiness. When you finally decide to take a wife, you'll find it difficult to find one if every woman thinks of you as a jester or a Don Juan."

I laughed and clapped my hand on Sidney's shoulder.

"A wife? Don't be absurd. We're going to be the bachelor warriors of socialism, tilting at capitalist windmills when we're older than Quixote."

Sidney shuddered. "Good Lord, I hope not!"

At the vestry hall, I wandered through the growing crowd and looked at the people with pleasure. For a socialist lecture on a winter's afternoon, the size of the audience was impressive. I noted with approval two young men in working man's clothes. The Fabian Society could use more recruits from the class that its policies are supposed to benefit.

I soon found Sidney talking to a brown-haired woman of about forty years of age who was wearing a fine wool coat that looked as if it might have recently been brushed. She was every inch as tall as Sidney and she listened to his explanation with an expression of suppressed amusement. Her most striking feature was a pair of luminous green eyes.

"The name comes from the Roman general Quintus Fabius," said Sidney. "He was called Fabius the Delayer because he bided his time until the precise moment came to strike. In the end, he defeated Hannibal at Zama."

"I believe Zama was won by Scipio Africanus," said the woman. Her voice had a refined Irish accent.

Sidney's eyes were wide, but I couldn't be sure if he was bothered more by being contradicted by a woman or by getting his history wrong.

"Er—you may be right," Sidney stammered. "In any event, one of our founders thought that delay would be a necessary strategy for a group of socialists. Hence the Fabian Society."

I stepped to Sidney's side and touched his elbow.

"I think we should start soon."

"Oh, yes." He turned back to the woman. "You'll have to excuse me. I'm the main speaker."

The woman smiled at Sidney. "Of course."

Sidney would have walked away without introducing me, but I grasped his elbow with an iron grip and gestured at the woman with a movement of my head.

"Forgive me," said Sidney. "Bernard, this is Miss Charlotte Payne-Townshend. Miss Payne-Townshend, this is Bernard Shaw."

"Very pleased to meet you, Mr. Shaw," said Miss Payne-Townshend as Sidney hurried away.

"I don't believe I've seen you here before. Is this your first taste of society?"

"Meaning the Fabian Society? Yes, this is my first meeting. It is not what I expected."

"What did you expect? Bomb makers in the basement? Free love in the parlor? You're mistaking us for the anarchists. They rent the hall on Thursdays."

"Jokes. That's what I didn't expect. I was prepared for long involved explanations of political theory."

"That's Sidney's specialty. You might want to escape before he finishes. After every lecture Sidney finds the most beautiful woman in the room and asks for her impressions."

"Whereas a more dedicated socialist like yourself would never dream of flirting with a pretty woman."

"On the contrary. I flirt with all women, pretty or not. It is part of my recruitment program."

"Ah. That explains the lack of women. I thought I had wandered into a gentleman's club by mistake."

"We have a shortage of Fabian women at present. Most of them fall in love with me and when they discover my heart is a rock, they throw themselves into anarchism, spiritualism, or the Thames."

I scanned her face for signs of indignation, but found only amusement.

"Mr. Shaw, are you always this vain?"

I inhaled and did my best to puff myself into a caricature of conceit.

"Always. And what of you, Miss Payne-Townshend? What brings you to the Fabian Society?"

"I want to lead a useful life. I am searching for the best way to do that."

This answer was so unexpected that I found myself at a loss for words for a moment.

"A useful life? Not a happy one?"

"If I find the best way to be useful in this world, I expect that happiness will take care of itself."

I wanted to continue this conversation, but Graham Wallas was beckoning me and I knew that it was time to introduce Sidney.

When Sidney concluded his lecture, I looked around for Miss Payne-Townshend. There was no sign of her in the lecture hall, so I hurried out the front door to the street. I found her waiting on the sidewalk, looking for a hansom cab.

"You had no questions for Mr. Webb? He is quite approachable. I'm the only Fabian who bites as much as I bark."

"Economic theory is very new to me, Mr. Shaw. Mr. Webb has given me a great deal of food for thought. Please congratulate him for me. I thought his talk was a great success."

I saw a cab approaching, pulled by a great dappled mare. I stepped into the street and signaled it. As the two-wheeler stopped, I opened the door and offered Miss Payne-Townshend my hand. She took it and climbed into the cab.

"Thank you, Mr. Shaw. I am having an at-home next Tuesday and I was wondering if you would come. If you are not averse to dining with dilatants."

"I always dine with dilatants for the same reason that Christ dined with sinners: it is there that I am most needed. I must warn you, though. I am a strict vegetarian and teetotaler."

"If you get too thirsty, you have my permission to turn the wine into water."

The cab pulled away before I could reply. I stood in the street for a long moment thinking that she had somehow gotten the better of me. It was a novel sensation. Perhaps this is the secret to success with women: let them have the victory in every conversation.

ELEVEN

Dear Miss Darling,

Work has once again proven a great solace. If I keep busy, I seldom think of the Great Man and any Great Opportunities that I have let pass by. I have been a productive social investigator because of my need to fill every moment of the day with work.

After consulting with Charles Booth, I have decided to write a book on the co-operative movement. This is not a subject that is much discussed in London and I immediately sensed difficulties in obtaining sources of information.

Mary Booth seemed determined to help me. Or perhaps I had not disguised my unhappiness as well as I had thought. She smiled and took my hand. "I shall introduce you to Sidney Webb. He is a fountain of information on all things economic. In fact, he is giving a lecture on Saturday. I'll take you."

The following Saturday, Mary and I shared a hansom cab to the shabby vestry hall where the lecture was to be given. Mary explained that the lecture was sponsored by the Fabian Society, a group of socialist intellectuals who are making a name for themselves with their constant lecturing and pamphleteering.

The crowd (as best as I could tell from appearances) was a mixture of middle-class intellectuals and working people. There were perhaps forty audience members in all.

A red-bearded man eventually appeared at the lectern on the stage and offered a few humorous remarks by way of introducing Sidney Webb. Mr. Webb appeared from the wings of the stage and strolled to the lectern while looking at some notecards.

Mr. Webb is not physically impressive. Some of my less charitable sisters might simply dismiss him as a short, ugly man. His pince-nez and thick mustache give him an intellectual appearance which makes an odd contrast with his Cockney accent. I have simply never heard anyone discuss economic theory with quite that accent before.

Mr. Webb placed his note cards on the lectern and took a deep breath. He smiled at the audience and then began.

"If you saw a beggar or an orphaned child in the street, you might give that man or woman or child some money. That would be compassion. But if you were to learn that one-third of London lives in the direst poverty, you might be so outraged you would try to change the system that permits such misery. That would be justice."

I saw some in the audience nodding their heads in agreement.

"But it is only very recently that it became possible to know how many Londoners lived in poverty. We have seen the face of—"

Mr. Webb looked right at me and seemed to lose his place. One notecard fluttered to the floor. He coughed, picked it up and continued.

"We have seen the face of poverty on our streets for centuries, but the size and shape of the monster was always invisible. It is only now through the application of mathematics—of statistics—that we can look not at the poor, but at poverty itself. A new science is being born.

A social science. A science that will arm our compassion with the weapons of logic and reason."

There was much more in this vein, but I will not recount his entire lecture. As Mary Booth had predicted, there were no facts unfamiliar to me in Mr. Webb's lecture, yet he had the ability to make social investigation seem like one of the great events of our time. He believes that moral progress flows from the facts uncovered by our investigations and listening to him, I felt pride that I was part of this great endeavor.

After the lecture, Mary took me to Mr. Webb.

"Mr. Webb, what a wonderful speech," said Mary.

"Thank you, Mrs. Booth."

"Mr. Webb, allow me to introduce my friend Beatrice Potter. She has worked with Charles on his survey of the London poor."

Mr. Webb smiled at me and shook my hand.

"Then my lecture must be very old news to Miss Potter."

"Not at all, Mr. Webb," I said. "Your speech was illuminating. You explained the importance and implications of Mr. Booth's work with greater clarity than I ever could."

"Miss Potter also is a writer," said Mary. "You may have read her piece called 'Dock Life' in *Nineteenth Century* magazine."

"I did indeed. A fine piece of writing."

"She is now writing a history of the co-operative movement."

"Splendid! There is need for such a book."

"And I promised her that if she ran into difficulties, you were the man to see."

"I would be delighted to help in any small way that I can. I must warn you, though, that I am hardly an expert in the co-operative movement. I believe that co-operative associations are more common in the north of England, are they not?"

I nodded.

"Yes, that's very true. But I was hoping that some historical accounts might exist in the London libraries."

"They might, they very well might. I will do my best to help you, Miss Potter. I will indeed."

I count this meeting a success. Mr. Webb has promised to write to me and I have decided to reread *Fabian Essays* to reacquaint myself with Fabian theory.

In truth, I was much impressed with Mr. Webb's speech. He summarized the moral implications of social investigation in a more succinct fashion than anyone I have ever heard.

If he is this clear-headed on every topic, then he will be a valuable ally in our campaign against poverty.

Sincerely,
Beatrice Potter

TWELVE

From Oscar Wilde's secret journal:

I have met the monster at last. I have tamed the great beast that haunts Bosie's imagination and I have freed us both from worry and dread. I am writing of course about the ninth Marquis of Queensberry, Bosie's father. I had heard so many tales of his evil nature from Bosie that I had begun to believe he was a mythical creature.

Bosie and I were dining in the Domino Room at the Café Royal when I saw the Marquis being escorted to a table. No one in London has sideburns like the Marquis and I said to Bosie, "Is that your father?"

"It is," said Bosie. His tone of voice was fearful.

"Go and invite him to our table."

"No, Oscar!"

"Bosie, we must. Go fetch him."

At last, I persuaded Bosie to go and in a few moments he returned with his father who looked at me with the suspicious eye of a man who has been cheated once too often. If half of Bosie's tales are true, his father is a quarrelsome man who disagrees with anyone who spends sufficient time with him.

I therefore greeted the Marquis with excessive cheer and indicated what a very great pleasure and privilege it was to meet him. He deigned to shake my hand.

"What would you like to drink?" I said as the waiter stood quietly by. "I often have champagne this time of night, but when meeting new people, I am inclined to be adventurous."

"Scotch and water," said Queensbury.

"I'll have the same," I said.

"I'm not drinking Scotch," said Bosie.

"And a bottle of champagne for the boy," I said and discussed the vintage for a minute with the waiter.

Queensberry seemed impressed that I knew something about wine and I wondered what impression he had of me and where he had gained it.

"So, you've befriended my son," said Queensberry in a tone that made it sound like an accusation.

"I have," I said. "Your son is not without talent when it comes to poetry and I try to keep up with our younger poets."

"I've written verse myself," said Queensberry. "Although I prefer manlier arts. A real man can wield a pen and throw a punch."

"And take a punch, too, I should hope."

"Have you boxed, Mr. Wilde?"

"Alas, no. But I have wrestled in college. Sometimes with two or three opponents who charged into my room with the intent of humiliating me. I had to throw them bodily into the hall."

Queensberry smiled at this image.

"I am not particularly fierce," I said. "But no one can deny that I am large."

Queensberry chuckled at this. The waiter now arrived with our drinks. Queensberry lifted his glass.

"The manly arts!" He toasted.

I drank with him and sent a look at Bosie suggesting that he, too, should drink.

"I understand that you are trying to convert all of Britain and America to use your rules of boxing," I said. "How is this noble project succeeding?"

I had decided that the key to charming Queensberry was for me to be silent for once and to let him talk. It took very little to prompt a monologue on the sport of boxing and how to civilize it. I asked a few pertinent questions when Queensberry paused for breath. As his father continued to talk, Bosie kept looking at me expectantly; listening to his father was apparently one of his least favorite things to do in the world. I refused to look at him and kept my attention completely on Queensbury.

I was likewise deferential when we ate and my dinner selection echoed his. I drank when he drank and at last he seemed to notice.

"You can hold your liquor, Wilde," said Queensbury. "I'll give you that."

"When I was on a lecture tour in America, I was once the guest of honor at a banquet held at the bottom of a mineshaft in Colorado. The first course was whiskey, the second course was whiskey and for dessert we had whiskey. When I did not lapse into unconsciousness, the miners named the mine The Oscar in my honor."

Queensberry chuckled at this.

"I felt I was upholding the honor not only of England and Ireland, but perhaps all of Europe. The Americans seemed to feel that my accent may have indicated some effeminacy on my part, and I felt the need to disabuse them of that notion."

Queensberry nodded and smiled. After supper, he shook my hand warmly and took his leave.

Bosie was at last free to express his exasperation.

"Why did you do that?"

"I did it for us. For you. Life will be much simpler if your father does not hate me."

"You think you've charmed the dragon? That it no longer bites?"

"I have done my best and it did not bite me tonight. You wanted me to quarrel with your father and that I am disinclined to do. You must be an adult about these things."

This last remark was perhaps too much. Bosie stewed and fretted for the rest of the night and kept trying to tell me stories of his father's past abuses. I refused to hear these tales of woe.

"You will speak of pleasant things or I will go home to Tite Street and sleep in my own bed. I should do that anyway. I miss my sons."

Bosie refrained from further grumbling, but I had to promise him a holiday in Brighton to keep his mood from remaining dismal. It will have been worth it however, if I have avoided future problems with his father.

THIRTEEN

Dear Lion,

My illusions are shattered. You must think me a great fool for falling in love at my age. After fending off so many suitors for so many years purely to infuriate my mother, I become enraptured by the first charming man who crosses my path after my mother's death. Heartbreak is a new emotion for me and despite my intention to be a stoic, deeply painful and confusing. I thought that at my age I had my own emotions firmly in hand. How wrong I was.

In short, you were right about Dr. Munthe and I was wrong.

Although not completely wrong. In many ways he is an honorable and even heroic individual. He will drop everything and journey to the most remote Italian town if there is a rumor of cholera or typhus. As a doctor he is altogether admirable. He tells his rich patients that he will overcharge them for his services so that he can afford to charge his poor patients nothing. Surprisingly, they put up with this and even spread his fame to their friends. He is the most popular non-Italian doctor in Rome.

As a private individual he is eccentric, but charming. He keeps a wide variety of animals: dogs (several), cats (the number varies by the week), a mongoose (I liked it) and even a baboon (it frightened me). He works long hours which sometimes leaves him exhausted and irritable. But if you suggest that he cut down on the number of patients he sees, he recounts his dream of one day owning a villa on the isle of Capri where once stood the home of the Emperor

Tiberius. Dr. Munthe claims this is the most beautiful locale in the world.

The part of your judgement on Dr. Munthe that was accurate concerns his relations with women. You were correct when you called him "a charming monster of vanity." He certainly enjoys the attentions of numerous women who all seem to feel that the bachelor doctor can be enticed to marry again. He flirts with them and corresponds with them and enjoys dinners and excursions to the countryside with them. He may even encourage their illusions about him. He certainly gives the impression that greater intimacies will soon follow without ever allowing the friendship to progress. More than one woman is still waiting for the doctor to declare his love, believing that it is only his work which keeps him from being the lover she dreams of. There may even be a member of the Swedish royal family among the horde waiting for the doctor to propose.

It was a chance encounter of seeing the doctor at a restaurant with another woman that finally opened my eyes. I bribed the waiter for a true account of how often the doctor dines with single women and knew the answer even before the waiter had opened his mouth. Perhaps I should have asked him how often he is bribed to answer that very question.

I feel very foolish indeed. I am surprisingly naïve about some elementary aspects of life, considering how much of the world I have explored and how many people I can count among my acquaintances. I have met ambassadors who have seen less of Europe than I have, yet all my travel has left me ignorant of the human heart, my own most of all.

Now that I am back in England, I have begun a program of self-education in the hope of making myself into a person who can do some good in the world. If I cannot be happy, I can at least be useful.

London is the place for such study; there are innumerable societies and political organizations that attempt to educate the public through lectures and debates. I recently attended one such lecture sponsored by the Fabian Society and was surprised to find myself amused as much as informed.

The main speaker was introduced by a red-bearded Irishman named Shaw who is apparently the self-appointed jester of the Fabian Society. He seems to believe that any cause worth promoting also is worth mocking, albeit in an affectionate manner. I would say that he is as vain as Dr. Munthe except that Mr. Shaw would undoubtedly claim that he is vainer; self-mockery disguised as boasting is part of his arsenal of jokes.

I off-handedly invited him to one of my at-homes and to my surprise he showed up. He drank only rainwater and told anyone holding a glass of wine that temperance would increase their vigor tenfold and that abstaining from meat would make the timidest man as ferocious as a tiger. It is hard to know in which causes he truly believes when he promotes them all so facetiously.

Do not assume that I have any romantic interest in Mr. Shaw just because he is an Irishman. I merely have a fondness for hearing the rhythms of speech of my native land and Mr. Shaw has not tried to suppress his natural accent as many Irish do when making their way in London. Because we are both Dubliners, we have a natural affinity, just as any two nationals have an affinity for each other when meeting in a strange land.

So, I will plant myself in London for a while and give up roaming the earth like the Wandering Jew or the Flying Dutchman. I hope this will give me the opportunity to see more of you and Robert. I will keep you informed about the doings of the Fabian Society as I know you sympathize with the socialists.

All my love to Robert.

Sincerely,
Charlotte

FOURTEEN

From Oscar Wilde's secret journal:

Our little holiday in Brighton has been cursed by influenza. Bosie fell ill almost as soon as we had crossed the threshold of our room in the Grand Hotel and I have had to accept the role of nurse. Although his fever and vomiting testify to the reality of his illness, Bosie's theatrical moans and intermittent weeping are most likely exaggerations designed to solicit maximum sympathy. I don't really mind; although his vomiting is repulsive and the odor of illness fills the room, I rather enjoy the opportunity to show my devotion.

I was sitting on the edge of Bosie's bed, wiping his forehead with a cool cloth.

"I'm sorry, Oscar," he said with a feeble attempt at a smile. "I must disgust you."

"Illness is never pleasant, but you could never disgust me, dear boy. You have a body of ivory and hair of wheat." I ran my fingers through his hair. "You'll soon feel better."

I pulled a slim volume from my traveling bag and then sat again on the edge of the bed.

"Shall I read you some of my poetry?"

Bosie shook his head. "Tell me a story. One I haven't heard. Something new."

"Ah. A challenge." It took me a long moment to summon inspiration, but as always it came at my call.

A fable: A myth of ancient Greece. Once there were three brothers who lived in Athens. They were young and strong and handsome, but they all lived at home because they were not yet married. Their father had been a priest of Athena and he had taught his sons to be very devout and they prayed to the goddess every day and sacrificed to her every week.

Bosie propped his head on his hand and some of his distress left his face.

One day, the oldest son was chopping wood when a tall figure appeared before him, glowing like the sun. He fell to his knees in terror, but she said: "Be not afraid. I am the goddess Athena whom you worship daily. You and your brothers are the most devout of all my followers, as was your father before you. Bring your brothers here quickly so that I may reward you all."

The oldest brother did as she bade and brought his brothers to the clearing where the goddess stood in all her glory. She said to them: "You live apart from the city and none of you has married. So, I will offer you three women that you may wed. One of you may marry the most beautiful woman in the world. One of you may marry the cleverest woman in the world. And one of you may marry the most loving woman in the world."

Hearing this, the oldest brother said, "I will take as my wife the most beautiful woman in the world." In an instant, he was transported to a pleasant cottage where a woman of unsurpassed beauty awaited him. Her hair was the color of sunbeams and her eyes were the blue of forest pools when the sunlight sparkles on the water. She was tall and slender, and the sight of her face caused an excitement to fill his body and love to fill his mind.

He stumbled forward and took her hand and when she seemed not afraid, he kissed her red-lipped mouth. For many days the two were happy. The oldest brother could scarcely stand to be parted from his wife for an instant and he followed her around the house when she was home or went with her on the forest paths when she went to pick berries or searched for wild honey. All day, he would hold her hand, or touch her body, or would kiss her lips and face.

As the months passed, she seemed to find his attentions wearisome and she begged for some time alone. But her beauty held him enthralled and her protests only increased his devotion. At last, she began to loath his touch and the thought of solitude began to seem like paradise to her. So, one day, when they were hunting for berries in the woods, she picked some unwholesome berries that her mother had told her never to eat and that evening she put these berries in her husband's food. He ate his dinner and was poisoned and was dead before dawn the next day. His wife buried his body behind her cottage, and she sang as she dug his grave because the solitude was to her the very essence of bliss.

I could see a smile on Bosie's face and he seemed to be suppressing a giggle.

When the second brother saw his oldest brother vanish in a blaze of golden light, he stepped toward the goddess and said, "I will have for my wife the cleverest woman in the world."

In an instant he was transported to a house in the city and he found waiting within a beautiful woman with a clear voice and a clever mind. The second brother asked his wife what he should do in the city and she advised him to become a merchant. She told him where he could buy pottery for little money and where he could sell it for much more. The second brother followed his wife's advice and soon began to make money. As the days passed, he found that whenever he followed her advice, he profited, and he soon began to grow rich. But as his purse grew heavier, he found a resentment growing in his heart. "I am nearly as clever as she is," he said to himself. And indeed, he had learned much by following her advice and had become the cleverest merchant in the city. "Why must she tell me what to do every day?" he began to mutter. "Am I not the man of the house?"

And the second brother built himself a mansion so large that he could hide from his wife whenever he wished for solitude. But his wife had formed the habit of giving him advice whether he wished it or no and she would wait for him in the mornings beside the front door to give him suggestions for that day's trades. The second brother's pride now bristled whenever she gave him advice and one morning he snapped: "Be silent woman! And be gone! I know how to do my job."

When the second brother returned home that night, he found no one at home but the servants. He asked them where his wife had gone, but they could not tell him. "Doubtless she will be back when her temper has cooled," he said to himself.

But his wife did not return, and the second brother was forced to conduct his business without her advice. At first, he prospered, but soon new merchants appeared in the city and they brought with them unfamiliar goods from far-away lands and the second brother did not know the value of these items. He overpaid for some of these goods and bid too little for others and soon began to lose money. The second brother took ever-more desperate gambles in the hope of regaining his fortune, but his judgement was poor and at last he lost everything and was reduced to selling his labor to whatever farmer would pay him. And he passed out of history and out of this story.

When the second brother disappeared in a flash of light, the goddess gazed at the youngest brother and said: "What is left for you is the most loving woman in all the world. Will you have her for your wife?"

"No thank you," said the youngest brother. "Let her marry who she will. I will not have her."

"And why would a mortal refuse such a gift from the gods?" demanded Athena.

"You have told me she is the most loving woman in the world," said the youngest brother. "Now I know her secret. There is no mystery to her. I prefer a woman whose secret I do not know. I would like a woman whose secrets take a lifetime to reveal. I may be trading happiness for mere adventure, but this is my choice."

"Now I have met the wisest man in the world," said the goddess. "It will be as you wish. I predict that you will find a woman whose secrets take a lifetime to reveal. But you may find they bring you happiness and heartache in equal measure."

"I will have it so," said the youngest brother.

The goddess vanished and the youngest brother walked back to his house. In time the youngest brother married. He found that his wife inspired in him love and anger and fear and joy and sorrow and contentment. Each of these he felt in turn and each of these feelings he inspired in her and both were satisfied. For each had found in the other infinite complexity and every day offered the possibility of surprise.

I brought my gaze back from the hills of Greece where I could see the youngest brother growing old with his bride and looked at Bosie. He was sleeping. His golden head was a vision on the pillow.

I drew the covers up to his chest.

Then I found my notebook in my traveling case and sat in an armchair to write down this tale. This trip has not been wasted if it produces such stories as these.

FIFTEEN

Dear Miss Darling:

Mr. Webb has fallen in love with me. I knew he would. It was inevitable. But I will tolerate the awkwardness that has invaded our friendship for the sake of our mutual work.

You probably suspect from what I just wrote that I am enormously conceited about my beauty. I don't believe I am any more conceited than any of my sisters, but I am aware that the type of woman I am—a freethinker, a social investigator, a woman who is confident or at least can feign confidence when required—is enormously attractive to a certain type of man and we are rendered even more valuable by our rarity. Mr. Webb has confessed that he has "never met anyone like me" and while he may have said this as romantic flattery, I know that it may be the literal truth. Mary Booth is probably the person most like me that he has met, and she is both older and married. If Mr. Webb has his heart set on marrying a socialist and a social investigator, he may find his prospects quite limited. And so, I concluded on our third meeting—or perhaps even as early as our second—that Mr. Webb would likely fall in love with me and that I would have to exercise all my charm to keep his friendship while rejecting his advances.

Mr. Webb is an odd mixture of confidence and timidity. Of his own abilities as a writer and a public speaker he is as confident as Disraeli. He speaks and reads both French and German because although his parents were poor shopkeepers, they managed to save enough to send their sons to study in Switzerland and Germany. He is a self-made man who studied at night at the University of London and King's College, won several competitive exams and earned scholarships for even more study. He has been called to the Bar and rose through hard work and sheer ability to a minor post in the Foreign Office. He is one of leading members of the Fabian Society and is perhaps their best writer. His tract *Facts for Socialists* sold twenty times the number of copies that the Fabians expected.

But I believe he is very inexperienced with women and his confidence vanishes when the conversation turns from political economy to affairs of the heart. Not that this happens very often. Some women may enjoy all the male attention that they can garner, but I get no pleasure from dashing men's hopes. I am all too aware of the pain of heartbreak and have no desire to inflict it on anyone else. I have tried to keep our conversations focused on our work and Mr. Webb is usually agreeable because he so enjoys being of use.

A word about the Fabians. I believe that I have mentioned before that they are not a mob of Jacobins and assassins. They merely desire to educate both the public and the political class in the necessity of doing away with capitalism. To this end, they write and lecture constantly and try to get the established political parties to adopt their policies. Permeation is an important word for the Fabians. They hope to permeate the parties with their ideas and so attain power without the necessity of any particular Fabian ever holding office. Getting credit for policy is unimportant to them if the correct policies are implemented. I find both their modesty and their industry to be admirable.

Mr. Webb represents the best of this little group. At our first luncheon at a modest restaurant, he impressed me with his breadth of knowledge and quick insight. I had brought along some maps related to Charles Booth's survey of the London poor and Mr. Webb looked them over and soon started to laugh.

"What is so funny?" I asked.

"Do you realize that this map destroys Thomas Malthus at a glance? Malthus argued that charity for the poor is self-defeating, because when the poor have enough to eat, they will breed like rabbits and their increased numbers will create an over-supply of labor which will drive down wages and thereby increase the numbers of the poor."

Mr. Webb showed me the map he was considering. He pointed to areas on it.

"But you have a map of London divided into areas marked by degrees of poverty and by birthrates. If what Malthus believed is true, then the poorest areas of London should have the lowest birthrates and the birthrates should increase as the populace becomes more prosperous. But the opposite is true! It is the poorest areas that have the highest birthrates, and the birthrate decreases as the wages of the population increase. Doubtless the poorest of the poor have no money for entertainment and so they amuse themselves in the oldest way they know, while their more prosperous cousins can afford a variety of entertainments."

Mr. Webb seemed delighted by this discovery and his enthusiasm was infectious.

"You've destroyed Malthus with one stroke! He's the excuse every rich man gives for refusing to help the poor.

When Scrooge talks about the surplus population, he is echoing Malthus. And now Malthus is exploded! Social investigation has knocked great gaping holes in his theories!"

How could I not like a man who so values my own work and who can see implications in it that I never imagined?

Mr. Webb endeavors to help me with my book on the co-operative movement, but I believe any facts he passed on to me were ones that he had gathered only a day or two before. The co-operative movement is associated with the farms in the north of England and the midlands and there is little awareness of it in London. But Mr. Webb was happy to hear my theory that the co-operative movement could prove useful as the economy changes from capitalism to socialism. Certainly, the farmers who jointly run stores in which to sell their produce are experienced in working with their neighbors for the common good, rather than competing with them in a way that drives down prices to their mutual ruin.

It was a necessity that I attend the Co-operative Congress in Glasgow and I impulsively invited Mr. Webb to come along. He accepted and we traveled to Scotland in a third-class train carriage, overly crowded with conference attendees and other travelers. The carriage was so crowded in fact, that there were seats only for the women and a few of the men. Most of the men were forced to stand, sit on the floor, or perch on their luggage as Mr. Webb did. Despite the discomfort, we chatted together and with other attendees for the entire trip and I gained an intimate knowledge of Mr. Webb's personal history as well as a feeling of comradeship with the various labor representatives who were going to the congress.

I will not bore you with detailed descriptions of the entire conference, but simply say that it was both informative and tiresome. Any organization with political ambitions is inevitably full of internal conflict and these squabbles produce interminable debates. When the arguments proved too excruciating, I would excuse myself and find an individual to interview about his experience of co-operation.

In the evenings, I would walk the streets of Glasgow with Mr. Webb. We tended to stroll to the outskirts of the city because the center was crowded with an overabundance of drunken Scotsmen and raucous conference attendees who seemed to feel that the tedium of their days must be compensated for with bacchanalian nights.

We were walking across the great bridge that is variously known as the Glasgow Bridge, or the Telford Bridge from the architect who designed it, or the Jamaica Bridge from the name of a nearby street. It is a wide stone bridge and it afforded us an admirable view of a beautiful sunset. When we stopped to look at the orange and pink clouds, Mr. Webb took my hands in his.

"Miss Potter," he said with a trembling voice. "We have known each other but a short while, but I can truthfully say that I have never met any woman who has impressed me as you have. Your intelligence, your aims and your good heartedness make you as one woman in a million. Both my mind and my affections have been stirred as never before. Our sympathies and our aims are so—

"Mr. Webb," I said, interrupting him. "Please do not go on. I respect you as a comrade and co-worker, but that is all.

If you value our friendship, say no more. I have given up all hopes for personal happiness. I have dedicated my life to my work."

"But why? Surely work and happiness are not opposed. One can have both. In fact, I am sure that personal happiness would inspire us to work harder. Common labor can become a joy if we were to have the right person by our side."

"I have reasons I do not wish to discuss. If you respect me and value our friendship as you claim, then you will avoid this topic and talk only of our work. In fact, I must insist on this. If you cannot meet these conditions, I will end our friendship and break all contact with you."

Mr. Webb looked alarmed at this prospect. "No. Do not say that. I can be a friend and a co-worker. I just—"

"Say no more, Mr. Webb. Let us enjoy the sunset."

We watched the sky for some minutes, but I doubt if either of us enjoyed it very much. Our friendship is now strained and yet I am loath to end it because Mr. Webb is so very useful to me and he is such a good-hearted soul.

The trip back from Scotland was a good deal less enjoyable than the trip going north.

What am I to do? I have extracted from Mr. Webb a promise to avoid the topic of his personal feelings and I hope that this will correct his behavior, but I have my doubts. We will have to wait and see if our work suffers, or if we can prove useful to each other's work without making each other miserable.

Sincerely,
Beatrice Potter

SIXTEEN

From Oscar Wilde's secret journal:

My Brighton holiday has become a nightmare.

No sooner did Bosie recover his health than I fell ill.

My hopes that he would sympathize because of his fresh experience with sickness were quickly dashed. He soon found me disgusting (his word) and made plans to amuse himself elsewhere.

As I lay in bed—exhausted from a recent bout of vomiting—Bosie scowled at the mirror as he buttoned his shirt cuffs.

"I've got a smudge of mud on my cuff! How could this have happened?"

He grabbed a towel and began frantically rubbing the offensive cuff.

"This is intolerable! I've been nowhere near mud or dirt. I always keep well away from passing horses or cabs. Whenever we walk together, I take the wall and you face the street. How could I get mud on my cuff?"

Bosie glanced at me. I was motionless in bed, waiting for nausea to subside.

"Oscar, you look like a corpse. A bloated, sweaty corpse."

"Thank you, I'm sure," I managed to say.

Bosie held up the offending cuff again.

"I think it's the staff. Some waiter or chambermaid who resents their lot in life. Who snuck in here while we were sleeping and smudged my shirt? They do that, you know. Petty revenge. The lower orders. They don't have the courage for a real revolution, so they carry out their little tricks in secret. To humiliate us. I'd complain to the management, but they'd only deny it."

"It was you," I said in a voice that was little more than a whisper. "Last night. You were drunk. You fell against a wall. Coming home. The wall was muddy."

"Did I? I have no memory of that. Oh well."

Bosie threw down the towel and began struggling with his tie.

"Stay with me."

I was angry with myself for the imploring tone in my voice, but illness had sapped my pride as well as my dignity.

"I'll be back this afternoon."

"I have nothing to drink."

"I'll have the hotel send up some lemonade. You'll be fine."

"Bosie stay. I stayed when you were ill."

"Yes. And look what happened to you."

He pulled open a drawer and held up my wallet. "I need a few notes. Oscar." He helped himself to my money. I made no word of protest.

"I'll be back this afternoon," said Bosie at the doorway. Try to feel better."

I heard the door closing. I couldn't decide if I wanted Bosie to return or to stay away forever.

All day I lay in bed, feeling the fever burn in me. I got up in the afternoon to use the bathroom and to splash water on my face and then staggered back to bed as a spell of dizziness overcame me.

Waves of self-recrimination swept over me. If I were home in Tite Street Constance would be there to nurse me. She would bring a cool towel for my head and would read to me from the newspaper or from whatever book I chose. She would forbid Cyril and Vyvyan from entering the room for fear of making them ill. They would wave at me from the doorway. I would wave back and my heart would fill with joy knowing that they were my sons.

I have wasted so much money on Bosie and so much time. Wasting money is bad, but wasting time is worse because time cannot be replenished. Why is my will so weak?

Such were the thoughts that chased one another through my feverish brain until sleep at last returned.

I woke in the dark burning with thirst. I could see some faint light in the window, but little else.

I started to sit up, but dizziness swept through me and I had to grab the edge of the bed to steady myself. I had packed some slippers, but in the dark I could not see my traveling case and I padded barefoot to the bathroom.

There was no drinking glass in the bathroom. Where could it have gone? Bosie might have misplaced it, but I could not find it anywhere in my room. I would have to go downstairs.

A gaslight burned low in the hallway. I hesitated. I knew I must look frightful in bare feet and with my sweat-matted hair and an expression of dull agony on my face. I almost retreated to my room, but the thirst burned my throat and I knew it was likely I would only encounter the hotel staff in the halls.

I padded slowly down the stairs, clutching the railing lest dizziness overcome me again. An ache throbbed between my ears and I wondered if I would have the strength to climb back to my third-story room.

At the bottom of the stairs, I could see a light burning in the hotel's sitting room. I walked to the doorway and peered inside.

Bosie was sitting in an armchair with a magazine in his hands and an open bottle at his feet. An empty glass rested on the table beside him.

"What time is it?" I asked.

Bosie casually looked up as if seeing me in a hotel sitting room in the wee hours was an everyday occurrence.

"It is one in the morning. Do you want some brandy?"

"No. I don't want brandy. I need some water."

"Well, don't look at me. I don't have any."

I stepped into the room. "What are you doing here?"

"I have a room here."

"You said you'd return in the afternoon."

Bosie turned a page in his magazine. "I was delayed. I think *Punch* needs a better artist, don't you? Who is this supposed to be—the Prime Minister?"

Bosie held up the magazine so that I could see the drawing.

"I need some water."

"Get it yourself, you lazy thing."

I could feel an anger growing inside me, hotter than my fever. "Why are you being so hateful?"

"I?" screeched Bosie. "I'm hateful? I've had an exhausting journey—to London and back in one day—on the most horrid trains. And I arrive at last at my hotel and I sit for one instant to glance at a magazine and recover my dignity and you appear like a wounded elephant, bellowing at me like I am a servant."

"You paid for the train with my money. You pay for this hotel with my money. You buy brandy with my money. And you have no gratitude. Get me some water."

Bosie threw the magazine at my face and I barely managed to block it with my hand.

"Get it yourself!" shrieked Bosie in a voice that I was sure could be heard all over Brighton. The look of fury on his face was so extreme that I was sure it was an expression seen mostly in asylums for the mad.

I staggered toward the hallway. By blind luck I found the kitchen and in the dim light found a glass that may or may not have been clean. I poured myself a glass of water. As I drank, I could feel my dignity flooding back into my body as if I was gulping something more essential than mere water. After I had drained the glass, I splashed some cooling water on my face.

I hurried back toward the stairs. I clutched the bannister and pulled myself up as fast as I could manage. My headache was gone, my dizziness was gone and I felt clearheaded for the first time in days.

I decided to lock myself in my room and not unlock the door until Bosie had left Brighton.

My foolishness has been made clear to me with a vividness that Saul on the road to Damascus would envy.

I will waste no more time and money on this spoiled child. I will return to my wife and sons and my work. I will repent of my foolishness and dedicate myself to my art.

I feel I have been set free.

I sense somehow that I have had a narrow escape. Although my reason tells me that I would have sacrificed nothing more than my self-respect had I reconciled with Bosie, I nevertheless have a feeling that the Angel of Death has passed over the Grand Hotel and that he would have alighted had he sensed Bosie in my room.

My illness seems to have made me morbid.

I will return to Tite Street and my family tomorrow and all my thoughts will be wholesome.

SEVENTEEN

Dear Miss Potter,

I very much enjoyed our trip to Glasgow, and I trust that you did as well. But I am haunted by our conversation on the bridge and all that was left unsaid.

I do believe that unless we help each other in the work of social reform that any love between us would count for nothing in the world. But to try to suppress the love in one's own nature is a folly for which I have no name.

There is no one except Shaw who has worked as hard for the Fabian Society as I have. And not even Shaw has my mania for the endless details and boring subtleties of economic theory. I know Marx better than the Archbishop of Canterbury knows his Bible. In short, I am a hopeless drudge. But even I know it would be a tragic mistake to sacrifice everything to intellectual work. You would smother the warmest parts of your nature and destroy not only your happiness but eventually the generosity of your spirit as well. I would rather see you abandon social reform altogether than see you amputate the love that is in your soul. I cannot believe you would commit this emotional suicide.

I ask only that you give me a chance. That you keep an open mind and an open heart. And we will let things alone and attend to our work and see what happens.

Sincerely,
Sidney Webb

EIGHTEEN

Dear Mr. Webb,

I thought that I had made it clear that I do not wish to discuss the personal nature of our friendship. A continued discussion of this topic can only be more painful to me. We must be comrades, or we shall be nothing.

I now regard my life as an instrument of public service, nothing more. I can live without feeling if I have my work. As a socialist, I should think you should applaud my commitment.

This will be the first time I have granted friendship to a man who has desired something else. But the motive which has led me to depart from what I conceive to be the safe and honorable course, has not been that I think there is any probability of a closer tie, but that I regard our work of greater importance than our happiness and that I feel the enormous help we may be to each other. You must realize that nothing can follow but comradeship. And if I feel that you are dwelling too much on lower feeling—or that our work is suffering—then I will withdraw even that.

Let us prepare for our Fabian summer holiday and gather the materials that we will need for our writing and say no more of other matters.

Sincerely,
Beatrice Potter

NINETEEN

From Oscar Wilde's secret journal:

I have given up my endless pleasures and resumed my duties as husband and father. I now go to bed at a reasonable hour and I get up when other people do. I eat in moderation and I drink less. I even smoke less. I should be expected to conclude this paragraph with an ironic sentence that undermines conventional expectations; I could write "The simple life is so exhausting." Or: "Nothing destroys happiness like healthy habits."

But the truth is that I feel better for keeping regular hours and forsaking excessive food and drink is not such a hardship as one might think. Even the dull routine of regular work has its compensations.

I have always been able to summon artistic inspiration when I needed it, but long hours of concentration entice the Muse to offer me her best gifts. One can easily build a castle in one's mind, but to live in it fully takes time and effort. And only by inhabiting it fully can one truly get to know the other guests. In short, my new play is coming along splendidly, and I cannot wait to get it into rehearsals.

I am a little worried about the plot. Or rather, I am worried about what Constance might think of the plot. The lying husband with a dark secret and the saintly wife who suspects nothing—will Constance suspect that my fiction mirrors my actual life? I hope she will not, and it is too late to change the story now.

But perhaps I am worrying about nothing. Every play has a character with a secret. Mine would be an odd thing indeed if it lacked one.

I do miss Bosie. At least I miss the good Bosie who longed for my approval for his poetry and who was quick to laugh and to smile and to kiss.

But the good Bosie has been eclipsed by the bad Bosie too often for me to return to him. The temper. The sneering. The spendthrift ways.

No. I will polish *An Ideal Husband* and I will get it on the boards as fast as possible.

I have an inkling for another play. Just a wisp of an idea. After *An Ideal Husband* is staged, I will develop it in earnest.

TWENTY

From the unpublished memoir of Bernard Shaw:

I have spent the past week bicycling down the lanes of rural England as I attempted to find an appropriate property that could be rented for our annual Fabian summer house. There is nothing unusual about this except that I was accompanied by Sidney Webb and a woman. A strikingly beautiful woman.

When Webb first announced that he was helping a woman who was an expert in political economy and who was writing a book on the co-operative movement, I imagined the female equivalent of Sidney Webb himself, a respectable personage more renowned for brains than beauty. But Beatrice Potter is a tall commanding woman whose only apparent defect is the lack of a sense of humor. At least, she seems to find my flirtations and gallantries annoying. In truth, she seems just as formal and correct as Webb and I can guess what has caused his stiffness in their friendship.

When Webb had returned from Scotland, I met him one night at a Fabian meeting. I suspected that he wanted more from Miss Potter than a dry friendship and I immediately began teasing him in the most affectionate manner.

"How did the Cockney Casanova fare in the north?" I asked. "Were the Scottish climes conducive to flirtation? Will Glasgow replace Paris as the city of romance?"

The look on his face was all the answer I needed.

"It can't be as bad as all that," I said.

"I told her about our Fabian summer house and how we were going to look for it on bicycles. She said it sounded like great fun. But after our painful discussions in Scotland, I don't know if I should even mention our summer holiday."

Webb's gaze strayed from my face at that moment. I turned and saw that Miss Potter had entered the meeting and was walking in our direction. This was not the first Fabian meeting that she had attended, but her appearance was still a novelty.

I was suddenly inspired. I turned to Webb and said in my sternest voice, "Sidney, that is a ridiculous notion. You must have more consideration for the fairer sex."

I turned and pretended to see Miss Potter for the first time. At the same time, I made a gesture with one hand of the kind that one makes when shooing chickens and Webb was intelligent enough to walk away.

"Good evening, Miss Potter," I said. "Please forgive Mr. Webb. He has gotten the foolish idea that you should accompany us on our bicycle scouting trip for our Fabian summer house. He may not have realized that I intend to bicycle all the way to Suffolk, a strenuous journey that should only be undertaken by bicycle experts in the best of health. You'll have to forgive his enthusiasm. Shall I make your excuses to him?"

Miss Potter bristled with indignation. "What makes you think I am not fit for such a journey? I have seen women bicycling all over London."

"Yes, but the dirt lanes of Suffolk are far more taxing than the civilized thoroughfares of London. You do not want to be miles from the nearest hansom cab when exhaustion sets in."

Miss Potter's expression would have suited a defiant goddess. "What is my mark of weakness for you, Mr. Shaw? My sex or my class?"

"Must I choose?" I asked. "They both have their merits."

Miss Potter's eyes grew wide as if she could not believe my impertinence. "I will accompany you and Mr. Webb to Suffolk and neither my sex nor my birth will hinder me."

She strode away with a confidence that Joan of Arc would have envied.

Sidney soon returned to my side. He had overheard this whole exchange.

"Oh, well done," he said.

When Webb and Miss Potter showed up at our appointed rendezvous on bicycles, I could see that she had lost none of her determination to prove indefatigable. And if the pace of our excursion tired her that day, she concealed it with apparent grace and Webb was more often the one lagging.

It occurs to me that some readers may not have yet ridden a bicycle. If not, I highly recommend that you try. I say in all seriousness that it is one of the great inventions of the nineteenth century. It is a very pleasant method of exercise and it makes places quite distant suddenly accessible at no expense and the frequent crashes and falls you will endure will improve your tolerance for pain immensely and will likely be a source of great amusement to all who observe you. I scraped my knees and elbows and even my face on the gravel more times than I can remember and yet I always spring up ready for another race, or demonstration of how to ride with one's feet on the handlebars.

The country lanes of Suffolk are ideal places for bicycle jaunts. There is seldom much traffic of either humans or animals, and you can hardly journey a mile in any direction without encountering enough scenic beauty to inspire a gallery of landscape paintings. Occasionally, a horse in a field spots me and challenges me to a race by dashing parallel to me on his side of the fence. I always accept such challenges and inevitably lose the race, but I acknowledge the superiority of my opponent with a salute as I pedal away from the scene of my disgrace.

This was of course a scouting expedition and Webb had brought alone a selection of addresses where rental properties could be found. Not every place proved to be appropriate. One house was so large and grand that I would not have been surprised to see the Queen emerge from the front door and I scowled at Webb to chastise him for wasting our time. But he was staring at Miss Potter and never noticed my scalding gaze.

Webb and Miss Potter attempted to negotiate with one farmer's wife for the rental of a well-appointed farmhouse. But as I rested against a tree munching an apple, two boys— apparently her sons—began throwing rocks at me. When one young rascal's stone bounced off my jacket, I stood, aimed and let fly with the apple. It bounced off the ruffian's forehead and he ran wailing to his mother. She shouted abuse at me and may have thrown my own apple at me—it went flying over my head—as I made my escape on bicycle. Webb refused to speak to me for two hours.

Finally, late on a Friday afternoon, we arrived at a farmhouse that was a little larger than we required, but which seemed as pleasant and scenic a location as I have ever rented. Webb and I talked to Miss Willot, the sturdy gray-haired owner, in such a manner as to drive down her asking price.

"It is very pretty, of course," said Webb. "But it is somewhat larger than what we had in mind."

"Our resources are limited," I said. "And we simply don't need this many rooms."

"It is a little further from London than we would like," added Webb.

"Mr. Webb and I will arrive by bicycle," I explained.

"And it is further from the village than is convenient," said Webb.

"I am sorry that we have wasted your time," I said.

At this moment, Miss Potter entered from the backyard with an enormous smile on her face. "Mr. Webb, have you seen the gardens—they're magnificent!"

"We'll take it," said Webb to Miss Willot.

I could have struck them in my annoyance, but that would not have been a grand beginning to our summer adventure. I settled for grinding my teeth.

And so, in a couple of weeks we will be ensconced in a Suffolk farmhouse, trying to write political papers that will change the future of England and trying to amuse each other in ways that intelligent people so often fail to do. Miss Potter is the mystery element in this experiment; we have not seen her like before.

In truth, I am worried for Sidney Webb. I have seen him disappointed in love before and it has been painful to watch. Miss Potter may have the power to wound him deeper than any of the others because she has so much in common with him and seems his equal in brains and ability. The very qualities that make her such a suitable writing partner for Sidney, will make her inevitable rejection of him that much more agonizing.

If there is a way for me to prevent such a catastrophe, I have not thought of it. I will keep trying.

TWENTY-ONE

Dear Lion,

    I will not be able to visit you until late in summer as I have been invited on a strange holiday that I hope will be amusing. If nothing else, it should provide me with some unusual stories.

    It began when Mr. Shaw invited me to see Oscar Wilde's new play *An Ideal Husband* at the Haymarket. It is quite witty and I was laughing merrily when I turned to my side and saw Mr. Shaw scribbling away in a notebook. For a moment I had the absurd notion that he was trying to write down all the dialogue as it was spoken and so preserve a record of the play for his future use.

    "What are you doing?" I asked.

    He refused to answer and merely kept scribbling.

    During the interval I confronted him. "Why are you taking notes during the play?" I demanded.

    "I am a critic," he said. "I am reviewing this play for *The Saturday Review.*"

    I laughed out loud at this. I don't know why it struck me as absurd that I should be accompanying a critic to a play. Perhaps because I thought he had some romantic interest in me and now I realized that he merely needed someone to keep him company while he did his job.

    After the play was over, Mr. Shaw walked me home and he explained to me why Mr. Wilde's play was so clever. I cannot remember all his arguments except he said that Mr. Wilde had the gift of making playwriting seem easy and that Mr. Shaw suspected that he had to work very hard indeed to make the play seem like little more than witty remarks strung together.

When we had reached my door, Mr. Shaw's conversation turned a little more serious.

"Sidney Webb says that you have made generous contributions to the Fabian Society. The Executive Committee is quite keen to have you."

"I warn you," I said. "I'm squeamish. In case you want me to sign my name in blood."

"No, that's the Masons. They rent the hall on Fridays. I was thinking of our Fabian summer house. Thanks to Sidney's Napoleonic decisiveness, this year our cottage has more guest quarters than the Winter Palace at Saint Petersburg."

"Mr. Shaw, is this an invitation?"

"In the hopes of saving your political soul, it is. I will be ensconced by the first week of June and ready to receive guests within a week. I warn you—we can be a dreary lot—reading and scribbling for hours on end."

"I'll be leaving for Rome in a week and I'll be there until the second week of June. Would the third week suit you?"

"Admirably. That should be just enough time for me to varnish your memory with a coating of fantasy."

"You're talking blarney now, Mr. Shaw," I said. "Not socialism."

"No, not blarney at all."

And he kissed me.

This is not a real romance. I am playing at romance. My heart is not at stake. Mr. Shaw is too much of a leprechaun to be a real lover.

So, this summer will be a holiday with the socialists. Am I too old to be doing such adventuring? Maybe.

But if I don't do it now, when shall I ever?

Sincerely,
Charlotte

TWENTY-TWO

From the unpublished memoir of Bernard Shaw:

My plans for my annual Fabian summer holiday have
taken an odd turn. Oscar Wilde will join me, Sidney Webb
and any other leading Fabians who care to make the trip to
Suffolk, in renting a summer cottage outside London, where
we will spend some weeks reading, writing and conducting
bicycle excursions to any local destination worth a glance.

I had no inkling of what to expect when I received an
invitation to lunch from Frank Harris, the editor of the
Saturday Review. Harris is a hearty man-about-town who
haunts the Café Royal and feasts there with any journalist or
literary figure that he considers good company. I used to
dine with him there regularly despite the over-priced salads,
but his constant delight in second-rate bawdy stories grew
tiresome and I soon found excuses to stay away. But the
short letter he recently sent me piqued my curiosity and
I joined him at the restaurant the next afternoon. After
toasting me on the success of *Arms and the Man,* Harris
placed the glass on the table, leaned back in his chair and
gestured to me. "Now, Shaw, I've got a favor to ask of you."

"I can't review any more plays than I am already.
I'm full up. I'm a critic, a playwright, a Fabian and a vestry-
man—four professions that demand the undivided energy
of ten men to do them justice. This camel is refusing any
more straws."

I attacked my over-priced salad with renewed appetite.

"I wasn't going to ask you to write," said Harris. "I was wondering if you and Webb are renting a Fabian summer headquarters this year."

This remark caused me to stop eating and stare suspiciously at him. "Yes, Webb and I and a few others. We're talking about a cottage in Suffolk. Why do you ask?"

"Do you ever have guests?"

"All the time. Most of the Fabian junta drops in at one time or another. Why? Do you want an invitation? I warn you; we keep a Spartan household. Vegetarians and teetotalers all."

Harris laughed. "No, I wasn't thinking of me. I was hoping I could persuade you to invite Wilde. I've invited him to join us today."

"Wilde? Oscar Wilde?"

"Yes."

"Invite him to our Fabian summer house?"

"Yes, do you know him?"

"Our families have had some slight connection for years. When I came to London, my first taste of society was at Lady Wilde's at-homes. I was a shy and ignorant boy and was probably only tolerated for the sake my sister Lucy, whom Oscar and his brother both adored."

"But can I persuade you to invite him? One Irish genius helping another."

"Is there something wrong with his health?"

"No."

"Nervous exhaustion?"

"No."

"Creditors plaguing him?"

"No more than usual."

"Then why on earth would he want to join a group of ascetic socialists in the country?"

Harris hesitated for a moment before speaking. "It would do him good to get away from the city just now."

"You're going to have to give me some reason. I'll have to tell my Fabian household something."

"Very well. You can make any excuse you like, but the real reason is to get him away from bad companions."

"Bad companions? You sound like a governess in a three-volume novel."

"I'm not worried about his morals. What a man does behind closed doors is his own business. But Wilde is flirting with scandal or worse. It's not enough that a man be discreet. His companions must be discreet as well. That's as much as I will say."

"I see." I munched my salad in silence for a few moments to test Harris's resolve to say no more.

Harris finally added: "I'd like to get him away from his usual haunts to where he can't be found."

"But on what pretext shall I invite him? I can't very well say: 'Harris thinks you are on the road to ruin and asked me to delay your journey.'"

Harris poured the last of the red wine into his glass. "Well, I don't know. Can't you—"

Wilde was suddenly standing beside Harris. He was dressed in a light blue suit that looked like the most expensive apparel in the restaurant. He rested a hand on the back of Harris's chair while gazing with apparent disapproval at his wine glass.

"Drinking as usual, Harris. Is the life of an editor as demoralizing as that? Or are you treating a troubled conscience with liquor to prevent the ghosts of a thousand murdered pages from rising up and haunting you?"

"Sit down, Oscar."

Wilde waited until the waiter appeared and pulled out a chair for him.

"Are you hungry?" asked Harris.

"No, I have dined. But a glass of champagne would be very pleasant."

Harris signaled the waiter and then ordered a bottle of Perrier-Jouet Brut '89. When the waiter had hurried off, Harris gestured toward me. "I believe you know Bernard Shaw."

"Of course," said Wilde. "My belated congratulations on your review of my play. It was the most astute and

perceptive analysis of a play that I've ever read. What was it you said? 'In a certain sense Mr. Wilde is to me our only thorough playwright. He plays with everything: with wit, with philosophy, with drama, with actors and audience, with the whole theatre.'"

I raised my eyebrows at being quoted so accurately. If any other man had repeated such praise, I would have thought him hopelessly pompous. But Wilde's good humor somehow made the outrageous into something amusing.

I said: "I should have added 'and with critics as well.'"

Wilde shook his head. "One cannot really play with critics. One can only make humble offerings to the gods and hope that the lightning will strike another man's house."

"Well, I'm not throwing any thunderbolts this afternoon."

The waiter appeared with a bottle of champagne and fresh glasses. Wilde and Harris each accepted a glass, but I waved the offered glass away.

"What shall we talk about?" asked Wilde, after he had sampled the champagne.

"Shaw and I were discussing his Fabian friends," said Harris. "But I suppose that wouldn't interest you."

"You do me an injustice," said Wilde. "Have you forgotten my socialist essay?"

I suddenly saw a possible way to help Harris. "Of course. I remember. *The Soul of Man Under Socialism!*"

"I'm flattered," said Wilde.

"Not at all. I thought it a pity we couldn't include it in our collection *Fabian Essays*. We thought it might sell a few hundred volumes and suddenly half of England was reading it. It did so unexpectedly well that we are thinking of doing a second volume."

"I wish you much success," said Wilde.

I now exchanged a glance with Harris. "And I'm suddenly wondering if I could persuade you to contribute an original essay to it."

Wilde smiled but waved a dismissive hand. "Oh, I'm flattered, of course. But socialist theory is hardly my forte. *The Soul of Man* was written on a whim and is not an event I ever expect to repeat. You must have any number of experts who have a greater command of fact and theory than myself."

"But none who could write so well. An hour of reading the average essay on socialism usually puts even the most fanatical anarchist to sleep. Socialism has greater need of wit than dogma. And if you had any questions on political economy you might consider visiting me in Suffolk. Sidney Webb and two ladies and I are renting our annual summer cottage. You would be welcome."

Harris nodded. "I think that's a capital idea. A change of scene for you, Oscar."

"I think not. I have certain responsibilities it would be heartless of me to ignore. I am working on a new play and my characters are desperately curious to find out what is to become of them."

Harris pointed at me. "Bring them along. And gather material for a new play. Satirize the Fabians, if Shaw doesn't beat you to it."

I decided to try obvious flattery. "It would be quite a coup for us to count Oscar Wilde in our ranks."

Wilde smiled but shook his head. "I am most grateful for the offer, but I must decline. I do wish to finish the play and—"

"Oscar! Oscar!"

For once Wilde moved quickly, turning in his chair to scan the restaurant for the person calling his name. He spotted a blond young man on the other side of the restaurant with a glass of wine in his hand.

"Excuse me, gentlemen," said Wilde, rising from his chair and striding toward the blond, young man.

The young man was dressed in a wrinkled tan silk suit, but he wore no tie. Seated at his table were two young men with smirking expressions on their faces and wine glasses in their hands. I could see that they had already finished one bottle and were well on their way to finishing a second. The blond young man stood up as Wilde approached.

"Bosie, keep your voice down," commanded Wilde.

"Oscar, I need money," said the man called Bosie in a voice loud enough to cause heads to turn.

"My dear boy, may I remind you that you are in a public restaurant."

"I'm not likely to forget. Do you what they charge for brandy? It's robbery." Bosie stepped closer to Wilde and lowered his voice to a confidential tone. I couldn't hear what was said, but the man called Bosie began obviously pleading with Wilde about something. Wilde took a step backward and I could overhear their conversation again.

"I think you've had enough, dear boy."

"It is only by having too much that one can discover how much is enough. William Blake."

Wilde nodded. "I know. I was the one who quoted him to you. But since you've raised the point, let too much be enough."

The young man gestured toward his table. "I've got two friends with me. Come join us, Oscar."

Wilde took another backward step away from Bosie. "I'm through with you, Bosie. I mean it this time."

"All right, I'll send them away. We'll have dinner alone."

"This absurd cycle of quarreling, repentance and forgiveness must end. I cannot tolerate any more scenes. They not only embarrass me, but they also exhaust me. I can never work when you are with me."

Bosie's face crumpled like a child about to cry. "I'm sorry. Truly."

Wilde remained unmoved. "There are offenses beyond forgiveness."

Bosie reached for Wilde's hand, but he backed away. Bosie then made an imploring gesture with open hands. "Oscar, I love you. Sometimes I don't know why I do things. But even when I'm hateful, I love you."

Some of the coldness left Wilde's face. "I know. But it is not enough. If I give you some money, will you go back to your friends and not make a scene?"

"Only if you come with me."

Wilde had begun to pull his wallet from his pocket, but now he pushed back. "Do you want the money or not?"

Bosie hesitated for only a moment. "Yes."

Wilde took out his wallet and gave Bosie a few notes. "At which hotel are you staying?"

"Good-bye, Bosie." Wilde turned his back on Bosie and began to walk away.

"I'll find you, Oscar!"

Again, Bosie's voice had become annoyingly loud, but Wilde ignored him and returned to our table. This time Wilde did not wait for a waiter but seated himself and then pulled out a silver cigarette case. He quickly lit a cigarette and then rearranged himself in his chair and assumed a position of languor. After puffing out a smoke ring, he finally seemed to relax.

"I'm sorry you saw that, gentlemen. The only excuse I can make for my friend's conduct is his unhappy family. He has suffered and so I indulge him more than I should."

Harris shook his head. "For friendship's sake, let me warn you that you are a terrible judge of character."

"But I never judge anyone by their character. Youth and beauty are far more reliable." This quip seemed to restore Wilde's good humor.

"Think, Oscar. That's all I ask."

Wilde smiled at Harris. "I have and you are right. A change of scene would do me good." Oscar looked to me. "If your offer is still open, I will join you in Suffolk."

"Splendid. Sidney Webb will be delighted that I have made such an illustrious convert."

Oscar tapped cigarette ash into a saucer. "Don't say convert. Say sympathizer. I warn you: I am no more likely to remain faithful to one creed than a bee is likely to be true to a single flower. The garden of philosophy is large and should be thoroughly explored."

"The cancer in society is deadly and should be thoroughly cut out. I am in the business of manufacturing scalpels. I can have no complaints as long as you bring your tools when you visit my workshop."

Wilde smiled. "My cutting wit, you mean."

Harris looked from Oscar to me and back to Oscar. "I never know what to think when I talk to you. When should I take you seriously?"

"Whenever I am joking," I said and to my great surprise Wilde said the same thing simultaneously. We stared at each other in such shock that Harris finally laughed at our startled expressions.

Shortly thereafter we went our separate ways.

What should I make of this encounter? I would think that Wilde's money problems might be inspiring Harris's concern, but the success of Wilde's new play makes that unlikely. Perhaps I will learn more this summer.

And so, Oscar Wilde will visit the Fabians. A very strange business—but it might be amusing.

TWENTY-THREE

From the memoir of Robert Ross:

I accompanied Oscar to the train station today to see him off on his trip to the Fabian summer house. I think it is decidedly odd for him to be taking a holiday with the Fabians, but I have Frank Harris to thank for that which means that, ultimately, I am to blame.

Oscar still has not confided in me what caused his falling out with Bosie, but I am content that it has happened. I can easily imagine Bosie losing his temper over some trifle and carrying on for such a ridiculous length of time that eventually even Oscar was offended.

Constance thanked me as Oscar was gathering his pocket handkerchief and she seems to assume that I personally arranged Oscar's estrangement from Bosie and then prompted Shaw to lure Oscar to the wilds of Suffolk.

"The boys have been so happy to have him home," she said with a smile. "He's been writing every day."

"I'm sorry he's going away again," I said.

"As long as he's not with Bosie, I know he'll be writing," she said. "When he concentrates, he can finish a play in no time."

Oscar appeared with Cyril and Vyvyan trailing behind. He hugged his sons and kissed Constance.

"Be good boys and obey your mother," he commanded them. "Robbie, find me a carriage, please. A four-wheeler. I have rather a lot of traveling cases."

It took a long while to find a carriage large enough to handle Oscar's cases and portmanteaus, but at last they were loaded aboard, and we reclined inside. Oscar lit a cigarette.

"Robbie, I feel that I have escaped some strange fate. These last two weeks at home have been such a relief."

"What kind of fate?" I asked, puzzled by his tone.

"I don't know. But it is good to be writing again. Good to see Cyril and Vyvyan. Good to see Constance."

Oscar blew smoke at the ceiling and then put his hand on my knee. "This mood will pass as all moods do and I'll crave a return to you and our friends and all my old habits. But for now, let me abide with the Fabians and study their strange customs."

"They're not a primitive African tribe," I said.

"I'm not sure they are not stranger," said Oscar. "I have heard rumors of vegetarianism and all manner of odd habits. In case these rumors are true, I have packed a few boxes of chocolates. For emergencies."

I laughed. It was good to see the old cheerful Oscar back.

"What constitutes an emergency?" I asked.

"Dinner."

This time, we both laughed.

"I find it quite peculiar that Bernard Shaw and Frank Harris conspired to draw me from London," said Oscar with an appraising look at me.

"Yes, it is odd," I agreed.

"Well, I'm sure they have their reasons."

We soon arrived at the station and as the driver unloaded Oscar's traveling cases, Oscar said his good-byes on the sidewalk.

"When I return, I expect to have a new play," he said.

"I look forward to it," I said.

"Thank you, Robbie. For everything."

Even now I'm not sure how much Oscar guessed.

TWENTY-FOUR

From the unpublished memoir of Bernard Shaw:

I have arrived in Suffolk with Sidney Webb and Miss Potter and we are settled in our picturesque farmhouse. We have arrived late enough in spring for many flowers to be in bloom. Nearby fields are dotted with red poppies and cowslip and oxlip border the lane that leads to the farm. I have seen some purple flowers as well, but I can't remember if these are pasqueflowers or dog-violets.

It took some days to bicycle here and I have been slowly accumulating fragments of Miss Potter's biography. As a female social investigator, she is unusual, but she becomes even more remarkable when one is aware of her social position. She is the daughter of a wealthy railroad promoter and the eighth of nine sisters. All her older sisters have married and so she must have a formidable conscience to avoid their example and, instead, to dedicate herself to improving the world. She was a rent collector in Katherine Buildings, one of those government-sponsored blocks of flats dedicated to improving the lives of the poor. As rent collector, she was responsible for separating the industrious, sober members of the working class from their lazy, drunkard brethren and allowing only the former a place in her building. This must be a difficult task for those familiar with the working class; I find it hard to imagine how a woman of breeding could do such work. Miss Potter may have seen more of the East End than I have, despite all my soapbox speechifying. She is modest about her accomplishments, but she may be an even more extraordinary individual than Sidney Webb.

She is also a hardy soul to bicycle for so long a journey without complaint. Webb would ask to stop and rest on occasion, but Miss Potter only permitted herself to ask how much of the journey remained at the end of each day's ride. But we were all of us hot and weary when we arrived in the afternoon at the farm.

The farm is no longer in operation and I take it that the farmer died sometime in the past two years. The barn is unused, and we have stored our bicycles in it. Mrs. Willot has apparently found that renting the farm to Londoners every summer provides her with enough pocket money to get by.

The house itself is a sizable stone structure with thick ivy-covered walls. The kitchen and dining room are the center of the house and these are by far the largest rooms. There is a large parlor, but judging from the dust that has accumulated in the corners, it has not seen much use of late. The numerous bedrooms are all relatively small. If there were a master bedroom, I have no idea how to identify it. I have chosen an east-facing bedroom as I hope the rising sun will wake me in the mornings, although the bedroom windows are small and no light shines directly on the bed.

The dining room table where much of our writing will be done fulfills all my expectations. It is large and sturdy without being either excessively rough or obviously beautiful. It is composed of heavy smooth boards and will not move even when I lean all my weight upon it.

There is also a wooden table in the garden. This is where we first rested after arriving.

Webb had corresponded with Mrs. Willot and he had a map that showed a footpath through the trees and fields to the local village.

"We should have an expedition this afternoon to the village to buy food," I announced. I was far too tired to be eager for such an expedition, but I knew I would never stir from the farm unless I committed myself. "Vegetables, milk, cheese and bread."

That is just what Webb and I did. Miss Potter stayed at the farmhouse to put fresh sheets on the beds while we hiked to the village and then staggered back with carrying bags full of supplies.

I made a vegetable soup for that evening's supper and we ate it with brown bread at the table in the yard.

"We should hire a cook," said Miss Potter.

"It's not that bad," I said.

"I'm sorry. I'm not insulting your soup," she said and then scowled as she realized I was being facetious.

"Mrs. Willot said there are women in the village who would be willing to cook," said Webb. "We just need to find them and interview them."

"Be sure they are used to vegetarian cooking," I reminded him.

We were all bone-weary from our bicycle riding and we retired early that night. I opened the window as I always do to let in the fresh air, and I trusted that the window was high enough off the ground to discourage stray cats from exploring my room.

The next morning, we made porridge and as Webb and Miss Potter ate, I read to them from a socialist essay.

"The chief advantage that would result from the establishment of socialism is, undoubtedly, the fact that socialism would relieve us from that sordid necessity of living for others, which, in the present condition of things, presses so hard upon almost everyone. Now and then, in the century, a great man of science, like Darwin; a great poet like Keats; a supreme artist like Flaubert, has been able to isolate himself, to keep himself out of reach of the clamorous claims of others and so realize the perfection of what was in him, to his own incomparable gain and to the incomparable and lasting gain of the whole world."

Webb looked puzzled. "That is a new argument: socialism as a basis for individualism. It doesn't seem to be quite your style."

"It isn't," I said. It's from Wilde's essay *The Soul of Man Under Socialism.*

"Is he a socialist?" asked Miss Potter.

"Not yet, but I have hopes," I said. "And if we can refrain from descending upon him like a pack of wild missionaries discovering a lonely cannibal, we might be able to convert him.

"Very well," said Webb. "You and Miss Potter can supply the charm and I'll supply the doctrine."

That afternoon Webb and I hiked back to the village to purchase the supplies that we had forgotten the day before and to begin inquiries for a cook. We were directed to one pleasant young woman who lost all enthusiasm when told that we needed a vegetarian cook.

"No meat?" she said in an astonished voice. "If all you eat is bread then you don't need a cook."

I tried to assure her that vegetarians eat more than bread, but she resisted such radical ideas.

It was later in the week that the postman finally brought us our first batch of mail. Webb and I were having our lunch at the table in the garden when Miss Potter appeared with a handful of letters.

"A letter for Shaw. A letter for me from my sister. And two letters for Webb."

"Your charm and beauty must have converted the postman to get such a socialist distribution of mail."

Miss Potter always scowls when one mentions her beauty or hints that males may be attracted to her. I try to do it at least once a day.

The handwriting on the envelope that Sidney Webb was holding looked familiar.

"Who is that from?" I said reaching for the envelope.

"Bertha Newcombe," he said.

I pulled back my hand as if a snake had tried to bite it.

"What? Is she writing you now?"

"She wants my advice," said Webb, scanning the letter.

"She wants you to plead her case with me."

"She is a woman with a broken heart looking for a word of hope," he said.

"Don't give her one," I said. "A soft lie would be crueler than the hard truth."

"What do you consider to be the truth?" asked Miss Potter.

"The truth is she is wasting her affections on me. She has no idea what to do with me except that she would like to tie me like a pet dog to the leg of her easel and have me make love to her when she is tired of painting."

"She wants to marry you," said Webb.

"She wants to stretch a few delightful days until they become a lifetime of tedious years. I give a woman the gold of my personality and she insists on owning the dross. And when I point out the foolishness of this, she changes from Florence Nightingale into Grendel's Mother. Is this sensible? Sidney?"

"I am not experienced enough in affairs of the heart to advise you," said Webb. He was opening his other letter and avoided looking at either myself or Miss Potter.

I opened my own letter and saw immediately that it was from Miss Payne-Townshend.

"She can't wait until Friday! The green-eyed one is arriving today! She can't wait to see my impish face. She says my magnetic field would draw her here from the ends of the earth."

Miss Potter snatched the letter from my hand. "She does not say that!"

"She has gone to a great deal to avoid saying it, but her hand betrays her. The slight trembling with which she writes my name. That quavering 'S' is as eloquent as any ten-page confession of love."

Miss Potter was reading the letter. "She says she is recovering from a head cold. She probably sneezed."

"If she's caught cold, it's from too many midnight walks whispering my name to the stars."

Miss Potter scowled at me. "When you talk about socialism you are the most practical person. But whenever the subject is women your talk becomes nonsense."

"Dear sensible Miss Potter, how would you talk if your letter was from a favorite beau? Would you say anything at all? Would anyone know if that iceberg heart was melting?"

From Miss Potter's expression I wondered if I had gone too far, but Webb spoke up and changed the subject.

"Old Hutch is dead." He was staring at his letter.

"What?" I asked.

"Henry Hunt Hutchinson is dead. Old age and infirmity were too much for him. He has blown his brains out."

"Who was he?" asked Miss Potter.

"An eccentric solicitor. I never met him in the flesh. I only know him from the enormous cheques he used to send the Society. I have been appointed one of his trustees. He has left the Fabian Society ten thousand pounds."

"Ten thousand pounds?" I said in astonishment.

"Ten thousand pounds?" echoed Miss Potter.

Webb held up the letter. "That's what it says."

"Who would have thought the old man to have so much quid in him?" I said. "We're halfway to Utopia."

"We must spend this wisely," said Webb.

"We could sponsor a whole new series of lectures," I said. "Bring the Fabian doctrine to the far reaches of England."

"Maybe," said Webb. "I want to think on this. No hurry."

"On what train is Miss Payne-Townshend arriving?" asked Miss Potter.

"She doesn't say. However, her coming must be prepared for. I shall put on my good suit."

Webb asked: "Why? It looks exactly like that one."

"The cuffs are less frayed."

But before I could change, we heard the clatter of horses' hooves and a four-wheeler came into view.

TWENTY-FIVE

Dear Lion:

I have met the playwright Oscar Wilde. He is as charming and clever as one would imagine from seeing his plays.

I boarded a first-class railroad carriage for the journey to Suffolk and my Fabian holiday and I noticed Mr. Wilde reading a newspaper. I recognized him from his curtain speech at his play *An Ideal Husband*. It is perhaps not quite proper for a lady to introduce herself to a strange man, but I always have been unconventional and we were to be spending some time together at the Fabian summer house and so our meeting was inevitable.

"Mr. Wilde?" I asked. "May I talk to you? I am sorry for disturbing you when you are reading your newspaper."

"My dear lady," said Mr. Wilde with a smile. "Not interrupting newspaper readers is quite unforgiveable and contributes to the national plague of melancholy which afflicts so many of us. Left to my own devices, I might have read the entire front page and suffered any number of ghastly effects."

"My name is Charlotte Payne-Townshend and I am a friend of Bernard Shaw. I believe we share a destination. At any rate, I recognized you from the opening night of your latest play which I attended with Mr. Shaw."

"Miss Payne-Townshend, please sit down. I am forever in your debt. Obviously, your charming presence soothed the breast of the fiercest critic in London. You will have to attend all my openings."

I seated myself near Mr. Wilde and we talked for the entire trip to Suffolk. He is a tall man and a large one. I would not call him fat, but he is fleshy and some exercise would do him good. He dresses very well and he wore a suit of the palest gray color that I do not believe I have ever seen on another human being. He asked permission to smoke and once I had given it, he took out a silver cigarette case and smoked for the entire trip.

Mr. Wilde can be amusing without ever saying anything of importance. He is so fond of paradoxes and epigrams that it is hard to know what he really believes.

When the conversation inevitably turned to Ireland, Mr. Wilde and I were of one mind: Ireland is a wonderful country best left behind.

"May I be so rude as to ask how you managed to remove Ireland from your voice?" I asked.

"Oh, but I did not remove Ireland," he said with a smile. "I added Oxford."

A few weeks spent in Mr. Wilde's company should prove entertaining.

Sincerely,
Charlotte

TWENTY-SIX

From Oscar Wilde's secret journal:

I had been second-guessing my decision to accept Bernard Shaw's invitation even before I set out for Suffolk, but meeting Miss Payne-Townshend on the train did much to allay my fears. She is Irish lady of about forty and is hardly the usual sort that one would expect to find hobnobbing with the Marxists and radicals of the Fabian Society. She apparently has enough money to be a woman of leisure and she seems to have spent much of her life traveling around Europe in the best society. I fancy that I might know Paris better than Miss Payne-Townshend, but in any other European capital she would be the expert and I the novice.

Although she is undoubtedly a lady, I suspect she has a disposition that inclines her toward unconventional opinions. Her friendship with Mr. Shaw is evidence of this; he is famous for preaching against unearned incomes and yet his radicalism does not repel her as it would most members of her class. Her boldness in introducing herself to me on the train is another indication. Certainly, a woman traveling by herself would learn to disregard some inconvenient social conventions, but there are still a few who would frown at her daring.

We both recognized that the other was an odd choice for a Fabian summer party and Miss Payne-Townshend had the grace to find the humor in the situation.

"I once wrote an essay on socialism in a moment of political passion," I confessed. "I daresay that Mr. Shaw hopes I will repeat that feat and that I will become one of the stable of horses that he hopes will pull the Fabian Society down the road to political power."

"I take it that you have no intention of becoming any such thing," she said with a smile.

"The Fabian muse haunts the lecture hall. My muse dwells in the theatre. Mr. Shaw told me that he and his comrades spend their days reading, writing and bicycling and I found his emphasis on writing appealing. Suffolk is sufficiently distant from civilization that the theatres and restaurants of London will not be temptations. In short, I hope to complete a play and return to London ready for a new production."

I leaned toward Miss Payne-Townshend to imply confidentiality.

"I hope you will keep my secret from Mr. Shaw and his friends. It may be amusing to see them exercise all their persuasive powers on me."

Miss Payne Townshend smiled like a schoolgirl. "Your secret is safe with me."

"And what about you? What treasure do you hope to steal from the Fabian vault?"

"I want a useful life," she said.

She said this with such simplicity that my next jest died on my lips.

When we arrived at the station, Miss Payne-Townshend took charge with such confidence that I became her instant admirer. She hired a carriage and found men to transfer all our luggage from the train to the carriage and she determined that the driver knew the area sufficiently to get us to our destination without getting lost.

When we were relaxing in the carriage, I expressed my admiration.

"You did that so efficiently I believe you could supervise the building of a bridge over the English Channel."

"I've travelled around Europe with my mother so often that I could hire a carriage in French, German, or Italian," she said. "One only needs confidence."

"Indeed."

Twenty minutes later we arrived at a rustic farmhouse. Mr. Shaw was waiting for us. With him was a short man squinting through pince-nez and a strikingly tall auburn-haired woman with a beauty that could seem severe or inviting, depending on whether she was smiling or not.

"Hullo!" called Shaw.

"We just got your letter saying you were coming today," said the short man.

I climbed out of the carriage and offered Miss Payne-Townshend my hand. She climbed out of the carriage and smiled at Mr. Shaw.

Shaw took a moment to whisper some private greeting to her, then turned to me and shook my hand.

"Mr. Wilde, allow me to introduce you to Sidney Webb. He is named for Sidneous, the Etruscan god of committees. And this is Miss Beatrice Potter."

Miss Potter favored me with a smile. "We're delighted that you could join us. Mr. Shaw has told us so much about you."

"Everything good, I hope," I said.

"Of course," said Miss Potter.

"I am relieved," I said. "I live in fear of gaining a bad reputation. They are so hard to live up to."

"The only reputation I've given you is for saying things like that," said Shaw.

"Miss Potter, I didn't know the Fabian Society boasted any beautiful women."

Miss Potter looked thoroughly offended. "I assure you that I am just as serious a socialist as your friend Mr. Shaw."

"And I assure you that I can produce just as much Irish blarney as your friend Mr. Shaw," I said. "I am sorry if I offended."

Miss Potter looked chagrined. "No, I should apologize. I have never taken compliments gracefully."

"Flattery which is amusing to an Irish ear often annoys an English one."

The driver had by now unloaded a small pile of traveling cases and portmanteaus. Shaw looked at the growing pile in surprise.

"Charlotte, why so many?"

"Those are mine," I said. "The summer heat often requires a change of clothes."

Mr. Webb stepped in front of me. "Follow me, Mr. Wilde and I'll show you to your room. It overlooks the garden."

I followed Mr. Webb toward the house.

"And what wonders does the garden hold?" I asked. "Will dew-diamonded daffodils beckon to me in the morning sun? Do chrysanthemum and delphinium parade themselves in homage to the beauty of youths turned to statues by jealous gods?"

"No," said Mr. Webb. "But there's a thermometer outside your window."

This was a comic anti-climax so suited to a Shaw play that I laughed out loud.

TWENTY-SEVEN

Dear Lion,

    I have arrived in Suffolk and have a room of my own in the farmhouse that Mr. Shaw, Mr. Wilde, Mr. Webb and Miss Potter will call home for the next few weeks.

    I had met Mr. Webb and talked with him before, but my initial impressions are being confirmed by prolonged conversations with him. He is a very bookish man of the lower classes who has risen above his allotted station in life by intelligence and hard work. He is less flamboyant than Mr. Shaw and I suspect that he calculates very carefully what he says to me in order that I might continue my financial generosity toward the Fabian Society. Perhaps this cynical view does an injustice to a man who is naturally formal and polite, but his conversation is so relentlessly about Fabianism and political economy I can't help thinking that he regards every human being as merely a potential ally or foe. I believe he is essentially good-hearted, but he does frequently condescend toward the very people that his political policies would benefit. In short, he believes in working for the good of the laboring classes without having any great respect for their intelligence or wisdom.

    Miss Potter is from a station in life far above Mr. Webb's, but she has essentially arrived at the same intellectual destination that he has. In many ways, she is like a female version of Mr. Webb, although she would be shocked if I said this to her. I believe she takes life too seriously and she would be happier if she could develop her sense of humor. I suspect she has little tolerance for human weakness, in others or in herself and this contributes to her discontent with the world.

Mr. Shaw continues to play the romantic fool. After I arrived at the farmhouse with Mr. Wilde, Mr. Shaw helped me bring my cases to my room. It is a narrow, almost Spartan room, but there is a writing desk, albeit one of the smallest I have ever seen.

Let me recount some of the nonsense Mr. Shaw and I say to each other so that you can see how foolish I've become.

"Alone at last," he said. "Now I can say hello properly and hug you till all your ribs have cracked." He did indeed hug me and kiss me. "Look at those ears of yours. They don't look any larger, yet they heard me calling all the way to Rome. Amazing. Wondrous."

"I have been terribly wicked," I said.

"What did my angel do? Did you purchase the Vatican and give it to the poor? Is his Holiness roaming the streets looking for a flat?"

"Stop. I don't like jokes about my money. I can't help it if my father was rich."

"I am sorry. I interrupted your confession."

"I lied to Miss Potter. I told her it was guilt over my idle life that brought me here."

"Am I about to flattered? Are you going to turn the tables and shower me with compliments? Fill my head with such starlight and moonshine that I won't be able to do any useful work for a week?"

"I know better than to think that anything I could say could stop the writing machine. In fact, I shall help you increase your production."

I opened a case on the writing desk and revealed a typewriter. I took the typewriter out of the case and placed it on the desk. I took a sheet of paper from my suitcase and inserted it into the typewriter. I struck the keys with some dexterity, typed for half a minute and then passed the sheet to Mr. Shaw who read it aloud.

"I didn't like the thought of spending the whole summer idly watching you and Mr. Webb and Miss Potter scribbling away. So, I have been practicing my typing. I've gotten quite good."

Mr. Shaw smiled at me. "That is remarkable. But is scribbling truly spelled with a 'Z ?'"

I snatched the paper from him and found that the word was spelled correctly. He bowed to me.

"I apologize. I am astonished. I was afraid I was going to have to send my manuscripts to Miss Dickens in London to be typed. Miss Dickens is the granddaughter of the great novelist himself and should be used to prolific writers, but my blizzard of paper has left her secretly wishing I'd fall off my bicycle and break my writing arm."

"Your description of those bicycles frightens me," I said." They sound dangerous."

"And so they are."

"Do you ride them often?"

"We ride every afternoon, weather permitting. You'll adore it. In a fortnight you'll be as brown as a Chilean and as fit as a mountain climber."

"I don't have a bicycle."

Mr. Shaw smiled at me, beckoned me to follow and ran from the room. I followed him and he scampered out the kitchen door and dashed to the barn. When I entered, I found him holding a bicycle. Three other bicycles were leaning against the wall.

"I've bought you a second-hand Osmond. I told Webb that I refuse to perform any more spectacular accidents without a properly sympathetic nurse at hand. Miss Potter merely shakes her head when she sees me lying in a heap and says that it is my own fault for standing on my head when I should be looking where I am going."

I stepped closer to him.

"I missed the magic of your voice in Rome. When I read your letters, I could hear it, but I wanted it in my ears and not just my imagination. I had to see you."

His smile vanished. "Beware that word 'had.'"

"You needn't worry that I am going to compromise my independence," I said. It is a habit far too ingrained to change."

"Good. Two people can dance only when they stand on their own feet."

"And can you dance? You never told me."

"There was never a family as musically inclined as mine. My mother came to London in pursuit of her music teacher and she teaches music at a women's college. My sister Lucy is a professional singer. The Shaw hasn't been born whose soul doesn't swim in music."

"I didn't ask about music, I asked about dancing."

"The dance is the sister of music. In fact, I can hear it now."

"What?

"A waltz. A bit of foolishness I composed at the piano one evening. Someone must be playing it far away. Hear it?"

"No."

"It's getting louder. Dum, dum, dum, dum. Yes, it's definitely my tune. The Fabian Waltz. Dum, dum, dum, dum, dum . . ."

Mr. Shaw hummed a passable waltz. I am not a music critic as Mr. Shaw formerly was, but I cannot remember hearing the piece before. Mr. Shaw swept me into his arms and we waltzed through the dust motes dancing in the sunbeams that shone through the boards of the barn.

"I shall write a new play: *The Waltzing Socialist*. A green-eyed millionairess meets a devilishly dashing socialist vagabond and is entranced by his hypnotic waltzing."

"How will it end?" I asked.

"Tragically. He falls in love with Wagner and never waltzes again."

"You'll have to come up with a better ending than that."

"How do you think it should end?"

But at that moment he twirled me with such speed that I could only laugh.

Have you ever heard of a grown woman indulging in such nonsense? No one can accuse me of not having a sense of humor when I willingly participate in such foolishness.

But now I must learn to ride a bicycle. I have truly entered my second childhood.

Sincerely,
Charlotte

TWENTY-EIGHT

From Oscar Wilde's secret journal:

If tonight's meager supper was an indication of things to come, I may have made a tragic mistake in coming here. Mr. Shaw served us a vegetable soup with brown bread, a meal that Mr. Webb hinted was the same as the previous dinner he had eaten. There was no butter or honey for the bread and no salt or pepper for the soup. I am reminded of those Biblical hermits who lived in the wilderness and who subsisted mainly on locusts.

No one else mentioned the meagerness of the fare and I very much fear I have fallen among a strange group of ascetics who take pleasure in their own deprivations. This unnatural state of affairs cannot continue and eventually some must rebel against Mr. Shaw's austere regime or we will be reduced to devouring each other, like the luckless sailors in Gericault's *The Raft of the Medusa*.

Fortunately, my prophetic intuition warned me of this danger, and I have secreted in my belongings several boxes of Belgian chocolates which proved to be literally life-saving tonight. Often, I prefer the mildly bitter taste of dark chocolate, but after tonight's hellish repast, I craved the sweetness of milk chocolate and I ate a half dozen before my reason reasserted itself and I vowed to ration my provisions. Considering the number of days I expect to abide here and the number of chocolates remaining in each box, I may only eat one and a half chocolates each day. This is scarcely enough to sustain life and I must find a local source of some ambrosial pleasures.

Before supper Miss Payne-Townshend gave us all a display of her newfound skill at typing. It is exceedingly odd that a woman of her station should master such an arcane skill, but Mr. Webb and Miss Potter were impressed. Miss Payne-Townshend told us during supper how she was attempting to change her life.

"It's your own fault, you know. All you Fabians. You're worse than any clergyman for imposing a sense of guilt. You've ruined my life. My carefree good-for-nothing life. Good Society. The Right People. They never seemed so useless before. And worse than useless—boring. I'm not saying I wouldn't enjoy riding in the Italian hills again or sailing on the Bay of Naples. But endless weeks of idle gossip can be just as tiring as a speech on economic theory."

Miss Potter is probably the person of our group who is the closest to Miss Payne-Townshend's station in life and she immediately agreed.

"I know exactly what you mean. When I was young, my sisters and I were taken to London every year for the social season in the hope of finding us husbands. I was as breathless and giddy receiving an invitation as any girl could be. But I have seen so much and done so much and become such a different person that I now look on those years as wasted."

Miss Payne-Townshend then expressed her own admiration of Miss Potter.

"I don't think I could transform myself as you have. To work in the worst slums of London one day and then give evidence before Parliament the next—I don't know which would frighten me more."

"I am frequently terrified," said Miss Potter." But if I ever feel timid going into a roomful of people, I say to myself: 'You're the cleverest member of the one of the cleverest families of the cleverest class of the cleverest nation in the world, why should you be frightened?'"

Miss Payne-Townshend spent much of the meal discussing Mr. Shaw's book *The Quintessence of Ibsenism* with him. Miss Potter and Mr. Webb talked about the co-operative movement and the structure of a book that Miss Potter is writing. Like the food, the conversation of the Fabians is strange fare and it wasn't until Mr. Webb offered to read Karl Marx to Miss Potter that the conversation turned to anything resembling humor.

"We can read Marx for an hour or two each morning," said Mr. Webb. "And when Marx grows too tiresome, I have a book of poetry by Dante Gabriel Rossetti."

"I don't know that I appreciate poetry," said Miss Potter. "I always have the urge to translate it back into prose."

This struck me as one of the oddest things I have ever heard anyone say about poetry and I wondered why Miss Potter wishes to avoid hearing poetry from Mr. Webb.

"Do you remember me trying to teach you German by reading Marx?" Mr. Webb asked Mr. Shaw.

"One does not easily forget Cockney German," replied Mr. Shaw. "But Marx was never meant to be read. Marx was meant to be dropped on the heads of capitalists from the roofs of tall buildings."

This remark caused laughter and smiles. I am glad to see that the Fabians can joke about their own heroes.

After eating my chocolates in my room, I emptied my traveling bags and placed my clothes in a tall bureau. In the top drawer someone had placed a copy of *Fabian Essays in Socialism*. What a thoughtful gift. I began reading the book in bed and fell instantly to sleep.

The next morning, I awoke unusually early; it may have been the gnawing worm of hunger that woke me.

I looked out the window at the fingers of sunlight caressing the fields, but who shall appear but Mr. Webb. He used a stile to climb over a fence and then walked across the field and disappeared into the trees.

I know there are some exceedingly odd souls who walk in the mornings for their health, but a man strolling for pleasure would likely stick to the roads and lanes. Tramping across fields would not only be more difficult, but would greatly increase the chances of soiling one's shoes.

So, Mr. Webb has a destination. Where could he be going?

TWENTY-NINE

Dear Lion,

The best part of my day is the afternoon when four of us go exploring on bicycles. Mr. Shaw, Mr. Webb and Miss Potter spend the mornings writing and reading in such a dedicated fashion as to inspire my admiration. Mr. Wilde never emerges from his room until almost noon, but if he is embarrassed by his sloth, he hides it well.

I spend my mornings walking, or reading, or writing letters like this one. Mr. Shaw, Mr. Webb and Miss Potter take turns making breakfast and this usually results in overly-thick porridge (Mr. Shaw's favorite), apples and bread (Mr. Webb's preference), or some form of underdone or burnt pancakes or drop scones (Miss Potter is hopeless as a cook). I mentioned to Mr. Shaw that I could find and hire a local cook, but he claims to have the situation well in hand and I eagerly await the arrival of someone with skill in the kitchen.

It may be my imagination, but I suspect that Mr. Wilde also is less than happy with the quality of our meals. He smiles politely when food is discussed, but he eats little of the soup and it looks like he finds chewing the thick brown bread a chore.

"The vegetable soup is my own recipe," said Mr. Shaw.

"Yes," said Mr. Wilde. "I can taste the spirit of Fabianism."

After luncheon, everyone but Mr. Wilde sets out on bicycles to explore the countryside. I find exercise invigorating. Any inclination to sleep vanishes once I begin peddling.

Of course, Mr. Shaw had to teach me how to ride and his encouragement took the form of describing the horrific accidents that awaited me once I had mastered the craft of bicycling. He also predicted that mastery would arrive suddenly, and this is how it turned out to be.

"One does not gradually learn to ride," he said. "One is perfectly hopeless for a while and then suddenly one is miraculously riding as if you had been born on a bicycle. The switch happens in an instant and is permanent. The acquisition of this skill will make possible an endless number of excursions and an infinite number of accidents."

And so, it proved. After a morning of frustrated attempts, I sat on the bicycle after luncheon and discovered that I could ride as if I had been doing it all my life.

Riding past the farms of Suffolk is great fun. Cows look at us from their fields and farmers sometimes stare as if they have never seen a bicycle before. Perhaps they haven't.

Mr. Webb and Miss Potter ride in moderation; they neither race ahead nor fall behind, but keep a steady pace. Mr. Shaw, on the other hand, seems to be recreating his boyhood, or is inventing one he never had. He races ahead whenever possible and rides with his feet on the handlebars and loves to come up behind a cow whose back is to us and startle the dumb beast. He rides beside farmers' wagons and pets the horses and annoys the farmers who fear the consequences of having their horses startled.

This foolishness has resulted in one accident. We crested the top of a hill and looked at the downward slope before us. Mr. Shaw pushed off, then propped his feet on the handlebars and let gravity and the slope increase his speed until he was rocketing down the lane at the velocity of an express train. Unfortunately, a flock of geese appeared in the road at the bottom of the hill. Mr. Shaw noticed the flock a second too late and he took his feet off the handlebars and applied the brakes. The bicycle stopped instantly, and Mr. Shaw was propelled through the air, over the handlebars and into the lane. The geese flew around like mad things and the chorus of angry honking was so loud I thought the whole flock was going to attack him.

We hurried down the hill, fearing the worst. But Mr. Shaw was already on his feet, saying: "I'm all right."

In truth, his trouser knees were torn and I may have seen some blood on his knee, but Mr. Shaw was determined to be cheerful. He seemed far more concerned about his bicycle than his own health. Once he had determined that his bicycle was still fit to ride, he was much happier.

In the late afternoon, I use my typewriter to type up some of Mr. Shaw's manuscript. He is writing a play about Julius Caesar and Cleopatra, although he seems to be avoiding the historic romance between them.

This is the form my holiday has taken. It may not be as exciting as a cruise down the Danube, but I am helping in some slight way a few people who are trying to change the world for the better. This gives me a deeper satisfaction than any mere sightseeing could do.

Am I becoming a Fabian?

My mother would say that I am betraying my class, but her opinion would only spur me to go further down the road that I am traveling.

Sincerely,
Charlotte

THIRTY

From Oscar Wilde's secret journal:

The mealtime abominations have grown worse.
Mr. Shaw has hired a cook from the village who is less
talented in the kitchen than he is. Her name is Mrs. Gibbons
and she apparently thinks that vegetarian cooking means
simply boiling vegetables. She is hearty soul who talks
constantly about her children to anyone who comes within
earshot of the kitchen. She tries to be agreeable, so when
Mr. Shaw suggested that she cook macaroni for supper, she
did as she was told and we were served bowls of steaming
macaroni without butter or a sauce of any kind.

I suggested that I would like a sandwich for lunch.
She served us cucumber sandwiches made with Mr. Shaw's
horrid brown bread. I could barely make myself chew and
swallow one.

My supply of chocolates is quickly diminishing. If
starvation haunts this unhappy farm, I cannot restrain
myself from eating more than my daily ration of one and a
half chocolates and I am all too aware that I will soon face
a time when there are no chocolates at all.

In a strange turn of events, Miss Payne-Townshend
may be our salvation. One evening, while we were finishing
the remains of our meager fare, she spoke up.

"Bernard, I think we may need a new cook."

"Truly?" said Mr. Shaw. "I just hired Mrs. Gibbons."

"She is not suitable. I do not enjoy what she cooks and
I believe that Mr. Wilde agrees with me."

Mr. Shaw looked at me, obviously expecting me to deny Miss Payne-Townshend's statement.

"A slight improvement in the quality of our meals might be desirable," I said.

Mr. Shaw looked to Mr. Webb.

"Slight improvement. Quite possible," Mr. Webb said.

Mr. Shaw threw his piece of brown bread into his plate with an expression of disgust.

"Miss Potter and I have been discussing Old Hutch's bequest," said Mr. Webb, obviously trying to change the topic of conversation. "I know now what we should do with the money."

Mr. Webb paused for dramatic effect until Mr. Shaw looked visibly impatient.

"We will found a school," said Mr. Webb.

"A school?" said Mr. Shaw.

"A college," Mr. Webb explained. "Something along the lines of the Ecole Libre des Science Politiques in Paris. Or the Massachusetts Institute of Technology in America. A school for specialists. For experts in political economy."

"You've given up the idea of lectures?" asked Mr. Shaw.

"A school would provide something more lasting than lectures," said Miss Potter. "And we will be able to attract money from those who want to see what their donations buy and are reluctant to see their money vanish in a puff of oratory."

"I knew there was a practical reason," said Mr. Shaw.

"This isn't just a ploy to raise funds," said Mr. Webb. "I'd thought of a school before, but it was never within our reach. We need an institution to preserve and regularize the work we do. Even the most advanced book, the most advanced thinker becomes out of date within a few decades. But a university can metamorphose itself. It can collect, debate and refine the ideas of the moment into intelligent economic doctrine."

"A school of economics could do the kind of social investigation on a regular basis that is now done only by a few eccentric individuals like ourselves," said Miss Potter.

"Exactly," said Mr. Webb. "The spirit of reform shouldn't rest on the undependable inspiration of individuals, but should be embodied permanently in an institution."

"I think it is an inspired idea," said Miss Payne-Townshend.

"Isn't it?" said Mr. Webb. "Of course, there will be a colossal amount of work putting it together, but I won't mind that. And there will be a frightful number of important people that will we have to recruit to support the idea."

"Not to mention the other Hutchinson trustees to convince," said Mr. Shaw.

"We have them to dinner and then devour them," said Miss Potter. "I have played hostess for my father even since my mother died and I dare say I can give as fine a dinner party as anyone in London. More than one man has asked when I was returning to the social scene. Well, now I shall. But with a purpose."

"How ruthless you are!" I said. "Like an attractive spider, you will lure your victims closer and closer until they are entangled in your web."

Mr. Webb barked out a laugh. "Pun! Pun!"

Miss Potter looked at me with suspicion. "You don't approve of our plan?"

I smiled at her. "I daresay your school will do no more harm than any other because most people seem incapable of learning anything. But I wonder if there is a place in it for the arts?"

"The arts? No," said Mr. Webb. "This will be a school of economics. I think the average Englishman cares more about the arts than is good for him."

"Mr. Webb, I must disagree," I said. "We live in the age of the Philistine. The greatest artists and thinkers of our time are kept from the stage by censors who believe it is more important to write plays that do good than it is to write good plays."

"He is right, Sidney," said Mr. Shaw. "You wouldn't have said that if you had been a theatre critic and watched audiences pay to see plays that would be considered unusually cruel punishment by the convicts at Wormwood Scrubs. The combined efforts of our playwrights, critics and managers are to keep the theatre in the eighteenth century even as we are about to enter the twentieth. No, Sidney. In no subject is an Englishman as ignorant as in the arts."

"Except economics," said Mr. Webb. "If you ask an Englishman who is this country's greatest actor, he will answer without hesitation Henry Irving—even if he has never once seen Irving perform. If you ask him who was our greatest playwright, he will answer Shakespeare. But if you ask him who is this country's greatest economist, he will look at you as if you had asked him to describe the backside of the moon. No matter what his position in society, he will know more about the theatre than he will about the economic system that determines whether he lives in luxury or dies in the workhouse. And this is what we must change. Imagine the progress society could make if our economists were as popular as our matinee idols. And if the talk in restaurants wasn't whether Tree could outshine Irving, but whether Marx would serve us better than Malthus."

"It is evident that you have done a great deal of hard thinking this morning," I said. "In fact, your toil has left me quite exhausted."

"Perhaps we should ask Mrs. Gibbons to make tea," said Miss Payne-Townshend.

"Tea would be heavenly," I said.

Miss Payne-Townshend supervised the making and distribution of the tea. As she was handing me my cup, she whispered, "I'll have a new cook by the end of the week." And then she winked at me.

My affection and respect for Miss Payne-Townshend grows by the hour.

I dreamed I was surrounded by a sea of cakes and pastries. But when I bent to seize one, it retreated from me by some magical means. I tried to grab a different cake and it, too, slid away beyond my reach. Hunger swelled in my belly and I felt so frustrated that I feared I would weep.

I awoke covered in sweat. As I sat in bed, trying to remember where I was, I heard a creaking noise from outside my window.

I went to the window and peered out. The sun was just showing his face above the distant trees.

Sidney Webb was climbing the stile. He descended on the other side of the fence and walked across the field.

Where can he be going?

THIRTY-ONE

From the unpublished memoir of Bernard Shaw:

Sidney Webb now has his heart set on founding a school with Hutch's money. This is a noble endeavor, but I wonder if the other Hutchinson trustees will be agreeable. Hutch wanted the money to go to Fabian activities and hitherto now no one would have named higher education as an activity especially associated with the Society.

But I shall not be one to pop Sidney's balloon. I will let him encounter obstacles and overcome them or fail on his own. He will be the stronger for his success and the wiser for his failures. And he may even surprise me with what he can accomplish.

I took two days off from our summer holiday to return by train to London for a meeting of the Health Committee of the St. Pancras vestry. I felt I had to attend; I miss one-third of vestry meetings as it is and I cannot miss more without admitting my irresponsibility to both the voters and my conscience.

I fear Miss Payne-Townshend will be bored without me and I asked Wilde to look after her and he agreed. Mr. Webb and Miss Potter will be fine plotting their subversion of the Hutchinson bequest and whatever other mischief Sidney can come up with for the good of the nation.

The vestrymen are overall as fine a collection of sober, hard-working citizens as has ever been assembled for the purposes of good government. That is to say that they are wholly ignorant of all political theory and have only one idea in their heads as to what constitutes good government: keeping the tax rates as low as possible. This makes efficient local government almost impossible because of lack of funds; no project no matter how worthy is possible if it costs money.

The Health Committee of which I am a part is distinguished by the chairmanship of the Reverend Ensor Walters, a Methodist minister who hopes to do some good in the world and sees purposes in the vestry other than keeping taxes low. He is a handsome young man and very amiable and he possesses a sense of humor, which makes him fonder of me than is perhaps good for him. I take contrary positions so often on the issues that I am regarded as a troublemaker by most of the committee.

The present issue before the committee was the question of spending money to construct a women's public lavatory on the Camden High Road. I knew this project would be irksome to most of the vestrymen and so it proved.

Bill Alders, a portly greengrocer, began the assault on the project by raising his hand and being recognized by the chairman.

"Mr. Chairman, a public lavatory for women would be a colossal waste of money because no real lady would ever use one. The only ones likely to use it are flower girls who need water for their violets."

"That sounds like a good reason to build one to me," I said. "The vestry supports public enterprise, does it not? Every flower girl who successfully sells violets is one less flower girl in the workhouse."

Bill Alders scowled at me, but I could see the Reverend Walters smiling.

"And I disagree with Mr. Alders' contention that no real lady would use a lavatory," I added. "If the demands of nature come hard upon a lady when she is in the Camden High Road, does Mr. Alders argue that she would foul the street like a horse rather than use a public lavatory?"

"Mr. Shaw!" exclaimed Mr. Alders. "You mock the honor of British women with your suppositions."

"No, Mr. Alders, you deny the intelligence of British women by claiming they will ignore a public lavatory when a pressing need is upon them. The honor of British women is not so delicate a thing that it can be destroyed or even stained by a public lavatory—or even by silly objections in a British vestry hall."

The Reverend Walters was now trying not to laugh.

"Gentlemen, there is a delegation of citizens from the neighborhood of the Camden High Road who wish to testify on this issue," said the Reverend. "Are there any objections to receiving them?"

I raised my hand.

"Are there any women in the delegation?" I asked.

"I don't believe so," said Reverend Walters.

"Then I move that the delegation not be received. The question before the committee concerns the health of women. A delegation that has no female members cannot say anything of relevance on this issue."

This statement caused an uproar as most of the committee disagreed with my logic.

The Reverend Walters raised his hand. "We will vote on whether to receive the delegation or not. All in favor . . ."

Many hands shot into the air.

"All opposed . . . "

I alone raised my hand.

"The committee has voted to receive the delegation."

The delegation turned out to be three men who owned stores or pubs on the Camden High Road. Their spokesman was a cobbler named Wallford, whose shop was located very close to the proposed site of the lavatory. Mr. Wallford was a burly man with a thick brown beard whose attitude suggested that the committee had entertained the idea of building a lavatory near his shop as a way of attacking him personally.

"You build a lavatory there and the value of all our properties will drop. No women will use it so it won't do no good, but the smell will drive away my customers and take away half the value of my property. Building a lavatory there would be the same as stealing half my money."

After five minutes of testifying in this vein, the committee members could ask questions. The Reverend Walters smiled as I raised my hand.

"Mr. Wallford, you truly believe that no women will use the lavatory?" I asked.

"Yessir, I do. That is, I believe they will not. My missus says she'd not use a public lavatory if her life depended on it. I don't believe any women would."

"And what about the lavatory would drive down your property values?" I asked.

"It's the smell, sir," said Mr. Wallford. "No one likes to smell that. It makes a neighborhood unpopular, it does."

"Why would there be a smell from a lavatory that no one uses? The smell you are referring to comes from human waste, does it not? If no one uses the lavatory, there won't be a smell, will there?"

Mr. Wallford looked puzzled. He remained silent.

"Mr. Wallford, how often do you clean up the horse dung that fouls the Camden High Road?" I asked.

"That's not my job," he said. "We've got street cleaners for that."

"So, animal waste can foul the Camden High Road in front of your shop all day long and you will do nothing about it, is that right?"

"It's not my job," he repeated.

"But doesn't the smell of horse dung drive away your customers? Doesn't it drive down the value of your property? I have walked on the Camden High Road and the odor of horse dung can be quite strong."

"People are used to horse dung," he argued. "We smell that every day."

"So, the British nose is used to horse dung, but is still so sensitive to the smell from the wastes of the human female that traffic on the Camden High Road would cease if a lavatory were constructed? Is it that the smell from the wastes of the British female is more repugnant than mere horse dung? How much more offensive is the smell of the wastes of the British female than horse dung to you, sir? Is it twice as offensive? Ten times as offensive?"

Mr. Wallford stammered, but no true words were emitted. Several committee members joined Reverend Walters in laughing at the witness.

"What do you think makes the wastes of the British female so especially offensive to you?" I asked. "Is it their diet? If we made the lavatory accessible to only those females who could swear that they have not eaten onions or radishes, would that satisfy you?"

Reverend Walters soon took pity on the witness and dismissed him and his delegation. No one else seemed inclined to testify. In the end, the Reverend Walters joined with me in voting for the construction of a lavatory, but the committee voted it down.

By the next evening, I had returned to Suffolk by train. I explained my adventures in local politics to my summerhouse friends over supper.

"You concern yourself with the construction of lavatories?" said Mr. Wilde. "I would find that kind of government work low and sordid."

"Lavatories must be constructed and public lavatories must be constructed with government money," I said. "There is nothing low or sordid about meeting public needs."

"But instead of attending a vestry meeting and dealing with these commonplace matters that any public-spirited citizen might master, you could have stayed here and crafted a play that would make your name echo down the ages. Surely, that would be a better use of your precious hours."

Miss Potter looked so offended by Mr. Wilde's argument that she leaned across the table toward him.

"What could be of more value than improving the world for everyone? The names of most of those who have built the good things of our world are forgotten, but their work lives on. Most of most of the men who fought slavery, who battled poverty, who expanded the franchise are forgotten. Did they live in vain? I don't think so. We profit from their work although we know not their names. I hope I live long enough to do some lasting good in the world. Whether anyone remembers me for it is immaterial."

Sidney Webb pointed a finger at Mr. Wilde.

"If mankind ever arrives at Utopia, it will not be through a thunderclap of revolution. It will happen through a slow accumulation of progressive taxation, improved public schools, free public hospitals and even women's public lavatories. Good government earns its practitioners no glory, but mankind rises to the future through their efforts."

"You have entered a temple of good government," I said to Mr. Wilde. "Mock not the gods here or be scorned as a heretic and blasphemer."

"I can see that," said Mr. Wilde.

"I'm sorry. Mr. Wilde is our guest, and I shouldn't attack him," said Miss Potter. "My apologies, Mr. Wilde."

"No apologies are necessary," said Mr. Wilde. "Passion needs no excuse. Mr. Shaw is right: you are a priestess of political economy and as such you are entitled to scorn followers of other gods."

"I feel foolish," said Miss Potter with a sheepish smile.

"Passions make us foolish and passions make us strong," said Mr. Wilde.

Miss Payne-Townshend had been watching the debate with amusement, but now she got up and disappeared into the kitchen.

Mr. Webb leaned across the table to me and whispered: "Did you notice the soup?"

"It was much better than before," I admitted. "Is it your recipe?"

Mr. Webb shook his head, but Miss Payne-Townshend returned from the kitchen before he could say another word. She carried a chocolate cake on a plate.

"We will have dessert tonight," she announced.

"Charlotte, did you bake that?" I asked.

"No, it was baked by Mrs. Foster. I have replaced Mrs. Gibbons and I trust our meals will be the better for it."

Miss Payne-Townshend passed around pieces of cake and soon we were all agreeing that we had at last found a cook we could abide.

"How did you know that Mrs. Foster was a skilled vegetarian cook?" I asked.

"She is the widow of the local butcher. A butcher who suffered greatly from gout the last ten years of his life. She learned to cook without meat."

"And how did you find her?" asked Sidney.

"That will remain my secret. I may not know much about political economy, but I know how to run a household."

Miss Payne-Townshend seemed pleased with herself. It is a truth of human nature that everyone likes to be useful.

THIRTY-TWO

From Oscar Wilde's secret journal:

I kept my window open all night in the hope that the noise of Mr. Webb on the stile would awaken me. But it was the sound of Miss Potter's voice that woke me.

"Mr. Webb, where are you going?"

I jumped from bed and rushed to the window. I could see Mr. Webb at the stile and Miss Potter near the kitchen door of the house.

"I often wake with a headache," said Mr. Webb. "Walking helps to sooth it. I'll be back soon."

Mr. Webb climbed over the stile and set off across the field. Miss Potter returned to the kitchen.

I had slept in my trousers and now I threw on my shirt with all the speed I could muster. Only moments later I slipped out the front door of the farmhouse and hurried to the stile.

Mr. Webb was still visible at the edge of the trees as I climbed the stile. The field was not as muddy as I had feared, and the uneven ground was the only faint difficulty I encountered.

Mr. Webb followed a path through the woods that bordered the field and although I could not see him ahead of me, I thought it unlikely that he would stray from the path. I followed him and I soon discovered that my guess was correct. When I emerged from the woodland path after half a mile, I found myself at the edge of the village.

Mr. Webb was on the other side of the street entering a rustic tavern or restaurant.

I paused for a minute or two to catch my breath. Now that I knew Mr. Webb's destination, there was no need for hurry. Once I had recovered my wind, I strolled across the street and entered the establishment.

Mr. Webb was seated at a table by the wall. In front of him was a plate of ham and eggs.

I walked to his table and feigned surprise.

"Mr. Webb! I did not expect to find you here. But what is this? Is that ham on your plate? Are you ingesting the fruit of the hog? Could those shimmering golden circles be the unhatched progeny of chickens? Mr. Webb, I don't know what to say. To hear you preach the wonders of vegetarianism at the supper table and then to find you here ingesting the products of the slaughterhouse—well, there are simply no words that can express my shock and delight."

Mr. Webb did not seem overly embarrassed to be accused of hypocrisy.

"Sit down, Mr. Wilde."

I took a seat across the table from him.

"Please, you must call me Oscar. I think we are going to be great friends."

"First point, Oscar, is that I've never preached vegetarianism to anyone. That is a hobbyhorse that Mr. Shaw and Miss Potter choose to ride. I simply try to make myself agreeable at mealtimes and if people draw the wrong conclusions, am I to be blamed?"

"But you do admit to telling Miss Potter that you had a headache so you could slip into the village and partake of this carnivorous bacchanalia?"

"You've got me there, I suppose," he said. "I would appreciate it if you do not tell Miss Potter where I've gone these few mornings."

"Your secret is safe with me."

The proprietress of the restaurant now approached my table.

"Would you like some breakfast, sir?" she asked.

"I would indeed. Ham and eggs, please. A double portion. Fried in deception and sprinkled with sin."

The good lady seemed shocked by my order, but Mr. Webb merely shook his and smiled.

After breakfast, Mr. Webb and I strolled slowly back toward the farmhouse. My mood had greatly improved with the discovery of Mr. Webb's secret.

"Have you been getting much writing done?" asked Mr. Webb.

"The Almighty created work solely to give us the pleasure of shirking it," I replied. "But sometimes I feel so inspired that I simply must take pen to paper. I wrote an entire sentence yesterday and this morning has been so pleasant that I may repeat the feat this afternoon."

Mr. Webb looked at me with a skeptical eye. "Forgive me, but do you really believe what you say, or are you only trying to be clever?"

"I am always trying to be clever, but I find that I speak the truth no matter how hard I try to avoid it. Of all the temptations, speaking the truth is one of the most irresistible."

"You had a conversation with Miss Potter yesterday."

I nodded, but my tone suggested moral outrage.

"Mr. Webb, you are not asking me to betray a confidence?"

"No," he protested. "Certainly not."

"I am glad to hear it," I said. "I am only indiscreet on those desperate occasions when lives are at stake or boredom must be alleviated. But you may rest assured that Miss Potter esteems your friendship."

"It may be that I desire something more than friendship," said Mr. Webb in a voice that suggested he had broached this topic with Miss Potter and had been disappointed with her answer.

"Yes, Miss Potter has a face like Helen of Troy and a mind like Aristotle. She seems almost mythological."

"And it will take a Paris or Achilles to win her," said Mr. Webb.

"Greek heroes are scarce this season," I said in my most encouraging tone. "And you have one advantage that even Odysseus would envy."

"What is that?" asked Mr. Webb.

"Proximity," I replied. "You are here and your rivals are not."

"I lack the face of a lover," said Mr. Webb.

"But you have a fine mind and good heart. Like water on rock, over time those forces are irresistible to a woman with any sense. Your love is geological."

Mr. Webb laughed and his voice sounded more hopeful. "Mr. Wilde, you seem a fount of wisdom. You must be a happy man."

"You must call me Oscar," I said. "And I am far better at giving advice than taking it. Even advice from myself."

Mr. Webb laughed again.

I hope this is the first of many morning walks we will take together. I may even be willing to get up early if it leads to such breakfasts and such conversations.

THIRTY-THREE

Dear Miss Darling,

This summer has proved to be everything I had hoped and everything I had feared. I had hoped that Mr. Webb would be a useful friend as I tried to write my book on the co-operative movement and he has surpassed my expectations. He has an orderly mind and has made useful suggestions on the organization of my book, the amount of detail that I need and the structure of particularly troublesome chapters. Once I have written a chapter, he demonstrates that he is a fine editor, tidying and simplifying my overburdened paragraphs until the meaning is clear and is stated with the greatest force.

But the awkwardness that is the product of his love for me is ever-present and I must exercise a great diplomatic talent to avoid painful scenes. Because the mornings are reserved for work, I make sure there is enough to keep us both busy and insist that we remained disciplined and diligent for the sake of our common cause. After luncheon, I try to avoid being alone with Mr. Webb and our bicycle journeys provide a good excuse to keep company with Mr. Shaw and Miss Townshend.

But Mr. Webb's strong emotions cannot be bottled forever and my gratitude for his helpfulness has led to embarrassing situations. The other day was warm and pleasant. We spent the morning sitting under a tree in the yard with our manuscripts in our laps. A faint breeze alleviated the summer heat and bees buzzed among the flowers of the garden.

Mr. Webb passed me a chapter of my book that he had revised in red pen and my response was perhaps too enthusiastic.

"I had thought I had made a good start on the subject, but your experience and breadth of knowledge give the chapter a depth I could never have attained on my own," I said. "You must look through all the chapters I have written so far."

"It will be my pleasure," said Mr. Webb. And once we've revised the manuscript to our satisfaction, we should give it to Bernard to read."

"Is all Fabian writing a committee effort?"

"The best of it is. If one is only concerned with the quality of the writing, then the more good advice the better."

"Sidney, you inspire me," I said. "You are the kind of socialist I hope to become."

"I will do everything in my power to help you."

"Thank you," I said. "You don't know what a relief it is to have someone to share my work and to talk with about serious matters. The philosopher Herbert Spencer was a friend of my family and when I was a girl, he used to talk to me every time he visited. It would talk to me, but not as an adult talks to a child. He would talk to me as if I was a fellow philosopher and it wasn't until many years later that I discovered how rare it is for man to talk to a woman as if she had a mind exactly like his own. Thank you, Mr. Webb."

"Rossetti knew that feeling," said Mr. Webb. And then he quoted some lines from a poem: "O born with me somewhere that men forget and though in years of sight and sound unmet, Known for my soul's birth-partner well enough!"

Mr. Webb tried to kiss me and I had to raise my hand to prevent him.

"Mr. Webb, you forget our agreement."

"Miss Potter, I know that my appearance, my position and my class are all against me. But in time our common cause and our united hearts will see these differences as nothing."

"Mr. Webb, you have broken your promise. We were to be comrades only."

He hung his head. "Yes. I apologize."

"If you break it again, I will know that we cannot be co-workers and that our friendship is impossible."

I rose and went into the house and stayed there until luncheon.

During the meal, Miss Payne-Townshend discussed the news she had learned in the village. She had brought a newspaper back with her.

"Anything interesting in the paper?" asked Mr. Webb. "I always find politics fascinating."

"I find politics quite tiresome," said Mr. Wilde. "I find gossip so much more interesting and delightfully inaccurate."

"I did read that Joseph Chamberlain is getting married again," said Miss Payne-Townshend.

My heart skipped a beat. "Who is he marrying?" I managed to say without a quaver in my voice.

"Mary Endicott. She is the daughter of the American Secretary of War. From what I've heard, she is quite young and pretty."

I did not stay at the table for dessert, but retired to my room.

All the old yearnings that I thought were dead have come back to me, flooding my mind and heart. Why should my heart long for someone who is so clearly unsuitable? Why am I so foolish? Am I destined for unhappiness until I can make my mind command my heart?

These are the painful thoughts that I ponder on this beautiful day. The afternoon sunshine streams in my window and Mr. Shaw or Miss Payne-Townshend will soon summon me to go bicycle riding. I will go with them and smile and attempt to pedal away my pain.

Only you will know the truth.

Sincerely,
Beatrice

THIRTY-FOUR

From Oscar Wilde's secret journal:

The food is better and my mood has improved with it. Miss Payne-Townshend has hired a wonder-worker in the kitchen and I no longer drag myself to the table like a man condemned to the gallows.

I asked her how she had discovered such a wonderful cook when Mr. Shaw had failed. She said that she had talked to the two people most likely to know everyone in the village: the vicar and the publican. She had promised them a small reward if they could find her a skilled vegetarian cook and within a couple of days the barman had recommended Mrs. Foster. It surprises me that the rest of us failed at such an easy task; once she had explained her method, it seemed child's play. I suspect that while Mr. Shaw and I have literary minds and Mr. Webb and Miss Potter have economic minds, Miss Payne-Townshend's mind is purely practical. I thank the Almighty that it is.

The wonderful cook does not arrive until mid-day, but I have begun waking early and walking to the village with Mr. Webb for a breakfast of forbidden pleasures. Miss Potter may suspect what we are doing, but she has said nothing and I am not inclined to bring up the subject. It is so much more fun to believe we are transgressing than to discover that she approves of our illicit breakfasts. The little tavern where we eat is willing to prepare us sandwiches wrapped in waxed paper that we may take and eat at our leisure. I find these a delightful refreshment for the late afternoon when the Fabians are out risking death or dismemberment on their bicycles and I am alone with my work, trying to pull inspiration from the afternoon sunshine and cawing of the crows that haunt the trees near the back garden.

As much as I enjoy verbal sparring with Mr. Shaw, or teasing Miss Potter about her seriousness, I think I love the solitude of the late afternoons the most. I write or nap as the mood takes me and I daydream about the characters in my play as if they were old acquaintances whose exploits they are only now recounting. I listen to their voices in my head and I sometimes laugh aloud when one of them surprises me with a bit of wit. The creation of other minds, the pleasures of assuming a strange point of view, are the joys of writing that are perhaps least spoken of, but for me they are the most potent.

After writing a scene for my play, today I celebrated with an afternoon nap. When I awoke, I went to the window overlooking the garden and found that the Fabians had returned. Miss Payne-Townshend was typing at the table in the garden and Mr. Shaw sat in the chair with one bandaged leg propped up on a footstool. Mr. Shaw looked over Miss Payne-Townshend's shoulder at the page she was typing.

"Mind the punctuation," said Mr. Shaw.

"Don't is spelled with an apostrophe," said Miss Payne-Townshend.

"Don't required an apostrophe when it was a contraction of "do" and "not," said Mr. Shaw. "But it is now in such common usage that any intelligent English-speaking being can only regard it as a proper word in and of itself. Remove the apostrophe."

Miss Payne-Townshend looked at Mr. Shaw with a skeptical eye.

"Your publishers will think it unreasonable of you to expect them to conform to your eccentricities rather than the public's expectations."

"The reasonable man conforms to the world," said Mr. Shaw. "The unreasonable man expects the world to conform to him. Therefore, all progress depends on unreasonable men. Banish the apostrophe!"

I assume the apostrophe was banished, but I will never know for sure because I changed into my lightest-weight coat and strolled into the garden. Miss Payne-Townshend smiled at me and stopped typing.

"Oh, please don't stop typing on my account," I said. "Usually, the clatter of the typing machine is almost as annoying as the sound of the piano when played by a close relation. But your dexterity elevates typing to an art. It is positively Mozartesque."

"Thank you, Mr. Wilde," said Miss Payne-Townshend. "You don't type?"

"I never exercise," I said. I walked to Mr. Shaw who was working on a manuscript with pen in hand. "What on earth happened to your leg?"

"A bicycle catastrophe."

"He collided with Mr. Webb and a flock of sheep," said Miss Payne-Townshend.

"I flew through the air like an arrow and plummeted to earth like Icarus. Sheep rocketed skyward like nine pins."

"And you a vegetarian," I said.

Just then Miss Potter and Mr. Webb appeared carrying gaily painted mallets.

"Mr. Wilde, would you care to join us for a game of croquet?" asked Miss Potter.

"Croquet?" said Mr. Shaw with all the venom that he could muster.

"We have been very bad hosts, riding off each afternoon to leave Mr. Wilde to fend for himself," said Miss Potter.

"Please don't trouble yourself on my account," I said. "Croquet sounds suspiciously like one of those strenuous competitions that are used in public schools to destroy boys' characters."

Miss Potter looked disappointed.

"I thought it would be the one activity we could all enjoy."

"I think it is a wonderful idea," said Miss Payne-Townshend.

"Are you mad?" said Mr. Shaw. "A game that exercises neither the body nor the mind. It is an absolute perfection as a waste of time. The only activity I can think of that is more idiotic is smoking."

Of course, I immediately pulled out my silver cigarette case.

Really?" I said. "I had no idea it was as wonderful as that."

I took the mallet from Miss Potter and gave it a trial swing. I clucked my tongue to make a sound like a ball being struck.

Soon we were all gathered to take our opening shots. Miss Potter and Mr. Webb had placed the wickets around the lawn and Miss Payne-Townshend had distributed the mallets. The others took their shots before me, Mr. Shaw with ill-concealed grumbling.

I took out my cigarette case and opened it to extract a cigarette. I noticed Miss Potter watching me.

"Cigarette, Miss Potter?"

She surprised me by saying "Yes." I handed her a cigarette and lit it for her.

"I confess I am surprised, Miss Potter," I said. "A cigarette seems like an un-Fabian vice."

Miss Potter inhaled and blew a puff toward the sky.

"I began to smoke when I noticed that men liked to smoke. If women are to take our place as equals in society, we will have to grab the symbols as well as the reality of power."

Miss Potter swung her mallet and hit her ball.

"And do your Fabian friends agree with you?"

"Mr. Webb likes to smoke. We smoke together in the evenings. Mr. Shaw says that women shouldn't damage their lungs just because men are stupid enough to do so."

"That sounds like Mr. Shaw," I said. I hit my ball and then we ambled across the lawn.

"Did I see a photograph in your cigarette case?" asked Miss Potter.

I opened the case and showed her the photograph.

"My sons. Cyril and Vyvyan."

"How handsome they are. Where are they now?"

"They are with their mother. My only regret is that I don't spend more time with my boys."

"May I ask a personal question?" said Miss Potter. "It is because I do not know you very well that I feel that I can."

"Very good, Miss Potter. We will make an ironist out of you yet. Ask me anything. We are in an enchanted garden and what passes between us will tomorrow seem but a dream."

"Do you regret marrying?"

"I never regret my mistakes. They have the most delightful consequences. In this case, my two boys."

"Is your wife very beautiful?"

"Yes, she is," I said.

"And was it her beauty that made you love her?"

"Why this fascination with beauty, Miss Potter? Has some blind man been hinting that you are plain?"

"No. Nothing like that."

Miss Potter found her ball and she took her shot. It glided across the greensward as if guided by fairy folk and passed neatly through the wicket.

"No, of course not. You have found a paramour with the soul of Hamlet and the body of Caliban."

"Something like that. A child will drink poison if the bottle is pretty enough—and a woman will marry for the same reason. If I had listened to my heart, I would have married a man who did not respect me. Only my reason saved me and I hated myself for listening to it. And so, I prayed that I might meet a man who respected my work and valued my mind and could help and be helped by me. Was it Aesop who warned us to be careful of what we wish for because we might get it?"

"I see. The gods have given him every gift but beauty."

"Every gift but that."

"Ah, beauty! It is a mere accident of geometry, a pleasing configuration of planes and curves and yet we crave it as our soul's delight. Love, friendship and affection are the meat and drink of our souls, but beauty is the soul's champagne. Drink deep and it intoxicates."

"But one can't live only for beauty any more than one can drink only champagne," said Miss Potter.

"I must disagree," I said. "I frequently do both."

"I'm afraid I need something more substantial," said Miss Potter. "The Yorkshire pudding of the soul."

I took my shot, but it went wide of the wicket. I could see triumph slipping away.

It was at this moment that Mr. Webb chose to wave at us from the far corner of the yard where his ball had apparently strayed under some bushes. The sight of his smiling face prodded my dull mind into thinking.

"We are talking about Mr. Webb, are we not?"

"Yes," said Miss Potter with a weight of sadness in her voice.

"And does he love you?"

"Passionately."

"How fascinating. It must be like watching Karl Marx play Romeo. Once again I am reminded that all the world's a stage— but the play is badly cast."

"You must think I am a foolish idiot."

"Love reduces even the most intelligent people to idiocy. That is one reason why love is so necessary."

"I have never talked with any man as I have with Mr. Webb. But does one marry for talk?"

"If Paris had kidnapped the greatest female conversationalist in Greece, Troy would be standing today and Paris would be remembered as the wisest and happiest of its kings."

"But he didn't," said Miss Potter.

"No. He valued only beauty and saw only Helen. Like you, he thought that love must be tempests and whirlwinds, hurricanes of the heart. He didn't realize it also could be the slow bloom of a flower."

"I don't know what terrifies me more: the idea of marrying him or the thought that he might leave me. If you were I my position, Mr. Wilde, what would you do?"

"Had I been in your shoes, I could not have resisted the beautiful man who did not respect me. I could never deny myself the joy of a glorious sin or the acquired wisdom of a colossal folly."

Miss Potter did not like the sound of this and she frowned.

"You don't think very highly of morality," she said.

"On the contrary, I adore morality. It gives my sins their significance."

I shot again for the wicket and again my ball rolled past it.

"The croquet gods frown on me today," I said. "Like Sisyphus I shall be condemned to aim at the wicket for all eternity only to see my ball go rolling past."

"I have told you a secret, Mr. Wilde," said Miss Potter. "Now tell me one of yours."

I thought for a moment.

"You must swear that you will never reveal what I tell you to a living soul."

"On my honor, I will tell no one," said Miss Potter with great solemnity.

I stepped closer to her and leaned my head close to hers.

"I have been known to enjoy… golf."

"Golf?" she asked with astonishment in her voice.

I nodded. "Golf. I was introduced to the game a couple of years ago and briefly became an enthusiast. I became quite good at the game. I was willing to get up early to play and would hit the ball even in the hottest sun. I lost weight and went to bed early. My strength clearly improved because I could see the ball fly farther every week. I was becoming a healthy man. The game nearly ruined me."

"You have a strange definition of ruination, Mr. Wilde," said Miss Potter with a smile. "I don't believe you are serious."

"Everything I just told you is true. I learned that one vice can drive out all the others. That is the fate that I feared and at last had the strength to avoid. I think we can all agree that a man with only one vice is a bit of a bore."

"A man who can talk like you will never be a bore," she said.

"I should leave you before you discover any more of my secrets. No woman should ever thoroughly understand any man she isn't married to. And of course, if she thoroughly understood all men, she would probably never marry at all."

I strolled away and watched Miss Potter walk toward Mr. Webb.

I do not remember who won the croquet game, but I felt as if I was the victor.

THIRTY-FIVE

From the unpublished memoir of Bernard Shaw:

I will admit here and now that the croquet game put me in a foul humor. My mood was already tainted from the injury I had sustained in my latest bicycle fall. I believed that I had suffered quite enough accidents for one summer and the continuing appearance of animals and birds in my bicycle's path was more bad luck than any one bicycle enthusiast should have to tolerate. The women's insistence that everyone play croquet was more annoyance than I could handle and still retain my good manners.

"Why are you smiling?" I barked at Sidney Webb as he took his shot.

"Why are you scowling?" he replied.

"I was in the middle of writing a scene of my Julius Caesar play. I was inspired. The words were flowing like water. Cleopatra had just entered and the scene was building to a—"

"Yes, there's nothing as enjoyable as work. But look, Bernard, we've made the women happy."

Sidney gestured towards Miss Payne-Townshend and Miss Potter who seemed to be enjoying accurate shots. I growled in disgust as Sidney ambled away after his ball.

Miss Payne-Townshend noticed my scowl and walked toward me like a mother confronting her unhappy son at another child's birthday party.

"You are being very rude," she said.

"The Almighty finally grants me a moment of inspiration when common labor becomes a joy and you tear me from the workshop of my mind. And for what? A Beethoven symphony? A definitive Lear? Or at least a bicycle ride in Nature's bosom? No. For croquet! The pastime of rich and idle fools."

Miss Payne-Townshend now had a scowl that matched my own.

"For the sake of our friends, I will ignore that remark."

"It was not an insult. It was a sermon. God's sacred gift of time is far too precious to be squandered on the hobbies of those made stupid by money."

"Mr. Shaw, having money is not a sin."

"No but leading an idle and useless life is."

I was about to hit my ball, but Miss Payne-Townshend gave a mighty swing with her mallet that sent my ball sailing clear across the yard. She planted herself in front of me and leaned close to my face.

"You have no right to talk to me that way," she said in voice that was both quiet and intense. "It was easy for you! You had poverty and adversity to give you character; I had only luxury and comfort at every side. How was I to build character from that? I had my father's good example, but that was more than cancelled by my mother's bad example. Above all things, my mother wanted me to be a useless person! You don't know how long I fought her! How hard I had to work to develop any character at all!"

She paused for breath. After a long moment, I finally spoke.

"How did you know I was born poor?"

"All your suits have been worn about a thousand times too often."

I nodded my head because she spoke the truth.

"We must look for my ball," I said.

Miss Payne-Townshend accompanied me as we went to search the bushes.

"What did your mother want that was so terrible?" I asked.

"She wanted me to marry," she said. "Being the wife of the local Irish nob wasn't good enough for her and she dragged my family first to Dublin and then London in search of good society. My father was a man of business— what you would call a capitalist, but his grandest dream was to help the poor villages where we lived. My father wanted to build an eight-mile stretch of rail to connect the villages east of Skibbereen with Cork. Probably not a very grand dream by your standards, but it would have done so much to relieve the poverty in those villages. My mother killed my father's dream of a railroad and the disappointment killed my father."

Miss Payne-Townshend seemed near tears, but when she looked at me there was fury in her eyes.

"So, then the only way my mother could rise in society was by marrying my sister or myself to some great catch. She dragged us all over Europe in search of husbands. And because I hated her, I swore I would never marry. I did everything I could to become the opinionated, argumentative, book-reading spinster my mother abhorred."

Miss Payne-Townshend found my ball and pulled it from the bushes.

"But perhaps you're right," she said in a gentler tone. "I may have avoided becoming my mother's type of useless person by developing a useless type of my own."

"Nonsense!" I said. "It's a pilgrim heart you have. A questing soul seeking a safe harbor."

I held my arms wide. She came to me and I hugged her and kissed her.

"I've been an ogre," I said.

"Yes, you have."

"I shall apologize to you, Mr. Wilde and Miss Potter."

"Later," she said and kissed me again.

I looked for the others and saw Sidney standing alone with his mallet on the other side of the yard.

"Why isn't anyone talking to me?" he called.

THIRTY-SIX

From Oscar Wilde's secret journal:

Mr. Webb has found a source of chocolates in the village. Of course, they are not Belgian chocolates, and they may in fact be little more than cocoa and sugar, but they are chocolates and they may be purchased for a nominal sum. Our new cook provides excellent meals, but a sugary treat when one wakes in the night does produce sweet dreams.

I have been dreaming of a young man. Lean and lank and long of limb. He is no one I can remember meeting and yet he appears vividly to me in the dark, staring and beckoning.

I feel he is a harbinger of some change in my life. Am I to resume my old pleasures soon? We are far into August and the autumn approaches. My Fabian summer is waning, and that thought is bittersweet. I am a heretic among these socialists, although they do not recognize that yet. They are so alien to me with their disciplined minds and their burning desire to shoehorn more work into every day. They toil like ants yet are consumed with guilt over not doing more.

And yet I am fond of them. Miss Potter and Mr. Webb will write many books together, although they may not know that yet. If anyone will read their books is another matter.

If Mr. Shaw sticks to writing plays, he may find success and happiness. If he continues to dream of reforming the human race, he will face ultimate disappointment and perhaps despair. The Fabians are laboring for a people that they believe are as reasonable as they are. They will learn and the lesson will be bitter.

But even if the world remains the world, they may improve little corners of it. Tonight at dinner, Mr. Webb laid out the organizational plans for his economic school. His enthusiasm and that of Miss Potter should carry them far. If I had to guess, I would say that the most lasting result of our summer together will be the creation of their school.

Of course, I have my own entry in that race. I am almost finished with my play. Perhaps the very seriousness of the Fabians provoked me into writing this light-hearted confection, so much more trivial and airier than my other works. But I won't know until I return to London if it fulfills my hopes and floats on the summer breeze like a puff of thistledown.

THIRTY-SEVEN

From the unpublished memoir of Bernard Shaw:

I have had a strange and momentous day. Some moments of sacred intimacy with Charlotte may prove some of the happiest memories of our lives—if my instinctive villainy with women does not curse our romance as it has all the others. My heart swells with hope when I remember holding her in my arms, but my mind fears her scorn when it notes how I have turned every other lover against me.

After supper, I went to the garden and sat at the table to revise my manuscript. The heat of the day had diminished, but there was still an hour or two until sunset.

Charlotte came to the table and joined me.

"You didn't seem very enthusiastic about the plans for Mr. Webb's school," she said." Beatrice is getting cross with you."

"What I realize – and that Sidney doesn't – is that we won't be able to raise funds for a truly radical school. And if we can raise funds, it will only be by making so many compromises that the school will not be the instrument that Sidney envisions."

This argument seemed to mollify her.

"Oh. I see," she said.

"But of course, I will support the idea. If Hutch had left us only ten pounds and Sidney proposed a school, I'd stand by him for friendship's sake."

She smiled at me.

"So, the writing machine is really a sentimentalist."

"Nonsense. Sidney and I work well together. I knew the first time I heard him speak that this man had a mind I could work with."

"But must people be of use for you to be friends?"

"Of course. The closest friendships are always founded on mutual usefulness."

"Even your friendships with women?"

"Especially with women. All my love affairs end tragically because the women can't use me. They only wish to own me. Sidney demands more work from me than ten wives would, yet the tie grows stronger with every task he gives me. If you need me and love me, then task me."

"You might not like the task I set for you?"

"Is there something you want?"

"Make love to me."

This was not the answer I was expecting, but I refrained from showing any surprise.

"You talk love, but you never make love," said Charlotte. "A few kisses, but—am I embarrassing you?"

"No, of course not," I said. "Intelligent people can discuss anything."

"Yes, and at an eternal length."

"So, you've grown tired of my blarney."

"No. But why haven't you tried to make love to me? Is it because I am not foremost in your affections?"

"You mean, is there someone else? No. Of course, there are dozens of women who would fly to me from the four corners of England if I so much as crooked my little finger."

Charlotte looked skeptical of this statement.

"But you are my dear one," I said. "Your independence gives me peace."

"Then why won't you make love to me?"

"Well, if we're going to be frank, I have to say that I often find the sexual act distasteful. In its intensity and intimacy, it can be delightful, of course. But indulging in it releases such a torrent of lower feeling that the friendship between men and women is often irreparably harmed. Given the choice between an indulgent passion or an unrequited romance, I choose the later. On most occasions."

Charlotte nodded thoughtfully.

"That may be a very wise attitude to have. Or it may not. I really don't know. The only feeling I have on the subject is curiosity."

"Curiosity? You mean you have never made love with anyone?"

Charlotte shook her head.

"I have spent my life traveling in the best society. Men from all over Europe proposed to me. I spurned them all just to anger my mother. And when my mother finally died, I found spurning had become a habit. The independence that you see as strength is merely the habit of a lifetime."

The humor of the situation struck me and I laughed.

"My green-eyed millionairess feels sorry for herself! She has the most romantic Irishman in England at her feet and she counts herself lonely! Wait here!"

I hurried to the kitchen, grabbed a picnic blanket from the cupboard and returned to Charlotte.

"Come with me."

"Where are we going?" asked Charlotte.

"I know a bank where the wild thyme blows."

I led Charlotte toward the stile.

"But let me say from experience that the main drawback to a prolonged virginity is that one's expectations are raised absurdly high."

Charlotte nodded solemnly.

"Very well. I shall expect to be disappointed."

"Good," I said. "Then there is a chance that you may be delightfully surprised."

THIRTY-EIGHT

Dear Lion,

What a fool I am!

As you predicted, I have fallen in love with Bernard Shaw. How could you have been so wise, and I have been so blind? How can we live with ourselves every day and yet our hearts remain such a foreign land? How could I not know that play-acting a romance would become the real thing?

I am not sure if it is his humor or his seriousness that I love more. He can find a joke in almost anything and he can be most entertaining when he truly decides to make the effort. But at heart he is a serious man who is laboring to change the world, or at least the portion of it that he occupies, and this larger purpose makes him for me heroic. Life for him is not a series of pleasures to be enjoyed, but tasks to be accomplished and the result of his labor and that of his friends, will be a world that is fairer for all.

It is too late in life for me to become like him, but it is not too late for me to aid him as best I can. My task then is to make him see that we should be partners and that his purposes will be my own.

I am excited and I am happy.

I am nervous and very afraid.

If you were so clairvoyant that you could predict that I would fall in love, then tell me what my future holds? Where will I be a year from now? Who will be by my side?

Will I still be happy?

Will I still be in love?

I am writing as if I am a girl again. I don't know if I should rejoice in new-found youth or curse my foolish heart.

A month, a week, perhaps a day will reveal the answers I seek.

Keep me in your prayers.

Charlotte

THIRTY-NINE

From Oscar Wilde's secret journal:

Robbie sent me a bottle of champagne and this surprise was so joyous that the day seemed to be a holiday. I waited until the evening to bring the bottle out. Mr. Shaw and Miss Payne-Townshend were nowhere to be found, but Mr. Webb and Miss Potter were willing to sample this French miracle. We were sitting in the garden, toasting the stars and the fireflies, when Mr. Shaw and Miss Payne-Townshend returned. They were holding hands and walking so close that their shoulders rubbed together.

"My friend Robbie Ross sent me a bottle of champagne," I called. "I am corrupting your friends. I have initiated a socialist distribution of champagne and Mr. Webb approves.

Mr. Shaw smiled. "Good. Fine," he said.

Mr. Shaw and Miss Payne-Townshend did not stop to converse, but disappeared inside the farmhouse.

"They look happy," said Miss Potter.

"Indeed," I said. "Such extreme satisfaction is usually seen only on the faces of those who have done something wrong."

"I am worried for Charlotte," said Miss Potter. "I have known Mr. Shaw but a little while and yet I've heard he has a reputation for breaking hearts."

"It is not our affair," said Mr. Webb.

"Charlotte is our friend," replied Miss Potter. "She has contributed generously to the Fabian Society and may be regarded as our comrade in politics. Do we not have a responsibility to help her avoid unhappiness?"

"We do," I said. "For although it is nearly impossible to see the pits we are about to fall into, it is always easy to see the traps others are blundering towards. I often know how to solve the problems of everyone around me, although my own difficulties defy solution."

"Should one of us talk to her?" asked Miss Potter?

"It is not our affair," said Mr. Webb.

"Perhaps we should warn Mr. Shaw that breaking the heart of so estimable a woman risks forfeiting the good will of all of us," I said. "I say this merely to contribute to the conversation because I have no intention of doing any such thing."

Miss Potter looked at me with scorn. "Mr. Wilde, do you always find the difficulties of others amusing?"

"Life would be very tedious if I did not," I said. "But you will discover, I hope, that amusement and concern are not antagonistic emotions, but are complimentary."

"Mr. Webb, what do you think?" asked Miss Potter.

"I think Miss Payne-Townshend has survived and thrived as an independent woman for many years without any help from us," he replied. "And until she asks for advice, I intend to avoid giving it."

"Sidney, you are one of those noble, good-hearted, sensible souls who delights in smothering the joys of gossip," I said. "Petty vices should not be dismissed lightly. If carefully cultivated, they may grow into major ones."

"If you're going to be ironical, then I am going to bed," said Mr. Webb, putting down his glass. "Shaw always tells me to search his jokes for hidden truths. But I'm not sure I like the truths you hide in your jokes."

"If there are truths hidden in my jests, it is not I that has put them there, but life," I said. "Your quarrel is with her. I have often thought that life is over-generous with ironies. Perhaps it is to atone for being so miserly with happiness."

There was more that was said that evening, but I choose to end my account of it with my best bit of wit.

The next morning, I once again joined Mr. Webb in a walk to the village. The sun was barely up, but it was already pleasantly warm.

"The summer is galloping toward autumn," I said. "I can feel our time growing short."

"Is your life in the city so hectic that you dread returning?" asked Mr. Webb.

"I dread it and I love it," I replied. "Each of my moods leaves me craving its opposite. This summer holiday will be rendered even more perfect if I am compelled to leave it before I am ready. Pleasures are more exquisite when they leave us unsatisfied."

"You're being ironical again and when the conversation goes in that direction, I can't keep up," said Mr. Webb. "I just hope your time here was well spent and that you accomplished what you needed to."

"Sidney, you'll be happier if you stop looking at life as a series of tasks that need to be completed," I said.

Mr. Webb shook his head. "I'm not sure that's true. I enjoy getting things done and I've never noticed that lazy people were much happier than their busy brothers. If you have a philosophy, Oscar, it's probably: be true to yourself. Am I right?"

"You are not wrong," I said.

"Then to be true to myself, I must stay busy," said Mr. Webb. "It's the way I am made."

"Well said. You are the ant from the fable, and I am the grasshopper."

Mr. Webb frowned. "I hope not. When winter comes, the grasshopper starves to death."

"Winter will never come," I declared. "I shall charm the sun into tarrying with me."

But the sun did not tarry that day. It rose quickly, reminding me that time will not pause. My Fabian adventure is almost over.

FORTY

Dear Lion,

I had thought that Mr. Shaw and I had been discreet, but some recent conversations have proved how wrong I was. Miss Potter sought me out this morning when I was enjoying a walk in the garden and soon began to talk of serious things.

"Miss Payne-Townshend, may I risk our friendship by talking of things that are none of my affair?" she asked.

"If this is going to be that kind of talk, perhaps you had best call me Charlotte," I replied.

"Thank you, Charlotte. First, let me say that Mr. Webb assures me that there is no more dedicated Fabian than Mr. Shaw. He has worked--"

I interrupted her. "Is this going to be a warning not to risk my happiness on a philanderer?"

Miss Potter seemed disconcerted at being so obvious. I suppose it is," she said.

"Mr. Shaw told me himself that several women have made themselves unhappy over him," I said.

"I see," said Miss Potter. "At least he is honest."

"I believe he is," I said. "And I should say that much of Mr. Shaw's appeal is not personal. It is his purpose—which he shares with you and Mr. Webb—that makes him so extraordinary to me."

"It is the novelty of the Fabian Society that makes you find us so unusual," replied Miss Potter.

"I don't think so," I said. "I have met quite a lot of people in my life. In fact, that seems to have been my life's work--meeting people. My mother dragged me around Europe in search of a husband for me and after her death I continued my travels in search of a purpose. And so, I can state that there are very few people in the world with your sense of mission."

"I fear you have an overly-romantic idea of what it is we do," said Miss Potter. "Much of my work is numbingly tedious."

"I suspect much of the work the world needs done is tedious," I replied. "That is the nature of work and says nothing about the cause to which the work is dedicated."

"I can see you know your own mind," said Miss Potter. "I will not trouble you again with my concerns."

Miss Potter began to walk away, but I was not finished with our conversation. "We are talking of matters of the heart and so let me state that I think it would be best if you made your mind up about Mr. Webb and not pull him toward you with one hand while pushing him away with the other. His agony is palpable."

Miss Potter turned to me with a distressed expression. "I don't know where you could have gotten the idea that Mr. Webb cares for me."

"His love is as obvious as an ocean," I said. "He positively glows with it."

"Perhaps he does," said Miss Potter. "But I am not obligated to return that emotion."

"No, but if you truly esteem him as a friend you will consider his happiness," I replied. "And right now, you are doing everything you can to make him as miserable as possible."

Miss Potter stiffened. "Mr. Webb and I are doing valuable work together," she protested. "He is a fine editor and writing critic."

"And there is no one else in the world who could perform those tasks for you?" I asked. "His attentions must be very flattering. But if you are his true friend as you claim, you should let him go."

Miss Potter said nothing, but nodded silently. I could not tell if she was nodding in agreement or merely acknowledging that she understood my meaning.

After Miss Potter left me, I went in search of Mr. Wilde and I found him sitting with his back against a tree, a manuscript in his lap and a pencil in his hand. I snuck up behind the tree and then stepped before him.

"You always talk as if you are the King of Idleness, Mr. Wilde, yet I find you working as hard as Mr. Webb."

Mr. Wilde smiled at this accusation. "It's true I am a dreadful hypocrite. No matter how desperately I clutch at indolence, artistic inspiration always finds me out. Work has its own temptations that my weak will is helpless to resist."

"Have you finished the play you were hoping to write?" I asked.

"Almost. It is a light-hearted confection, so much sillier and more trivial than my other plays."

"Now you have me curious," I confessed.

"You will have to be patient and wait to see it performed," he said. "For although I hate anyone to deny my curiosity in any way, I do expect patience in others."

"How very noble of you," I said.

"Yes, it is only by holding others to a higher standard than we hold ourselves that society maintains any standards at all. Hypocrisy is the foundation of all modern morality. Without it we would be lost."

"Would you mind if I sat down?" I asked.

Mr. Wilde took off his jacket and spread it on the ground for me to sit on. I sat and leaned against the tree. "Has Miss Potter been pestering you about your friendship with Mr. Shaw?" he asked.

"So, she talked about me with you," I said. "I'm not sure I like being discussed when I am not present."

"There is only one thing worse than being talked about and that is not being talked about. But you may be assured that we all had your happiness as our theme. I suspect Miss Potter's concern for your peace of mind springs from her own experience of heartbreak. She hopes you will avoid the abyss that she has fallen into on occasion."

"And what is your opinion of the dangers of love?" I asked. "Is it something about which one should be cautious?"

"If one is capable of being cautious then one cannot be said to be in love," replied Mr. Wilde. "Love demands that we risk our health, our happiness, our very souls."

"That sounds a little frightening," I replied.

"Indeed," said Mr. Wilde. "Romeo and Othello both teach us that love can be a fearful, terrible thing."

"Thankfully, it is an exceptional love that ends in murder or suicide," I said.

"True. It often in ends in one lover proving unworthy. Or more often--both. Love thus prepares us for one of the great truths of life: that it is often disappointing."

"I think that people who find life disappointing are disappointed in some aspect of themselves," I said.

"That is far too wise a comment for a beautiful summer morning," said Mr. Wilde. "You must promise to talk only nonsense for the next hour."

"I should leave you to your work," I said.

"Please stay, dear lady," said Mr. Wilde. "My inspiration has fled, thank heaven and now I can stop wasting the afternoon with work and get down to the important business of being amusing."

These are the conversations that make up my days. Have you ever heard the like? They seem to be equal parts wisdom and whimsy. I will miss Mr. Wilde when the summer is over, and I have a feeling that I will never have another season like this one. That is a melancholy thought.

But I have only to search out Mr. Wilde again to be cajoled from my somber mood.

Sincerely,
Charlotte Payne-Townshend

FORTY-ONE

From the unpublished memoir of Bernard Shaw:

This may have been the strangest night of my life. Even now I am shaking. I may have been the victim of nothing more than a bad dream and yet I feel as if I have been given a glimpse of Hell itself.

I must write down all my confused recollections and make sense of what has happened.

It began in the evening, when I went to the parlor and stretched out on the divan and closed my eyes. We have seldom used the parlor and I don't know what impulse drove me there except a mild sleepiness.

After a few minutes I felt a hand on my forehead.

"What angel is this that disturbs my rest?"

"Your own true guardian angel," said Charlotte's voice.

"For a guardian angel you've strangely derelict in your duty. I looked for you all afternoon."

"I wanted to think."

"About what?"

"If you must know, I was thinking about marriage. What would you say if I told you that you are the only man I would ever consider marrying?"

I felt a shock pass through me as if from electricity and I sat up on the divan.

"I would ask if you knew the cost of passage to Nepal."

"Nepal?"

"Where I could preach socialism to the Sherpas until this madness has left you. What has become of the woman who would never give up her independence?"

"She is looking at life in a new way. After yesterday—"

"Ah! The heart of the matter! Well, it is a common mistake to confuse the sexual instinct for love. This is even more common when the man and woman are friends and the man is a well-known London genius. But the sex attraction is merely the bait in the trap of marriage. Once the trap is closed the bait quickly evaporates."

Charlotte laughed heartily and long.

"You are the vainest thing. The sex attraction has nothing to do with my feelings.

"Of course it does."

"It doesn't. I was curious. My curiosity has been satisfied. And you were right—it is distasteful."

"It is?"

"Perhaps distasteful is too strong a word. Is uninteresting any better?"

"Not much. Was it something I did?"

"Oh no."

"Something I didn't do?"

"Not at all."

"Then it's nerves. That's all. Your first time—anyone would be—"

"Oh no. Your jokes put me quite at ease. I haven't laugh so hard in years."

"You're welcome, I'm sure. But you mustn't assume every experience will be like your first one any more than you would assume that every meal would make you sick after eating a bad egg. In fact, I shall prove it to you. I am at your disposal."

I took Charlotte's hand, but she looked at me with pity.

"I've wounded your vanity, haven't I? I am sorry."

"Not at all. I'm merely afraid you'll draw false conclusions from a poor example. Once I am fit, we shall conduct a series of experiments designed to prove—"

"There is no need for any experiments. I have learned something more important than any physical pleasure."

"And what is that?"

"I've learned there is no need to fear the sex instinct. All my life I feared it because I knew that it could tempt me to surrender my independence to the wrong man for the wrong reasons. But now I am amazed we invest such a curious act with such depth of feeling. Now that curiosity has been satisfied, fear has departed as well. I can at last think clearly about marriage and consider all those elements in human relations that don't evaporate after the trap is closed."

"You are the most extraordinary woman."

"Should I list the reasons we are uniquely suited for one another?"

"No. I have enough to ponder for one night."

"Then good-night. I am going to bed."

"Good-night."

I kissed her on the divan and then she went to the doorway and paused.

"Sweet dreams."

Charlotte disappeared down the hall.

I collapsed on the divan, my mind in a whirl. How could I prevent this romance from becoming a disaster? Would she forgive me if I stated that I had no intention of marrying anyone in the next decade?

I have no memory of falling asleep, but suddenly I heard Sidney's voice.

"Wake up, Bernard," said Sidney.

"What is it?"

I sat up on the divan. The light in the parlor was greenish and strange.

Miss Potter appeared and took her place by Sidney's side.

"Mr. Wilde has proposed we hold a séance," she said.

"A séance?" I said. "Don't be absurd."

Mr. Wilde strolled into the room. He wore a purple suit that I had never seen before and that looked ghastly in the greenish light.

"I assure you that a séance is quite the thing to do these days," he said. "It is hardly possible to attend a London dinner party without encountering guests from another plane. The fashionable Londoner communes with the dead more often than he sups with his own relations and with good reason. The deceased seldom linger for more than half an hour, they rarely borrow money and they never describe the achievements of their children for the length of time it would take to have my own. I look to the day when the dead are eligible for public office."

"And who is to be the medium?" I asked.

"I believe Mr. Webb will be a perfectly efficient medium," said Mr. Wilde. "He believes the future will arrive through him, why not the past?"

"And who are we to summon?" I asked.

"As a favor to you and Mr. Wilde, I propose to summon the spirit of Shakespeare," said Sidney.

"Everyone be seated," said Mr. Wilde.

We took our places around the parlor table. Despite my reservations, I felt compelled to take my place in the circle.

"Hold hands," said Miss Potter.

We clasped hands. Miss Potter was on one side of me and Mr. Wilde was on the other.

"Close your eyes," said Sidney.

I closed my eyes.

"Let us begin," I heard Mr. Wilde say.

"I call upon the spirits of the past to abide with us tonight," said Sidney's voice. "May the bard of Stratford-on-Avon share his wisdom and pain with the living gathered here."

"This is ridiculous," I said.

Miss Potter made a hushing sound.

"May the essence of England's genius appear before us now!" cried Sidney in a commanding voice. "Come to us now! Everyone!"

We all began to chant: "Come to us now! Come to us now!"

"It's humbug!" I cried. "I won't believe it!"

I opened my eyes.

There rose a great sound of clanking and a clatter of metal and a feeling of dread filled my breast. The clanking grew louder and seemed to come from the hall of the house. I feared that whatever was making the noise was drawing closer.

And so it proved. A glowing ghost appeared in the doorway of the parlor. It was in the shape of a man with a great mustache and bushy chin whiskers. The ghost was encumbered by a great chain that wrapped around its middle and dragged on the ground behind. Attached to the chain were books of all kinds: thick books and thin books and some that seemed little more than pamphlets.

The staring eyes of the ghost were fixed on mine and it chilled my soul to look on them.

"Who are you?" I asked the ghost.

"Ask me who I was," it said. Its voice seemed to come from a great distance.

"Who were you then?"

"In life I was the author Charles Dickens."

"Dickens?" said Sidney in an aggrieved tone. "Where is Shakespeare? We were calling for Shakespeare."

"He's busy," said the ghost in a voice that brooked no argument.

"Beware!" said Miss Potter. "This spirit may be a devil sent to tempt us."

"Oh, I hope so!" said Mr. Wilde.

"It's humbug still!" I cried.

The ghost took a step closer to me.

"Why do you doubt the evidence of your senses?"

"Because my imagination makes them cheats," I answered. "You may be a half-remembered bit of fiction, a bit of book, a piece of play, a Gothic fancy regurgitated by my buzzing brain. There's more of tome than of tomb about you."

The ghost raised its arms and rattled its chains and gave a great wail that shook the windows and made me want to crawl under the table.

"Do you believe in me or not!" it demanded of me.

"For the moment I must," I said. But why have you come to us?"

"Every man is given a gift from God and it is required of him that he pay his debt in service to his fellow man." The ghost stared off into space as if seeing its own past. "If that debt is not paid in life, it must be paid for after death."

"But what debt had you to pay?" I asked.

The ghost's eyes turned to stare into mine.

"The debt of art," it said. "The Almighty made my mind a philosopher's stone that touching paper transmuted it into gold. My pen was a lever that I used to lift the world a little closer to heaven. Every book, every story, every page was payment to my creator. Every lazy hour, every indolent day was a theft from mankind and God. I wear the chains I forged in life—the chains of idleness. Every link is a wasted hour, every coil an unwritten book."

The ghost stooped and grabbed a book that was bound to its chain.

"This might have moved men's hearts to pity, if only I had written it."

The ghost let the book fall and it grabbed another.

"This might have kindled rage against injustice, if I had not been too busy to do my true work."

The ghost let the second book fall and it tenderly picked up a slim volume from the end of its chain.

"And this might have made children laugh."

"Alas, poor ghost!" I said.

"Alas, poor mortals," said ghost. "Would you know the weight and length of the coils you bear yourselves?"

"No! Don't tell us!" cried Mr. Wilde.

"I am here to warn you that you have yet a chance of escaping my fate."

"Thank you," I said.

"You must take the path of industry. The solitary road of toil. Only by unremitting labor can you—"

"Liar!"

I turned and looked to the doorway. Standing in the doorframe was a female ghost wearing a dress that might have been in fashion forty years ago, but there were no chains binding it. It glowed with an eerie light, its features were contorted in rage. It jabbed an accusing finger.

"Even in death you are a fool and a liar!".

"Begone, woman and trouble me not!" yelled the ghost, but it stepped to the side of the room to put some distance between itself and its accuser.

"Who are you?" asked Miss Potter.

"Ask her who she was," advised Mr. Wilde.

"In life I was the wife of Charles Dickens," said the female ghost. But her eyes never strayed from the ghost.

The ghost moaned. "It is bad enough that you deceived yourself your whole life long," shouted the female ghost. "Must you fool yourself after death?"

"If I have wronged you, I have suffered," cried the ghost. "Leave me be!"

"You suffer, but you do not repent." The female ghost turned toward us. "Hell has no judge or jailer to explain to the damned their crimes. And so, they invent their own mythologies which flatter their consciences and permit them to indulge in the very sins which damned them in the first place."

The female ghost whirled and again pointed an accusing finger at the ghost.

"Idleness? Sloth? Who are you fooling? Your work was your god. Art was your mistress. You are damned for neglecting your wife and children and for loving only the progeny of your mind!"

"Lies! Lies!" cried the ghost. He hugged his chains to his body and fondled the books attached to them.

"And you persist in your folly," cried the female ghost. "Hell is full of unrepentant scribblers who glorify their sin by calling it art. Shakespeare writes his millionth play in torment, when all he needs do is to turn to Anne Hathaway to be in Paradise."

"You tempt me with lies!" cried the ghost. "My sloth was my sin!"

"Even now it is not too late!" shouted the female ghost. "Throw down your pen! Come with me!"

"No!" cried the ghost. "I am an artist. I belong to the world!"

"You belong to me! You are mine! Mine!"

"No!" shouted the ghost.

The female ghost screamed "Mine! Mine! Mine!" as she lunged at the ghost. As she clasped the chained figure there was a great thunderclap and a flash like lightning and for a long moment I could see nothing. The thunder seemed to roll and echo, but I could not tell if I was hearing it in my ears or only in my mind.

I opened my eyes and found myself on the floor beside the divan. There was no one in the room but me. How strange. If this was a dream, why was I shaking from head to foot? I will tell no one of this and will ponder what I have seen and heard. Is this a warning from beyond, or merely an eruption from the bottom of my soul?

Either way, it doesn't bode well for Charlotte's happiness.

FORTY-TWO

Dear Lion,

I have had a sobering conversation with Mr. Webb, which has made me look at my romance with Mr. Shaw in a more realistic light. Mr. Webb may not be Mr. Shaw's oldest friend, but he seems to be the closest friend that Mr. Shaw currently has. I came upon him in the garden this morning. He had papers spread out across the table. He seemed deep in thought, but he looked up when I approached.

"Ah, Miss Payne-Townshend, good morning," he said.

I tried to back away.

"I didn't mean to disturb you," I said.

"Stay, Miss Payne-Townshend, please. There's something absurd about working on an economics text in a garden this beautiful. I have not seen you all day. Will you sit down?"

I sat at the table with him.

"Is there some problem I can help you with?" he asked.

"I don't think I should burden—" I began.

"It's Bernard, isn't it?" he said.

I could only nod.

"I have been expecting trouble. Sooner or later, he exasperates all his women."

I did not like the sound of this.

"How many women has he had?"

"Probably more than you suspect but fewer than he boasts of," said Mr. Webb. "Bernard was a shy youth and became attractive to women late in life. That may be why he so enjoys being a flame for the moths. But please don't think

I am talking about the type of relation where the woman earns the label "mistress." Bernard often leaves a woman her honor while stealing her heart."

"How very odd. Mr. Webb, what is your advice to me?"

"The advice you don't want to hear: give him up. You're talking to me like this means you are at the stage when your love will change from a pleasure to a torment. Give him up."

My heart sank at this advice.

"If I were pursuing him solely for my own pleasure, I could perhaps find strength to do that. But you and Miss Potter and Mr. Shaw have awakened a Fabian conscience in me. I believe it may not only be my desire to marry Mr. Shaw—it may be my duty."

Mr. Webb looked very puzzled.

"I don't know what we could have said that would—"

I interrupted him.

"You awakened my conscience and it drew its own conclusions. But I am too old and too timid to start my life over and transform myself into a useful person. I would be condemned to a useless life of idle luxury except for the fantastic luck of meeting Mr. Shaw. I am good for nothing but running a household and he is good for everything but that. You probably think that devoting myself to a noble person is foolish when I could devote myself to a noble cause, but that is only because one is more apt to be disillusioned with a person than with a cause. But I don't think I have any more illusions left about Mr. Shaw. Except perhaps the illusion that he can be induced to marry at all."

Mr. Webb squinted at me through his pince-nez and thought for a long moment.

"Miss Townshend, I don't know what to say. As to the rightness or wrongness of your decision, I have no answer. I can only tell you what you must not do."

"And what is that?" I asked.

"Chase him. If you pursue him, he will flee; if you clutch him, he will struggle; if you trap him, he will vanish. I have seen it before. The only way to catch him is let him run away."

"That sounds suspiciously like an Oriental paradox."

"Perhaps. But it is the best advice I have. You've used up my store of wisdom."

"I hope it will be enough. Bernard and I are both strange individuals, but somehow, I feel we are perfectly suited for each other. Sooner or later, he must recognize that, won't he?"

"One would think so. But some men find wisdom too late."

And some men never find wisdom at all, I silently thought to myself.

I confess that I have mentioned the subject of marriage to Mr. Shaw. You might think of me as horribly foolish and unconventional to do so. But I am too old to be playing silly games about love and marriage and I do not feel like wasting months of my life on a romance that will not be permanent. If Mr. Shaw will not have me, I will know the worst at once. Very soon I will have my answer.

Sincerely,
Charlotte Payne-Townshend

FORTY-THREE

From the unpublished memoir of Bernard Shaw:

The worst has happened. I may have ruined our summer holiday for once and all.

It began in the evening, when I looked into the parlor and saw Charlotte sitting on the divan, staring out the window at the flowers of the garden.

I began to back out of the room. But before I could make my escape, Charlotte turned.

"Coward!" she cried.

I stopped and stared at her. "What?"

"I called you a coward. You weren't even going to speak to me."

"You looked so at peace I didn't wish to disturb you."

"Liar. A coward and a liar. You have been avoiding me. You are afraid I will demand an answer to the question I put to you last night."

"Charlotte, I still find it extraordinary that you would want to marry me, knowing what you do about me."

"Is it so extraordinary that a woman would care as little about the sexual act as you do?"

"It is not a case of the sex instinct alone. Most women have a desire for motherhood."

"I knew from a very young age that I would never want to be a mother. I never wanted there to be the slightest chance that a child of mine would have a childhood like mine."

"I see," I said.

"I believe that is one more feeling that we share. We are extraordinarily suited to one another."

"Charlotte, you must understand that in truth love is only a recreation to me. I am a writing machine and little more. I have said that before as a joke, but I say it now as a warning."

"I know that," she said in a softer tone. "It is because I want to tend the writing machine that I want to marry you. Oddly enough, I think you are something like a genius, despite your habit of announcing that you are. You will find the profession of genius easier with a companion—a sympathetic friend who will take care of the mundane tasks of running the household and leave you to devote yourself to your work. If you are not as productive when we are together as when we are apart, it is your own fault. You insist on talking sentimental nonsense for hours.

I assure it isn't necessary. But even if you don't believe me, marriage would soon put things right. No man continues to woo the woman he sees at breakfast every morning."

"That is the most unromantic attitude toward marriage I've ever heard. If you railed against marriage as a sham or a trap, I could sympathize. But to propose a union of souls with the manner of a horse breeder selecting a mare and a stud—"

Charlotte interrupted me with great energy. "I am merely adopting the realistic attitude toward marriage that most people are forced to adopt around the time of their first wedding anniversary. You may accuse me of premature common sense if you like, but that attitude ill becomes a man who claims to be the champion of clear thinking."

"Did my gallantries mean nothing to you? I thought we were whispering warm words of love together in the fields of Venus and instead I find you in Vulcan's workshop coldly assembling a steam engine for two!"

These words truly upset her. Charlotte became angry in a way that I had never seen before.

"When Henrik Ibsen or Bernard Shaw looks at life and marriage without illusions, they are geniuses. When a mere woman does the same, she is a monster! I can abide your vanity, Mr. Shaw, but not your hypocrisy!"

That taunt stung my temper.

"There isn't a man in England who is as honest with women as I. You knew from the first that I was as likely to marry as the statue of Nelson in Trafalgar Square. I've said on numerous occasions that I would rather fly to ends of the earth than be bullied, blackmailed, cajoled or wheedled into sacrificing my sacred independence. And you smiled and laughed and said that you agreed. Hypocrisy—thy name is woman!"

Charlotte stared at me for a long moment, but she apparently decided that shouting did not become us because when she spoke her tone was icy.

"You are right of course. I genius always is. Independence is far too sacred a thing to ever relinquish. I must have been mad. Well, there is a remedy. I shall leave in the morning."

And she did. Someone—perhaps Sidney—walked to the village early in the morning because by mid-morning a carriage had arrived to take Charlotte to the train station.

I watched her ride away with a heavy heart. I have felt this sadness many times before, but there is another feeling in my heart that is novel. Is this regret I feel?

I review the words we last spoke to one another in my mind and I would take back much of what I said. I spoke the truth and yet I feel that my words did not represent all of what my heart holds.

Damnation! I was so eloquent in my anger. Why could I not have given voice to softer thoughts?

I will write to her. It may not be too late to salvage the friendship.

FORTY-FOUR

Dear Miss Darling:

My Fabian summer is almost over, and I am already looking back on it with nostalgia. I have learned to mix work and pleasure without one weakening the other. Mr. Webb and Mr. Shaw have taught me much about the discipline of writing and Mr. Webb especially has demonstrated many writing skills that I will probably use for the rest of my life.

Miss Payne-Townshend departed earlier this week and we all suppose that she had an argument with Mr. Shaw. Mr. Shaw is apparently one of those charming souls who amuses all the women who fall into orbit around him, but who then exasperates any one of them who tries to claim him as her own. I don't know who is more foolish: Miss Payne-Townshend for trying to marry this socialist sprite, or Mr. Shaw for letting this practical-minded Irish millionairess slip through his fingers.

Her absence has made any gathering of those who remain feel incomplete and our routines feel strained and awkward. Mr. Shaw proposed a picnic today, which seemed to me to be most uncharacteristic of him and I wondered if he was trying to distract himself from the pain of missing Miss Payne-Townshend.

But we were all agreeable and Mrs. Foster packed a fine luncheon in our basket. We all followed Mr. Shaw to a nearby field where we spread our blankets and sat down to enjoy the day.

As I unpacked our picnic lunch, I handed Mr. Shaw a letter that had arrived for him. Mr. Shaw looked at the envelope and threw it to the ground.

"Damnation! It's postmarked Paris. The letters I sent to her will miss her. How can I write to her if she won't stay in one place? I don't understand this mania for travel. It's not as if she hasn't seen everything in Europe five times before. What can she find in Paris she can't find in England?"

"Your absence," I said.

Mr. Shaw scowled at me. He sat down and bit into an apple.

"Ridiculous. Does she think I'll lay siege to her London flat? I have so much work to do that even when I am in London, I'm fifteen years in arrears in my social calls."

"A pity you can't borrow from me," said Mr. Wilde. "I'm twenty years ahead in mine."

"How often do you write to Miss Payne-Townshend?" asked Mr. Webb.

"No more than once a day," said Mr. Shaw. He picked up Miss Payne-Townshend's letter, opened it and read it. After a minute he again threw the letter down in a fury.

"Damnation! How did such a sensible woman become so contrary and perverse?"

"She spent a holiday with you," I said.

Mr. Webb poked my foot with his and silently shook his head. I believe he wanted me to refrain from pressing on Mr. Shaw's nerve.

Soon Mr. Shaw, Mr. Webb and I went to wander in the woods. We left Mr. Wilde relaxing on the blanket.

On the other side of the tree-lined hill, we found a small river and we followed its bank until we came to a ruined mill that was so lovely that I decided we should return to Mr. Wilde and bring him to observe it. As we emerged from the trees, I thought I saw Mr. Wilde slip some pages of a manuscript into the book that he was reading.

Mr. Webb was the first to return to the picnic blanket.

"Oscar!" he called. "We've found a ruined mill by the river."

"Destroyed by a fire," added Mr. Shaw. "Probably fifty years ago."

"You should see it," I said. "It's quite picturesque."

We all sat on the blanket and I passed out sandwiches.

"I'm sure it is," said Mr. Wilde. "Everything around here is quite picturesque. It has become exquisitely tedious."

"I thought you were the great disciple of beauty," said Mr. Shaw.

"Even the most devoted disciple craves some variety of experience," said Mr. Wilde. "This endless succession of dazzling landscapes leaves me craving a muddy London street on a foggy winter's morning. Nature is quite an artist in her own way, but she simply doesn't know when to leave well enough alone."

"Well, she certainly hasn't left well enough alone here," said Mr. Shaw. "The ruins of the mill are so glorious and inspiring I feel a play coming on."

Mr. Wilde got to his feet.

"You surprise me, Mr. Shaw. I thought a sensible socialist would see only the remains of an economic enterprise, or a lesson on the value of fire insurance. Show me this inspiration. Perhaps I will see evidence of a forgotten crime or the epilogue of an ancient tragedy. Who will say whose vision is clearer?"

Mr. Wilde strolled toward the woods.

"I will," said Mr. Shaw and he followed Mr. Wilde.

"I've finished drafting a letter to the London County Council about our school proposal," said Mr. Webb.

"Good," I said. "I'll read it tonight."

"When we are back in London, I assume I will see you at Society meetings. And if you need help with your book, I shall be at your service. But for the most part, perhaps we should limit our contact to letters."

I felt a sudden pang at this statement.

"But why?" I asked.

"It would be best for me," said Mr. Webb. "It has become obvious that I was foolish to think that we could be more than friends. I entirely understand and respect your decision, but it would be best for me if we limit our personal meetings."

I felt stunned. His decision was an inevitable development, of course and yet I was taken utterly by surprise.

Mr. Webb lay on his back on the blanket and stared at the clouds.

"Such a beautiful day," he said.

"Sidney . . . " I began.

"Shhh. It's all right. What does that cloud remind you of? To me it looks either like a camel or the profile of Frederick Engels."

I was trying to decide how to respond to Mr. Webb's decision when Mr. Shaw came tearing out of the woods. He raced to us as if devils were chasing him. Mr. Webb sat up in alarm.

"What's wrong?" he asked.

Mr. Shaw began pawing among the plates of food.

"Where's Wilde's book? Ahh!"

Mr. Shaw found Mr. Wilde's book and he pulled manuscript pages from it.

"I saw him slip these pages in it," said Mr. Shaw. "It must be his socialist essay. Aren't you curious how it's turned out?"

"Bernard, put it back," said Mr. Webb.

"This may be the new socialist gospel. Or an attack on the upper classes so witty that next season an unearned income will be a social indiscretion."

Mr. Shaw handed the pages to Mr. Webb.

"But if you don't wish to read it, you may put it back."

Mr. Webb looked to me, but I made no sign. At last, Mr. Webb unfolded the pages and read them aloud.

"Jack: When one is placed in the position of guardian one has to adopt a very high moral tone on all subjects. It's one's duty to do so. And as a high moral tone can hardly be said to conduce very much to either one's health or one's happiness, in order to come up to town I have always pretended to have a younger brother of the name of Ernest, who lives in the Albany and gets into the most dreadful scrapes. That, my dear Algy, is the whole truth pure and simple."

Mr. Shaw nearly shouted his outrage: "He's writing a play!"

Mr. Wilde now appeared from behind us. He had apparently emerged from the trees while we were engrossed in his pages.

"Yes, a delightful little farce to illustrate the most profound of philosophies: that we must treat the serious things in life lightly and take the trivial things in life seriously. It will be my greatest triumph yet and when it is produced I will reserve tickets for you all. But until then I regard my manuscript as private and personal."

Mr. Webb handed some pages to Mr. Wilde.

"I'm sorry," said Sidney. "I beg your forgiveness."

But Mr. Shaw was still fuming. "A play? All these weeks we thought you were writing a Fabian essay. This is the most ungrateful breach of etiquette I've ever seen."

Mr. Wilde looked indignant. "I never promised to write an essay. And you never made that a condition of your hospitality."

"But we assumed—"

Mr. Wilde interrupted. "I specifically warned you that socialist prose is not my forte. I am not at fault if you didn't listen."

"But can't we persuade you to work on a socialist essay in the short time we have left?" I asked. "We will be returning to London in a week and I would like to think we were able to persuade you to contribute to mankind's most noble endeavor."

"But that is exactly what I have been doing," said Mr. Wilde. "Once you see my play performed you will have to agree that my time was far better spent creating this incomparable work of art rather than writing a trivial economic essay. It is through art and art alone, that we can realize our perfection."

I could not let a statement of such obvious foolishness stand. "Art has its place of course, but our foremost duty is to our fellow man."

Mr. Wilde shook his head.

"The illiterate farm boy who carves his name in a tree shares an impulse with the mighty Shakespeare: they both wish to write their name on the world and say: 'I was here. I had talent enough to do this!' Egoism is the engine that drives all mankind."

"But can't your egoism be satisfied by expressing the noblest parts of your nature in a way that will help mankind?" I pleaded.

"I honor all parts of my nature, the base as well as the noble. And it may very well be that the monuments my selfishness erects to itself will outlast the pavilions your virtue constructs for others. It may be that my life of vice will benefit generations of mankind while your life of virtue merely keeps yourself amused. You may condemn me as a selfish artist, but the same verdict should then fall on Michelangelo and Leonardo da Vinci. I am content to stand in the dock with them."

Mr. Webb now stepped to my side. "The work of the most selfish artist might benefit mankind, but that doesn't mean he helps art more than the reformer. A hundred years from now, if your plays are still being performed, audiences will sit and theatres and applaud your genius. They may say 'What a witty fellow he is!' Or "What a great writer!' But never for one moment will they think of all those who labored to give them the money and leisure to enjoy your play."

"Yes!" I cried, taking up Mr. Webb's theme. "A person who works sixteen hours a day, six days a week, for pauper's wages will never appreciate art. Every person who enjoys a play owes a debt to a countless throng of reformers and revolutionaries who have struggled since the beginning of history to dissolve the class barriers, increase the wages and create the freedom that makes enjoyment of art possible for everyone and not just a tiny jaded privileged class."

"You may create Art," said Mr. Webb.

"But we create the audience!" I concluded.

Mr. Wilde stared in astonishment at us. He looked to Mr. Shaw. "Their minds have fused. They have but one brain."

Mr. Shaw nodded. "That is what they have been creating this summer. A single consciousness. Potter-Webb. A Webb of Potters."

I found this foolishness annoying, so I spoke up. "There is one thing that I don't understand, Mr. Wilde. If you believe that art is so superior to socialism, then how did you come to write *The Soul of Man Under Socialism* in the first place?

"It was for the only reason that I ever write anything: I was inspired. A friend invited me to hear a Fabian speaker at Willis's restaurant and lo and behold! The main speaker was my old acquaintance Bernard Shaw."

Mr. Wilde now smiled at Mr. Shaw.

"I knew you had a reputation as a platform orator, but nothing prepared me for that night. So eloquent were you that the words caught the ear of the Socialist Muse and she paused in her flight and alighted next to your podium. Proving that she has a sense of humor—or at least a sense of irony—she surveyed the throng and picked perhaps the most unlikely man in the crowd to kiss. This sturdy, matronly muse was not at all my usual preference, but when the muse kisses one, one must kiss back. In memory of the occasion, I have Algernon ask Jack to dine with him at Willis's in the first act of my play. It is less than a footnote to history, but it amuses me to pay invisible tributes."

Mr. Shaw handed Mr. Wilde the remaining pages of his play. "Thus, am I repaid for my bad manners."

Mr. Wilde smiled. "Apology accepted. Well, this mental stimulation has left me fatigued and hungry. Miss Potter, are there anymore sandwiches—"

Mr. Wilde trailed off as he spotted something in the distance. I turned and saw a young man striding through the grass toward us. He had blond hair and an expression of extreme distress on his face.

Mr. Wilde's face grew grim. He strode out to meet the young man some distance from our picnic blanket.

"Bosie, what are you doing here?" he asked.

"Your wife told me you were here," said the blond young man." The cook told me you had gone to the river."

"You have no right to be here. This is an unacceptable intrusion."

"Please don't make me go." The young man's tone was so full of distress that he sounded as if he had been weeping and was about to commence again.

"I have nothing to say to you," said Mr. Wilde.

"Oscar, please . . . "

"You must leave at once."

"My brother's dead!" This came out as a wail of despair and the blond young man did begin to weep and Mr. Wilde took him in his arms.

"What? How?" asked Mr. Wilde.

"Francis. He's dead."

"My poor boy. How?"

The young man pulled away from Mr. Wilde and tried to wipe the tears from his eyes.

"Shot."

"A hunting accident?" asked Mr. Wilde.

"That's what they're saying. But I don't know. Oh God, Oscar, I don't know!"

The young man gave in completely to his grief and Mr. Wilde led him away from us and murmured gently in his ear.

"My dear sweet boy, how terrible for you. You must tell me everything."

Mr. Webb and Mr. Shaw watched these proceedings with downcast expressions. Mr. Shaw waited until Mr. Wilde and the young man were distant figures on the far side of the field before speaking.

"I suspect that we will be saying good-bye to Mr. Wilde today."

Mr. Webb spoke up. "Follow him, Bernard. They may need you."

Mr. Shaw nodded and hurried off in the direction that Mr. Wilde had gone.

When Mr. Shaw had left, Mr. Webb and I sat on the picnic blanket and began putting the remains of our lunch into the basket.

"We were wasting our time with Mr. Wilde," I said. "His sympathies may be socialist, but he hasn't the temperament."

"No," said Mr. Webb. When the food was packed away, he helped me fold the blanket.

It was as Mr. Shaw predicted: Mr. Wilde packed his things and left with his young friend. The young man's name was Lord Alfred Douglas and his brother was Francis, the private secretary to Lord Rosebery, the Prime Minister. Francis had been shot while climbing over a fence on a hunting trip; it isn't clear if this was an accident or some attempt to disguise suicide as an accident. The whole event seems very odd.

But there was no doubt that young Lord Douglas was in very great distress and it is to Mr. Wilde's credit that he has changed his plans to comfort his friend. They must be very close for Lord Douglas to rush to Mr. Wilde for consolation instead of to a member of his own family.

And so, my Fabian summer draws to a bittersweet close.

Mr. Webb is polite and correct in all his dealings with me, but he also has the formality of the recently heartbroken. I suppose our friendship was doomed from the start. He cannot be content with merely that and I would be unhappy with more.

But I also am aware of how much I have achieved with his help. I pray that I may keep his friendship for the sake of his work and mine.

Sincerely,
Beatrice Potter

FORTY-FIVE

From the unpublished memoir of Bernard Shaw:

I am writing under a tree next to my bicycle as Sidney Webb searches this village for some refreshment.

The trip back to London is a melancholy one. When Mr. Wilde departed with his young friend, much of the joy of the summer seemed to leave with him. After a couple of days of trying to work in surroundings that had suddenly become too quiet, I suggested to Sidney Webb and Miss Potter that we leave. To my surprise, they readily agreed.

Miss Potter decided to return to London by train, leaving me to wonder what had recently passed between her and Sidney. On the long bicycle ride back to London, Sydney declined to talk much about Miss Potter. Instead, he rambled on and on about his plans for an economic school until even I was thoroughly sick of the subject.

If I consider what we have accomplished, then perhaps we should count this summer as a success. Sidney has solid plans for the school that he intends to launch while I have almost finished my Julius Caesar play. Miss Potter has made much progress on her book on the co-operative movement. Even Mr. Wilde has completed a play, although perhaps I should review it before considering it a triumph.

But nothing feels like success. We are all of us in a somber mood and I think disappointment in love is the unspoken topic that haunts our conversations. Sidney's disappointment was predictable and perhaps inevitable, but I still ponder what I could have said to Charlotte that would have preserved our friendship after I had declined her offer of marriage.

I write to her daily although her habit of flitting from city to city means that my letters are constantly being returned to me as undeliverable.

Why am I a tormenter of women? I am as honest as I know how to be and yet women inevitably end up feeling betrayed by me.

And how does Sidney Webb find happiness? He is as good-hearted and hard-working a man as I have ever met and yet handsome scoundrels like Edward Aveling (who drove Eleanor Marx to suicide) find women flocking to them while Sidney bicycles back to London with only an Irish jester in a ragged suit for company.

Nature plants discontent in our hearts to drive humanity to improve its own condition; does this discontent mean happiness can only be caught in fleeting moments?

Sidney returns with two bottles of ginger beer. We will drink them and then flee from our troubles as fast as our legs can pump the pedals.

FORTY-SIX

From the memoir of Robert Ross:

"I know you harbor some secret grudge against Bosie," said Oscar. "But I do not wish to hear a word against him."

"You've described his failings far more eloquently than I ever could," I reminded him.

"Perhaps I have," admitted Oscar. "But if I have accused him, I also surely have the right to forgive him. He is quite heartbroken over his brother's death."

Oscar and I were eating at Kettner's. It was a Tuesday night, and it was late and the dining room was almost empty.

Although we had exchanged letters, this was the first time I had seen him in person since he had returned from his Fabian holiday. Oscar complained about the Fabian dinner menus, but I secretly suspect that he has enjoyed himself; he was certainly proud that he had completed another play over the summer.

The Importance of Being Earnest was now in rehearsals at the St. James Theatre. If this new play is a triumph, Oscar will have two plays running simultaneously in London *(An Ideal Husband* continues its run at the Haymarket). He will undoubtedly be the premier playwright of the age. While I would rejoice in his success, my intuition warns me that too much good fortune leads to hubris and hubris presages calamity.

I was distressed to hear that Oscar and Bosie were reunited and all my good work was undone. If Bosie had pleaded with Oscar, or tried to seduce him once again, Oscar could have remained firm. But the death of Francis, Lord Drumlanrig has broken Bosie's heart and Oscar's sympathetic nature could not resist trying to assuage his grief.

I should note that Oscar is famous for assuaging grief and comforting the afflicted. When the socialist and artist William Morris was on his deathbed, the visitor he most enjoyed was Oscar.

And so, Oscar and Bosie have returned to their usual haunts and habits and once again Bosie spends Oscar's money as if it flowed from an unquenchable spring.

"I hear that Queensberry has been going from restaurant to restaurant looking for you," I said.

"I charmed that lion, but the lion did not stay charmed," said Oscar. "The man is mad."

"It's the death of his heir that's made him so," I said. "There's rumors that Francis killed himself to avoid a Uranian scandal. Everyone says that Lord Rosebery is one of us and Francis was his secretary. Queensberry must think that driving you away will protect Bosie."

"What nonsense," said Oscar. "Did you know that Queensberry came to my house? He had one of his boxers as a companion. He insulted me and threatened me and told me to stay away from Bosie and I had to warn him that I would call the police if he did not leave. It was the most appalling breach of manners I have ever seen. The man is an utter brute. Bosie is in constant danger."

I silently disagreed. A perceptive man could see that Bosie was a danger to Oscar. Bosie bragged that he tormented his father with insulting letters and postcards. It seemed to me that baiting a man as notably vindictive as Queensberry was the height of folly. Queensberry might want to thrash his insolent son, but he would gladly destroy Oscar.

"Oscar, I saw Constance yesterday."

Oscar looked startled. Constance had told me that Oscar had not seen her since he had returned to London. He had checked into a hotel without even a stop at Tite Street. I wondered if he was now abandoning even the pretense of being married. Had Oscar lost all feeling for his own wife and sons?

"How is the lovely Constance?" asked Oscar in an even tone.

"She needs money, Oscar," I said. I tried to avoid sounding like I was accusing him of something.

"I have perhaps been a little negligent," Oscar confessed. "I will send her something. Unless you would care to deliver it?"

There was no accusation in Oscar's tone, but I sensed a subtle warning that I was interfering in his domestic affairs.

"No. I do not need to be a messenger," I said.

"You've been a good friend, Robbie," said Oscar with a smile. "To us both."

"What will you do now?" I asked. "Attend the rehearsals?"

"No. I think I will take a little holiday in Algeria. I hear that the beggar boys there have exquisite profiles."

I had mixed feelings about this news. Going to North Africa would put Oscar beyond Queensberry's reach which was all to the good. But how much indulgence could Oscar afford before his new play opened? That Constance had to have me ask for money was not a good sign. And going abroad with Bosie was a guarantee of extravagance.

But If Oscar could stay away from Queensberry long enough, Bosie was sure to eventually cause a scene so offensive that Oscar would break with him again. Bosie could no more refrain from being childish and obnoxious than his father could refrain from being a brute. Once Oscar had broken with Bosie, Queensberry would cease being a threat.

"Maybe a trip to Algeria is just the thing," I said. "Go with Bosie."

"Shall we finish with a strawberry parfait?" asked Oscar. "I fancy something light."

FORTY-SEVEN

From Oscar Wilde's secret journal:

I had just returned from Algeria when I encountered Frank Harris at the Café Royal. He asked how my rehearsals were progressing and I asked who would be there on opening night.

"I suppose Bernard Shaw will be reviewing my play," I said.

"I couldn't get Shaw to agree to it," said Harris. "He says he's not writing at present."

This was utterly unacceptable. When I remembered how perceptive Shaw had been in his review of *An Ideal Husband,* I decided no one else could fill his seat at the St. James Theatre.

"Where does Mr. Shaw live?" I asked.

I found the Fitzroy Square address given to me by Frank Harris. The Shaws occupied the second and third floors of the building and when I knocked on the door on the second floor, it was opened not by a servant, but by a tall woman of advanced age who had a fierce face and a square jaw.

"Good afternoon, Madam," I said with my hat in hand. "My name is Oscar Wilde. I am looking for Mr. Bernard Shaw."

"You're Irish," said the woman. She spoke with a Dublin brogue.

"I have that honor," I said. I was a little surprised

because often people fail to hear the rhythms of Ireland in my voice.

"Are you related to William Wilde, the surgeon?" she asked.

"He was my father," I said.

"He operated on my husband once," she said.

"With success, I hope," I said, but the woman had retreated from the doorway.

"Sonny!" I heard her call. She took a step back toward me. "I'm Elizabeth Shaw. Please come in."

She took me into a parlor that had a faint look of neglect, as if it was seldom used. The furniture looked old and faded.

"Please, sit down, Mr. Wilde," said Mrs. Shaw. "Sonny will be right down."

"You're from Dublin, Mrs. Shaw," I observed.

"Left many years ago and never went back," she said. There was no hint of nostalgia in her voice, no regrets or wistfulness.

Shaw appeared in the doorway, dressed in red woolen pants and a wrinkled white shirt.

"Ireland does not exist in vain as long as it produces people with the good sense to leave her," he said.

Mrs. Shaw scowled as if Shaw's wit was an imposition she had to put up with.

"I'll leave you two alone," she said. She turned and nodded to me in a formal fashion. "A pleasure to meet you, Mr. Wilde."

"And you, madam," I said as she slowly walked away.

"Wilde! I didn't expect to see you in the city," said Shaw. "I thought we had bored you enough in the country."

"You mustn't judge me too harshly, Bernard," I said. "I know you wanted a socialist essay and that I am a disappointment to you. But I am a goose that lays only golden eggs. It is quite unreasonable to expect me to lay breakfast eggs as well. Now, I am here because of an alarming rumor. Frank Harris tells me you won't be reviewing *The Importance of Being Earnest.*"

"That's right," said Shaw. "I am having problems laying eggs myself at the moment, golden or any other kind."

"I understand. The muses are fickle. When they desert me, I am left quite bereft. I can do nothing but eat and sleep and make amusing conversation."

"I am currently doing even less than that."

"Then perhaps it would be best if you postponed your attendance at my play."

"You are afraid I'll spoil the banquet like Banquo's ghost," said Shaw with a smile. I was glad to see he hadn't lost his sense of humor.

"The bloody specter of a lost Fabian romance moaning in the stalls could prove distracting to the actors."

"I see you've been exchanging letters with Miss Payne-Townshend."

"She sent me one delightful letter. She is a most intelligence correspondent and charmingly indiscreet. The irony of the grand socialist forming an alliance with a millionairess was too sweet not to be savored."

"Well, it's apparently too ironic to come to fruition. I haven't heard from her since we parted."

"Have you written to her?" I asked.

"Of course."

"A penitent letter?"

Mr. Shaw looked offended.

"Of course not. In our dispute I was entirely in the right."

"All the more reason for you to take the initiative. Doubtless her guilt keeps her silent. It is up to you—the magnanimous man of words—to bridge the chasm of silence. Quickly—you must take up pen and paper at once. Go!"

Mr. Shaw fetched paper and a pen. He sat down, waited for me to take a seat and looked at me suspiciously.

"Write what I tell you," I said.

"No. You are being perfectly foolish."

"Good. I'll wager your romances would last longer if they had more of my foolishness and less of your wisdom. Write: My dearest Charlotte. I write to you as a broken man. When you packed your bags and departed Suffolk you inadvertently packed up my heart and happiness as well. The passage of time has done nothing but show me how right you were in every particular of our quarrel and how completely I was in the wrong. I hope you can forgive a foolish and pompous man—

"Pompous?" said Shaw. "Arrogance I will admit to. Pomposity never."

"It is always better to admit to faults you do not have than remind her of the ones you do. Now, do be quiet until

I have finished. The muse is kissing me, and I must kiss back. Where was I?"

"I hope you can forgive this foolish and repentant man."

"Repentant will do, I suppose. Now write: My one hope is to see your glorious face again and read forgiveness in your shining countenance."

I thought I heard Mr. Shaw mutter: "Now that's pompous."

I ignored the comment and said: "Write to me at once, for your silence breaks my heart. Your most unworthy suitor, Bernard."

When Mr. Shaw had finished, he looked at me and said: "This letter would be regarded as ridiculous by a girl of seventeen."

"In love letters, ostentatious emotion is the expected thing. And your willingness to risk your dignity will be regarded as evidence of your devotion. You needn't thank me. A glowing review of *Earnest* is all that I require."

I stood and smiled down on him. "Now, I must be off. There is a rehearsal this afternoon. And I find that if I am absent for even one rehearsal, the performances become distressingly lifelike. I think people should nearly as artificial on stage as they are in life, but these modern actors seem to have forgotten how to act. Well, if Miss Payne-Townshend's reply restores your good humor, I trust I will see you at the St. James Theatre. Good-day, Bernard."

I took my leave and felt so wonderful for doing a good deed that I strolled nearly two whole blocks before becoming fatigued and summoning a hansom cab.

FORTY-EIGHT

Dear Miss Darling,

I have returned to Box House and the care of my father. After such a summer of wit and work, bicycles and books, this seems a dreary lot. I know I must appear to be a spoiled rich girl to complain when so many toil ceaselessly for the necessities of life, but this summer was so rich in what I value most that even a privileged life seems a weariness.

My sisters noticed my downcast spirits and quite against my will, they arranged a dinner party to cheer me up. If that was not bad enough, they also invited a handsome bachelor to make my acquaintance.

"I am done with romance," I told my sister Mary as I dressed for the party. "The sooner you all accept that, the happier we will all be."

"Lizzie Gainsworth says he is quite charming," said Mary. "And he's traveled a lot. If nothing else, you can talk about that."

I had no great faith in Lizzie Gainsworth's opinion of men, but when Mary escorted me into the parlor, I saw a very handsome man conversing with my father. He was perhaps thirty-five years of age, with a clean-shaven face and black hair and a strong jaw. His eyes were bright and his smile was sincere and attractive.

"Papa, may I interrupt?" said Mary. "Mr. Fields, I would like to introduce my sister Beatrice. Beatrice, this is Mr. Andrew Fields."

"Miss Potter, a pleasure to make your acquaintance." said Mr. Fields.

He took my hand and despite all my reservations, I believe my pulse quickened.

"The pleasure is mine, Mr. Fields," I replied.

"Are you the same Beatrice Potter who writes for *Nineteenth Century* magazine?" he asked.

"I am," I admitted.

"Well, then I am in luck. To attend a dinner party and meet a pioneer in social investigation. Who could have predicted that?"

Of course, I immediately suspected that Mary had discussed my interests with Mr. Fields before the party, but when I cornered Mary, she denied that she had.

"I have never spoken to Mr. Fields before tonight," said Mary. "I merely heard that there was a new bachelor living in Wellman's Cottage and I sent him an invitation by post. Lizzie said he was handsome, but you know how she is. She will declare that any man who can walk without a cane is a new Hercules. Any man who reads more than *Punch* is an English Aristotle."

Mr. Fields soon requested a walk around our gardens before dinner and I found myself revealing thoughts and feelings that I had never disclosed to my own family.

"My sisters don't understand that my work can be both dull and tiring and yet immensely satisfying," I said. "I attended the Co-Operative Congress in Glasgow and you cannot imagine a more boring congregation of petty quarreling men. And yet I learned so much that was useful for my book. Much of this work is hard and dreary and yet it must be done for the good of society."

He nodded and I added, "I'm sorry. I am talking too much."

"Not at all," he said. "Most women have done very little and so they know very little of the world. And all they can talk of are books and music. I am afraid I don't have time for books and music and so my conversational possibilities are limited. I am grateful to meet a woman who is interested in politics and has opinions on the issues of the day."

"What is it that keeps you so busy, Mr. Fields?" I asked.

"I own a company that manufactures matches," he said.

And with that, he pulled a box of matches from his pocket and handed it to me. "Field's Matches," he said. "That's me. One simple product that the whole world can use."

It was at this moment that Mary appeared and announced that dinner was ready.

Mr. Fields was the center of all attention at dinner and not merely mine.

My father (who finds talking laborious since his stroke) asked him, "Mr. Fields, I knew your father many years ago. He once mentioned that he hoped you would ship your matches to America. Has this prophecy been fulfilled?"

"Not yet," Mr. Fields answered. "But we are negotiating with an American firm and I am hopeful that within a year, we will be lighting fires all across America."

It was at this moment that I remembered some facts about matches and I took the box from my pocket and pulled out a match.

"Mr. Fields, is this match made from white phosphorus?" I asked.

"Yes," he answered. He looked puzzled at my question. Doubtless, he did not expect a woman to be familiar with any details of the manufacture of his product.

"Not red phosphorus?" I inquired.

"Red phosphorus is more expensive," he explained.

"But safer," I said. "White phosphorus collects in the jawbones and gums of factory workers who have to work with it."

"Are you an expert in matches?" he asked with a hint of irritation in his voice.

"When I was a rent collector in Katherine Buildings, I was taken to see a woman who had worked in a matchstick factory, but was now sick and could not pay her rent. There were rumors that so much phosphorus could build up in an afflicted jawbone that it would glow in the dark. I dismissed such talk as foolishness. But it was true. Her son showed me that in the dark she could open her mouth and a faint green light would glow from the necrotic bone. She died soon after our meeting."

Every dinner guest looked at Mr. Fields with new hostility.

"Using red phosphorus is too expensive," he said. "My factory must make a profit."

"The Salvation Army runs a matchstick factory that uses only red phosphorus," I said. "Men who value profits over the health of their workers deserve neither profits nor workers."

I decided I could not continue to eat with this man.
I stood, but turned in the doorway and looked at Mr. Fields.

"Do you still like women with political opinions?" I asked.

Mr. Fields made no answer, and I left the room. Mary later told me that he soon made an excuse to depart.

I then issued an instruction to Mary. "No more matchmakers!"

I believe Mary now regards me as unmarriageable. I intend to encourage this impression.

I have returned to working on my manuscript. But without Mr. Webb's help, this task now seems drudgery.

I seem to be sinking into a swamp of self-pity. Forgive me. I shall try to be more joyous in my next epistle.

Sincerely,
Beatrice Potter

FORTY-NINE

From the unpublished memoir of Bernard Shaw:

I met Sidney Webb for luncheon today, although he declined to eat at a vegetarian restaurant and insisted on dining where he could get a cutlet. What has made him so disagreeable suddenly?

The restaurant he selected gloried in the name The Kettle which I thought ridiculous. I soon discovered that I disliked other aspects of the restaurant as well.

"Look at those waiters," I said to Sidney. "They flit from table to table like bees in a garden. A poor dinner guest can barely have a moment of conversation before a waiter is back asking if we need more wine or butter."

"I believe that's called good service," said Sidney. "How should waiters behave?"

"In a dignified way. The waiters at the Café Royal move in a stately manner."

"That's because the waiters at the Café Royal are all over fifty and they wear those floor-length aprons that nearly entangle the waiter when he walks. They have to walk slowly to keep from tripping."

"Well, it makes the waiters move in a dignified manner and I appreciate it."

"The only thing I've ever heard you say about the Café Royal is that their salads are over-priced."

"And so they are. One does not preclude the other."

"I'm sorry my restaurant choice does not meet with your approval," said Sidney. "But I suspect there must be another reason for you being so disagreeable."

"I am amiability itself. What reason could I have for being disagreeable?"

"You are lonely."

Sidney said this so matter-of-factly that I was taken aback.

"Nonsense."

"Very well, it is nonsense," said Sidney. "But I wanted to talk to you because I've made a decision. I've decided to run for the London County Council. I'm running for the Deptford seat as a candidate for the Progressives. The trade unions will back me and the workingman's clubs and the Women's Liberal Association."

"Public politics?" I said. "And why are you doing that?"

"You inspired me. With your talk of your vestry work."

"I recall mostly describing my defeats. Shaw supports road construction and road construction is defeated. Shaw supports drainage and drainage is defeated. Shaw supports women's lavatories and lavatories are defeated. I cannot conceive of a less inspiring collection of political tales."

"You were in the thick of it and fighting for what you believed in. We live in the most staggeringly large and prosperous metropolis in the world. The proper government could do wonders to improve people's lives."

"That is what makes government work so frustrating," I said. "The potential to do so much good and the constant failure to reach that potential."

"Well, I'd like to get into the thick of it myself and feel that triumph or frustration."

"What does Miss Potter think of your decision?" I asked.

"I have not told her," he said. "I have seen little of her since our return."

"Are you still working together on your school plan?" I asked.

"Yes. I have already convinced most of the Hutchinson trustees as to the rightness of my plan. I may consult Miss Potter if I encounter other obstacles."

That told me all I needed to know about the state of their friendship; there was no need to embarrass Sidney by asking direct questions.

"And what of Miss Payne-Townshend?" asked Sidney. "Do you write to her?"

"Why does everyone take such an interest in our friendship?" I asked. "Would you believe that Wilde came to my house specifically to dictate a letter that I should send to Charlotte under my name."

"And did you send it?" asked Sidney.

"No. It was too penitent and sentimental. I've sent her a new letter of my own that I hope will repair our friendship."

"I suspect that Wilde might be skilled at dealing with affairs of the heart."

"Then you should go to him for advice," I said. "Maybe he'll make you a happy man."

"You're in a foul humor," said Sidney.

I could not disagree, so I paid for the meal.

FIFTY

Dear Mr. Shaw,

 I am writing this letter to you from a train en route to Paris. But I shall not linger there long; I am returning to England and will then press on to Ireland. My sister and her husband have invited me to stay with them near Dublin.

 Sadly, I must decline your kind invitation to return to London and type your Himalaya of manuscript. I suggest that you write to an agency and engage however many secretaries that it takes to keep up with the writing machine.

 You say that I will never find anyone whose company is as stimulating as yours. That may be true, but there is more to friendship than mental stimulation. You told me yourself that friendship is built on mutual usefulness, but you will not allow yourself to use or need anyone. You regard yourself as a fountain of genius indifferently showering anyone who comes near. That makes you a splendid natural wonder, but a decidedly poor friend. As a socialist, I'm sure you'll approve of my spending my time visiting those who need and want me—and not wasting it visiting natural wonders I have already seen.

Sincerely,
Charlotte Payne-Townshend

FIFTY-ONE

From Oscar Wilde's secret journal:

The premier of *The Importance Being Earnest* did not begin with auspicious omens. When I tried to check out of the Avondale Hotel, Mr. Grant, the clerk, looked at me apologetically.

"I'm sorry, Mr. Wilde," he said. "I've been told to hold your things until your account has been settled."

"That is a bother," I said. I did not make a scene. It was not Mr. Grant's fault that the hotel's managers honor their accountants more than their guests.

I walked to the St. James Theatre along streets dappled with snow. A London snowfall is a rare thing. What does it portend? I know of no superstitions linking snow and theatres, but it feels like there should be such a thing.

At the theatre, George Alexander approached me with a grim expression on his face.

"Mr. Wilde, I've just heard from one of the actors that the Marquis of Queensberry is planning on disrupting our opening night's performance," he said. "I think we have no choice but to cancel his ticket."

"Yes," I said. "That seems wise."

"With your permission, I'd like to ask a few police constables to be present."

"You have my permission and my blessing," I said. "But we shouldn't wait for trouble to begin. Queensberry should be arrested at once."

"I don't think Queensberry can be arrested for merely planning to disrupt the play," said Mr. Alexander.

"If the authorities must wait for a crime to actually be committed, then they must trail hopelessly behind evil like the man at the circus who follows the elephants with a bucket and broom."

Mr. Alexander did not disagree, but he shrugged to indicate there was nothing he could do.

FIFTY-TWO

Dear Miss Darling,

I returned to the theatre with my sister Mary to see the opening night of Mr. Wilde's play *The Importance of Being Earnest*. Although I attended the theatre often in my youth, it has been many years since I had seen a play and my acquaintance with the playwright made the evening even more special.

We arrived in London to find the remains of a snowstorm dotting the streets with white. This is a rare enough occurrence to be remarked upon by all and here and there children were conducting snowball fights.

On the sidewalk outside the theatre, I spotted Mr. Shaw who was standing with a mustachioed man he introduced as Frank Harris. Mr. Shaw greeted me with such enthusiasm that I believe he too misses our summer camaraderie. He soon turned the talk to Mr. Wilde and his play.

"I owe it to Wilde to see his play and I owe it to myself to see the product of one of our leading dramatists," he said. "And yet, I have mixed feelings. If the play is bad, I will be disappointed and if the play is good, I may be envious."

"I am surprised that any artist would admit to envy," I said.

"Artistic envy is merely admiration plus ambition," he replied. "I want to be made envious. I long for it. It is a sign that the play has taught me something."

I wanted to hear more, but there was the sound of a disturbance. We turned and saw two police constables blocking the path of two men. One of men clutched a bag of vegetables and he said, "I paid for a ticket. I demand entrance."

"Your ticket has been cancelled," said one of the constables. "You'll not be let in. We'll not be having a disturbance. Best move along."

The man with the vegetables began to curse and sputter, but the constables were implacable and eventually the angry men left.

Does Mr. Wilde have enemies? This seems very odd. He has always seemed to me to be the most amiable of men. What could he have done to provoke such enmity?

Soon Mary and I took our seats, and the play began. I shall not recount the plot to you. Even if I could remember it, the plot was not the chief focus of the evening. It was the language of the characters that provided the entertainment. Mr. Wilde had created characters who spoke as he did, with epigrams and amusing ironies.

I shall give one example only. When Lady Bracknell, the disapproving mother of a young woman in the play, learns that her daughter is to be married, she states: "To speak frankly, I am not in favor of long engagements. They give people the opportunity of finding out each other's character before marriage, which I think is never advisable."

Of course, these lines were greeted with gales of laughter.

The play was a great success and the applause at the end of the night was loud and prolonged. After the actors had taken their bows, Mr. Wilde appeared on the stage, but he said no words and merely bowed as well.

I waited in the theatre lobby for a long time to see Mr. Wilde. It seemed every member of the audience wanted to congratulate him, and other actors sought him out to shake his hand once again.

"Wilde, I've never seen an opening like this," said Mr. Alexander, the actor who played Jack Worthing. "This is the best opening of my career!"

"Yes, the muses seem to have rained blessings upon me and everyone in my vicinity is getting wet," said Mr. Wilde.

"The play will run for years!" shouted Mr. Alexander. "You will be a rich man!"

But at that moment Mr. Wilde spotted me and he broke away from Mr. Alexander.

"Miss Potter, I am so glad you could come," he said. "Are you here with Mr. Webb?"

"No, I came with my sister Mary," I said. "Congratulations. It was wonderful. But I was surprised that you didn't speak to the audience after the play. You are famous for that."

"The performances were so perfect that any additional words from me would have been gilding the lily," he replied. "How are you, Miss Potter? Have you adjusted to the simplicity of the city after our summer of rural sophistication?"

"I have not," I confessed. "I miss our bicycle rides. Our simple suppers. Most of all I miss our conversations. Who can talk like you and Mr. Shaw and Mr. Webb?"

"Miss Potter, you are a very clever person," said Mr. Wilde. "And one of the disadvantages of being a very clever person is that one finds less clever people rather dull.

What the gods bestow with one hand, they take away with the other."

I wished I could have talked to Mr. Wilde all night, but there was a crowd clamoring to congratulate him and Mary was waiting.

So, this is one result of our summer: a successful play. I am happy for Mr. Wilde. At least one of our merry band has found happiness and good fortune.

Sincerely,
Beatrice Potter

FIFTY-THREE

Dearest Robbie,

Since I saw you something has happened. Bosie's father has left a card at my club with hideous words on it. I don't see anything now but a criminal prosecution. My whole life seems ruined by this man. The tower of ivory is assailed by the foul thing. On the sand is my life spilt. I don't know what to do. If you could come here at 11:30 please do so tonight. I mar your life by trespassing ever on your love and kindness. I have asked Bosie to come tomorrow.

Ever Yours,
Oscar

FIFTY-FOUR

From the memoir of Robert Ross:

I found Oscar pacing the floor of his room at the Avondale Hotel. His collar was undone, a cigarette was in his mouth and the air reeked of smoke. There was an open bottle of sherry on a table and a glass that was half full.

"I don't know what to do," he said. "Perhaps I should go directly to the police and have Queensberry arrested."

"Calm down," I said. "What has he done?"

Oscar reached into his pocket and pulled out a card. "He left this for me at his club."

Oscar handed me the card. It was a calling card from the Marquis of Queensberry, but there were scrawled words on the back. The handwriting was very poor.

"What does it say?" I asked.

"I'm not sure about the early part of the sentence or phrase," said Oscar. "But I can read the word sodomite."

I stared at the card.

"He's spelled it wrong. S-O-M-D-O-M-I-T-E."

"Yes, he's illiterate as well as a brute," said Oscar.

"What's before it?" I asked. "That's a P, I think."

"Posing sodomite or posing as a sodomite," said Oscar. "Does it matter? It's a deadly insult, either way."

"Yes," I said for lack of anything better to say.

"The porter at the club saw this. That makes it a public insult," said Oscar. "We can have him in the courts."

"You could tear it up," I said. "No one will know."

"The porter saw it," Oscar insisted.

"But could he read it? We can barely read it. It might be best to forget the whole thing."

Oscar filled his sherry glass to the brim and took a drink.

"Queensberry has placed himself in our power now."

"Maybe," I said. "But a lawsuit is a serious matter."

"Bosie will be here in the morning," said Oscar. He suddenly noticed my empty hands. "I've been very rude. Please forgive me, my dear friend. Would you like a drink?"

"A small one, Oscar."

Oscar found a glass and filled it with sherry.

"Thank you," I said.

"Yes, Bosie will be here in the morning. He'll know what to do."

I could not think of a worse person to offer advice than Bosie. I stepped closer to Oscar and put my hand on his shoulder.

"If you want to forget about the whole affair, tear the card up tonight. Tear it up now."

"Bosie will want to discuss this," he said.

"This is not Bosie's decision. It is yours. Only you can sue for libel."

"Queensberry is Bosie's father."

"That is not a reason for letting him decide for you. That is a reason for ignoring Bosie's advice. He has motives and grievances that are not yours. He wants to hurt his father and that is all he wants. If this gets into the courts, your name will be dragged through the mud."

"If I do nothing, Queensberry will hound me forever."

"You don't know that. He is a man of many quarrels. He may find some new enemy to harass. Don't think about Queensberry or Bosie. Think of what is best for you."

Oscar sat and drank his sherry.

"I'll discuss it with Bosie in the morning."

I knew how that discussion would turn out. I knelt before him and put my hand on his knee.

"Oscar, end your obsession with Bosie. Give him up. He brings to your life nothing but trouble and strife. He is not the only one who loves you."

Oscar looked at me and smiled. He touched my cheek.

"Dear Robbie. So loyal and devoted. I don't deserve you. But I am captive to my fascinations and no one fascinates me like Bosie. Your consolation is to know that a foolish love is its own punishment."

I stood up and shook my head.

"At least see a barrister. Oscar, promise me you'll consult a barrister before taking any action. That is advice any friend would give you. Promise me."

Oscar seemed touched by my concern. "Very well, Robbie. I will see Mr. Humphries. He has helped me before."

That was the best I could do for him that night.

The next morning, Bosie joined Oscar and me for breakfast. I found his jubilation at the possibility of seeing his father arrested for libel to be indecent.

"Imagine the look on his face when the police show up to arrest him!" said Bosie, eyes gleaming. "He'll be cursing like a sailor. His prizefighter friends won't be able to help him."

"You will want the advice of a solicitor before any arrests are made," I said, directing my remarks to Oscar. "Humphries will have questions for you and you must answer them honestly."

"What are you going on about?" asked Bosie, taking an enormous bite out of a piece of toast. I had little appetite, but the thought of his father's name being dragged through the mud apparently made Bosie ravenous.

"Humphries will have to ask you if there is any truth to your father's accusations."

Bosie looked as if he thought my suggestion was ridiculous. "Oscar is a gentleman. No solicitor is going to question his morals."

"It will be his duty to do so," I said.

Oscar had been in somber mood this morning and he said quietly: "I think Robbie may be correct on this point. It will be his professional duty to ask awkward questions."

"You must answer them honestly," I said with as much force as I would muster to Oscar.

"Don't be silly," said Bosie. "Humphries is a solicitor, not a priest. We're not going to confession."

"Lying to your solicitor is as foolish as lying to your doctor," I said. "He cannot give you good advice if he doesn't know all the facts."

"You have very curious views on what is appropriate conversation between gentlemen," said Bosie, attempting to make a joke of my advice. Both of us were watching Oscar's face to see whose view he favored. I sensed that Bosie's humorous tone masked a growing irritation at my interference in what he regarded as his own affairs.

If Humphries persuaded Oscar that a lawsuit was unwise,
I expected Bosie's subsequent tantrums to be volcanic.
His greatest dream seemed to be to see his father in prison.

"We will see what Mr. Humphries wants to know,"
said Oscar enigmatically. He refused to commit himself to
either Bosie's or my point of view.

Later that day, Oscar, Bosie and Humphries went to
the Marlborough Street Police Station to have the Marquis
of Queensberry arrested for libel. When I caught up with
Oscar and Bosie later that night, I asked if they had told
Humphries the truth during their initial interview with him.

"Don't be absurd," said Bosie.

At once my heart was filled with foreboding.

FIFTY-FIVE

From the unpublished memoir of Bernard Shaw:

Frank Harris once again summoned me to the Café Royal for luncheon. I was surprised to see that there were no bottles of wine at his table and that Harris was drinking coffee. After greeting me and summoning the waiter for my order, Harris immediately began talking about Oscar Wilde.

"It's possible the Queen may request a command performance," said Harris. "You must have been the only man in London who didn't like *The Importance of Being Earnest*. Every other review was so full of praise, they could have been written by Oscar himself."

"Even a farce must touch life at some points, or it is just a silly machine for generating laughter."

"I haven't laughed so hard in years," said Harris with a smile. "Wilde must be swimming in money now. And don't start arguing with him about the theatre when he gets here. He wants some help from me and I need to give him some advice. It'll help if you back me up."

"What's going on?" I asked.

Harris lowered his voice to a confidential tone. "It's a bad business. You heard about the death of the brother of Lord Alfred Douglas?"

"I was there when Douglas told Wilde about it."

"Well, there are whispers that it wasn't an accident. That he killed himself to avoid a scandal. The same sort of scandal that Wilde is flirting with. Of course, Douglas's father will do anything to prevent that. Queensberry has to be afraid he'll lose both sons."

Wilde chose that moment to appear with Lord Alfred Douglas. Wilde wore a blue suit with a carnation in his buttonhole. Lord Alfred wore a conservative gray suit.

"Speak of the devil and he shall appear," said Harris.

"I won't ask which of us you think is the devil," said Wilde. "Allow me to properly introduce Lord Alfred Douglas. I call him Bosie. Bosie this is Bernard Shaw. He is named for Bernarok, the Norse god of vegetarian debauchery."

I had to smile at this jest as I shook Lord Alfred's hand.

"A pleasure, sir," said Lord Alfred.

We all sat down. The waiter appeared, but Harris's somber mood prevailed. Oscar wanted only coffee. After the waiter had left, Oscar directed his first comment to me.

"I'm afraid I must talk some business with Frank, but I hope that you will stay and have a drink or dessert with me afterwards."

Harris looked at Oscar. "You may not want to stay after you hear my advice."

"You can't think that *Dorian Gray* is an immoral book?" said Oscar.

"Of course not," said Harris.

"Then why won't you testify to that?" said Lord Alfred.

Oscar put his hand on Lord Alfred's.

"Bosie, please . . . "

"Are you afraid of my father?" asked Lord Alfred.

"You're not helping things," said Oscar.

"You are truly going to bring a suit against the Marquis of Queensberry?" asked Harris.

"My father is the most vicious brute in London!" said Lord Alfred in a voice that was slightly too loud.

Oscar forcefully grabbed Lord Alfred's arm, and this was apparently so unusual that surprise showed in Lord Alfred's face and he was instantly silent.

"Be still!" commanded Oscar. When it became apparent that Lord Alfred would say no more, Oscar turned his attention back to Harris.

"The man left his card for me at my club with filthy and misspelled slanders on it. He plotted to disrupt the opening night of *Earnest* and was only prevented because he bragged of his plans to the wrong persons. He has harassed me for months and will do so forever unless I stop him. The only legal remedy I have is to press suit against him for libel. As a desperate man, he will try to destroy my reputation in any way he can including attacks based upon my works. I am simply asking you to testify to my integrity as an artist by saying in court that *The Picture of Dorian Gray* is not an immoral book. As the editor of the *Saturday Review* you qualify as an expert."

Harris stared at Oscar as if searching for common sense in his face.

"Oscar, have you gone mad? If this gets into court, no one is going to give a damn about *Dorian Gray*. All they are going to care about is the evidence."

Oscar nodded. "Good. There is no—"

"Let me finish," said Harris. "Queensberry has been bragging at his club that he has sent private detectives to every hotel you have ever stayed at. And he's bragged that they've found things. So, I must ask you, was there any evidence for them to find?"

"No," said Oscar. "Of course not."

"There was never a scene that could have been witnessed by a chambermaid or a porter and misinterpreted?"

Lord Alfred looked alarmed. "We're not on trial here!"

"If this gets into court," said Harris, "Oscar will most definitely be on trial."

There was silence for a long moment as both Oscar and Lord Alfred considered this. When Harris spoke again, it was in a quieter tone.

"I'm talking sense. Oscar, if there is any evidence, or anything that looks like evidence, then you dare not press this case. Because if you, lose, the magistrates will turn around and prosecute you. And that will mean not only prison, but absolute ruin. I tell you; I know." Harris gestured to me. "Bernard, am I right?"

I looked Oscar in the eye. "If there is any evidence against you, you cannot go forward."

Oscar looked around at Harris and me. For the first time, he seemed uncertain.

"I am in too deep. I cannot drop the case now without seeming to admit my guilt."

"There is a way," said Harris. "It's not perfect, but it's the best you can do under the circumstances."

"What is it?" asked Oscar.

"You must go abroad," said Harris. "And take your wife and boys with you. And then you must write a letter to *The Times* explaining that you decided to drop the case because you knew that no British jury would find against a father whose motive was to protect his son."

Oscar pondered this a long moment and then looked to me.

"What do you think, Bernard?"

"It sounds very sensible to me," I said.

"Of course," said Harris, "You will have to sever your acquaintance with Lord Douglas."

"No!" shouted Lord Alfred. "He is trying to divide us! He wants to keep us apart."

Harris jabbed a finger at Lord Alfred. "Her Majesty's prisons will do a far better job of keeping you apart than I ever could and that is what will happen if you don't use your head."

"You don't know anything!" said Lord Alfred in a tone that reminded me of a petulant child. "We can't lose this case. I will take the stand and tell the world what kind of monster my father is. After they've heard my testimony no judge or jury in the country would decide against us."

Harris glared at Lord Alfred. "All the jury will see is a wretched brat who is obsessed with hatred for his father and will do anything to hurt him." Harris turned to Oscar. "He's as likely to hurt your case as help it."

"You don't know anything!" shouted Lord Alfred. "They'll believe me because I'll tell them the truth! Oscar is innocent and my father is mad!"

"Yes, it runs in the family," said Harris.

Lord Alfred stood up with such speed that he knocked his chair over. "Oscar, let's go," he said.

"Oscar, he's using you," said Harris. "You're a pawn in his war with his father."

Lord Alfred grabbed Oscar's arm and tugged.

"These men are no friends of yours. Come on!"

Oscar was too large for Lord Alfred to move. Oscar looked to me with an alarmed expression. "Bernard, what do you think I should—"

Bosie interrupted him. "He's not your friend! If you love me, come with me. Now!"

I reached out and put my hand over Oscar's.

"Oscar, you told me that my life could benefit from some your foolishness. Well, your life could benefit from some of my wisdom. You've been given advice as sage as any you're likely to get. Now, do the intelligent thing or be damned."

Lord Alfred tugged again Oscar's arm and Oscar began to move like a great barge that at last is budged by the pull of a tiny boat.

"They are not your friends," said Lord Alfred again.

The last look I saw on Oscar's face was as fearful and puzzled as an animal being led to the slaughter.

FIFTY-SIX

Dear Mr. Shaw,

For a long while, I have been pondering your failure to get the St. Pancras vestry to build women's lavatories. It has been obvious to me that mocking the foolishness of your opponents may be satisfying to you, but this is unlikely to change their opinions or get you the votes you need.

I have little experience of public affairs, but it occurs to me that you might appeal to their self-interest by explaining that a woman is more likely to linger in a store if she knows that there is a nearby remedy should a pressing need come upon her. Thus, a woman's lavatory could serve the public even if it is never used; its mere presence could increase the commerce in an area by reliving women's minds if not their bodies. In support of this idea, I have enclosed a short letter which you can show to any man you think might be persuaded by its logic.

I expect I will always admire the public-spiritedness of you and your Fabian friends. To devote oneself so wholeheartedly to the public interest with no hope of personal gain or even fame is a rare quality. The bond between us will fade with time, but you will always have my esteem.

Sincerely,
Charlotte Payne-Townshend

FIFTY-SEVEN

From the unpublished memoir of Bernard Shaw:

I spent election night with Sidney Webb at the Progressive headquarters in Deptford. This was a shabby second-floor room not far from the Foreign Cattle Market where butchering takes place. It was perhaps my imagination, but I thought the air was tainted with the bloody stockyard smell that always reaffirms my commitment to vegetarianism.

But the air of the upstairs room was more than tainted with the smoke of dozens of cigarettes. The room was crowded with representatives from all the organizations and working men's clubs that made up the Progressive's coalition. The noise of the throng made it difficult to hear the person sitting next to me and the drifting smoke from various cigarettes (and occasional cigars) made it difficult to breath. Many of the men spoke with accents as Cockney as Sidney and many wore workingman's clothes.

Sidney and I were squeezed into chairs in a corner next to a window that I had opened to get some breathable air. The combination of the smoky miasma in the room and blood-tinged air from the window had me feeling vaguely sick, but I tried to remain cheerful for Sidney's sake. Midnight had come and gone and I was growing weary, but the rest of the crowd was as loud and convivial as they ever had been.

"If you win, you'll be taking on a lot," I said. "The London County Council and running your school. It's a lot of work for one man."

"The London School of Economics and Political Science," said Sidney. "That's what we've decided to call it."

"The L.S.E.P.S.," I said.

"Yes, although perhaps we will shorten it to LSE," said Sidney with a smile. "And you're right. It will be a lot of work. Maybe too much. I may have to find someone to help with the school."

"Miss Potter?" I said.

"No, social investigation is her forte. Education and administration are outside her field of expertise."

"How is Miss Potter?" I asked. I had not touched on the subject until now out of consideration for Sidney.

"I believe she is well," he said. "She sent me a letter wishing me good luck with the election."

I nodded and waited for him to say more, but Sidney said nothing and we listened to the hum of other people's conversation for a moment.

"How is Miss Payne-Townshend?" Sidney finally asked.

"If endless wandering were a medical condition, I would urge her to seek treatment. She ricochets between Paris and Rome so often one would think she was a diplomat trying to settle a border dispute. Most of my letters miss her, but when one catches her, she honors me with a reply."

"And are you writing plays?" asked Sidney. His eyes, peering through his pince-nez, suddenly seemed very piercing.

"A little," I said.

"I believe it is important for happiness and health to keep busy and not to have time to brood on melancholy thoughts. I ran for the London County Council to keep as busy as possible."

I considered all that he was saying and leaving unsaid.

"And are you happy?" I asked.

"I've avoided despair," he said. "I believe that is an achievement."

There was yelling from below and the conversations in the room ceased as everyone tried to hear what was being shouted. There was the sound of boots thundering up the stairs and then a young man burst into the room and shouted: "Webb's won!"

There was a great cheer of triumph and then every head turned to Sidney and a half dozen large men with grinning faces reached for him and clutched his clothes.

"Steady on!" shouted Sidney.

But it was no use. The men grabbed him and hoisted him on high as easily as they could have lifted a bag of flour. In an instant Sidney was as horizontal as if he were laying in his own bed, but his face was mere inches from the ceiling. With a great deal of noise, the men spun him around and then hauled him toward the door.

"Mind the doorframe!" shouted Sidney and his nose was nearly scraped along the top of the door and only a quick twist of the head saved him.

"You can put me—" Sidney began, but the men carried him out of the room and down the stairs with a great clatter of boots and I failed to hear the end of his sentence.

I followed the jubilant mob down the stairs and into the street, all feelings of illness forgotten.

The crowd in the street was happily chanting "Webb! Webb! Webb!" as if they expected him to make a speech. But the young men who were parading Sidney were not to be denied their prize and they lifted Sidney higher and began pushing their way through the crowd.

"Bernard!" yelled Sidney in exasperation and he twisted his head enough to see me standing on the steps observing the spectacle.

"Enjoy it, Sidney!" I shouted, but it was impossible to tell if he heard me.

I watched Sidney floating, as if my magic, on a sea of hands and he was carried down the street and out of sight, held aloft by the will of the people he had pledged to serve.

FIFTY-EIGHT

Dear Miss Potter,

My work on the London County Council so consumes my time that it has been obvious to me for some weeks that I also cannot assume the directorship of the London School of Economics and Political Science. I am hard at work on the subcommittees for education and these will require large portions of my day if I am to fulfill my role as a responsible public servant. Of course, as a public servant, I can do a great deal of good by pointing public money toward the school; the money from the tax on beer and spirits is to be used for "technical education" and there is no reason the London School of Economics should not get its share.

The obvious other candidate for the directorship is of course Graham Wallas. He is a fine teacher, lecturer and Fabian. There are few men who are as good-hearted and honest as he. But after some consideration, he has refused the position as director and he has convinced me that this is the right decision. He has pointed out to me that he has no administrative experience and does not have the appropriate personality for a position of authority. And if I am honest, then I must admit that Wallas often is more impressive at the beginning of a project than in the latter stages. His enthusiasm seems to wane over time, and he may lack the dogged determination that pushes a project to completion despite numerous obstacles. I like Wallas personally and admire his many virtues, but I have come to believe he is not the man to run the London School of Economics and Political Science.

I have determined to ask William Hewins to assume the directorship. He is an expert on economic history at Pembroke College, Oxford and he has already agreed to lecture at the LSE on economic matters. Although I have not known him long, I believe he has the necessary ambition and energy to make the school a success.

But first we must convince him to accept the position and I am asking for your help in persuading him. We will need to convince him in short order and if he cannot be made to accept then we may have to abandon the school altogether as I cannot think of anyone else qualified to run it. Would you be available to meet with Mr. Hewins at his convenience during the coming week? I will write to him and invite him to meet with us in London this week if this is agreeable to you.

I hope this letter finds you in good health and that your manuscript on the co-operative movement is progressing. I believe my acquaintance with Oscar Wilde has made me fanciful because when I think of you, I now often picture a socialist muse floating behind you as you write. The muse looks rather like Eleanor Marx with a great mass of dark hair and a cigarette between two fingers. Whenever she blows smoke at the back of your head, inspiration apparently strikes because you scribble furiously and the pages rapidly fill with your neatly printed sentences.

Am I silly? Perhaps, but you must remember that I am as fond of Rosetti as I am of Marx. Mr. Wilde would argue that I must honor all sides of my nature, the foolish child as well as the adult committeeman.

But I suppose Mr. Hewins must see only the adult when he comes down to London. I would welcome any ideas of yours on how to persuade him.

Sincerely,
Sidney Webb

FIFTY-NINE

Dearest Charlotte,

Your advice on appealing to the commercial self-interest of the businessmen of the Camden High Road in the matter of women's lavatories seemed to me eminently sensible. The only addition I made to your plan was to use the Reverend Ensor Walters as my intermediary in wooing the other vestrymen. My reputation is such that most of the vestry is prepared to find my arguments humorous, but few are likely to find them convincing. The Reverend Walters was amused by my plan and persuaded by the logic of your arguments. He wasted no time in cornering other vestrymen for a quiet talk and soon convinced them that hordes of idle dowagers would descend upon the Camden High Road if only they could be sure that the needs of nature could be met.

In short, lavatory construction will begin in the spring. This may not mark the dawn of a socialist paradise, but to this luckless champion of the poor a minor victory feels as grand as a Roman triumph.

Thank you for your advice. Thousands of distressed bladders will find relief because of you and if I could work my will, the walls of the Camden High Road Lavatory would bear your name.

Tell me if you ever arrive at a location within a day's bicycle ride from London. After you have seen every castle, museum, alp and fjord in Europe, perhaps the green pastures of England will again appeal to you. I remain as strong and independent and busy as ever I was and

I welcome burdens that would crush Atlas or exhaust
Sisyphus, but I could find time for a walk with a friend at
twilight, or a bicycle ride past a sheep-strewn meadow.
I count this past summer the grandest of all that I have seen
and your companionship is first among the reasons why.

Yours,
Bernard

SIXTY

From Oscar Wilde's secret journal:

Success! The first day of the trial has gone better than I could have hoped, and my misgivings have proved to be mere night terrors, dispelled by the reality of day.

Before I ever set foot in court, Mr. Humphries had made me aware that the defense would allege that I committed immoral acts with many young men of low character. Private detectives hired by Queensberry have scoured London, searching for the young men that I have known and if I took the stand, as would be necessary, I would be cross-examined about my acquaintanceship with them. I therefore knew that our success would depend entirely upon my ability to lie consistently and convincingly to men who had every reason to doubt my testimony.

I disguised my misgivings for Constance's sake and was determined to be the picture of confidence on my first day in court. I dressed in a blue Chesterfield coat trimmed with velvet and I smiled as I kissed and hugged Cyril and Vyvyan before departing.

I had hired a carriage and pair and Bosie rode with me. At first, he was not good company. He was far too confident of victory and his carefree mood soon became irksome.

"After the trial we should go to Paris," he said. "Or maybe Italy. The damages my father will have to pay should cover our expenses."

"For God's sake, we haven't won it yet," I finally burst out in a tone of voice that expressed all my fears.

For once, Bosie was sensible enough not to argue with me and he took my hand in a way that reminded me of past moments of tenderness. Bosie has many childish faults, but he also can show love in the same simple manner of a child.

The pomp and solemnity of the courtroom made a great impression on me. The robes and the wigs of the barristers are as impressive in their own way as the miter of a cardinal or the raiment of a pope. The gravity of the occasion weighed upon my mood as I took my place beside Mr. Humphries.

The Old Bailey was crowded with spectators. Sir Edward Clarke, an associate of Mr. Humphries, told me that the crowd was made of both solicitors and reporters. I recognized several members of the press.

"The vultures are here," I said. "But on whom shall they feast?"

Mr. Clarke made no reply.

Queensberry sat at the defense table, his reddish side whiskers bristling, glaring hatred in my direction. I had an impulse to stick out my tongue at him, but I restrained myself and then tried to track the impulse to its source in my mind. To behave thus would be the height of folly. Why should it occur to me?

The Honorable Sir Richard Collins was to preside at the trial, but he took his time arriving and I felt a sense of relief when the proceedings were finally underway. I was committed. There would be no turning back.

In his opening statement, Mr. Clarke recounted my personal history to the jury and especially my friendship with Lord Alfred Douglas and the conflict with his father.

But he soon introduced the topic of Alfred Wood and the letter that Wood had once used to blackmail me. It was Mr. Clarke's strategy to be forthright about this episode in the sure knowledge that Mr. Carson, the counsel for the defense, would attempt to use this incident against me.

Mr. Clarke first called Willie Matthews, the hall porter at the Albemarle Club, to the stand and established the circumstances under which Queensberry left his abominable card for me.

Then Mr. Clarke called me to testify.

To testify in court is a novel sensation. If I was to state that I do not enjoy being the center of attention on most occasions, I would rightly be disbelieved. But testifying at a trial for a prolonged period is a far different business than entertaining friends over champagne at Kettner's. As I climbed to the witness box, I was acutely aware that all eyes were upon me and that not every glance was sympathetic. But I took a deep breath and remained as motionless as I could until Mr. Clarke began his questions.

He began simply and established the pertinent facts of my life, my artistic achievements and the history of my marriage. He had me recount my friendship with Lord Alfred Douglas and Lady Queensberry and my short but contentious acquaintanceship with Bosie's father. He had me describe young Alfred Wood's attempt to blackmail me with letters stolen from a coat that Bosie had carelessly lost.

Mr. Clarke concluded by asking me if there was any truth to the allegations that Queensberry had made.

I answered: "There is no truth whatsoever in any of them."

Mr. Clarke sat down.

Edward Carson rose from his place at the defense table and approached me. He was a clean-shaven man with a spare face that seemed to me to be humorless. We had once been fellow students at Trinity College in Dublin and there was more than a trace of Ireland in his voice. I had relaxed while being questioned by Mr. Clarke, but now I felt as a deer must feel when it spots a wolf across a field.

Mr. Carson began by disputing my age. I had stated that I was thirty-nine, but he proved that I was forty years of age. I had not meant to be inaccurate and I felt foolish that he had so quickly caught me in an untruth.

But Mr. Carson next tried to attack me on artistic grounds and here I was in my element. He often succeeded only in making himself look foolish.

"Here is one of your *Phrases and Philosophies for the Use of the Young*," said Mr. Carson, holding up a magazine. "'Wickedness is a myth invented by good people to account for the curious attractiveness of others.'"

This remark caused a good deal of laughter in the courtroom and I fancied that I saw a hint of a smile on the face of the judge.

"Yes." I said.

"Do you think that is true?"

"I rarely think that anything I write is true."

This caused another burst of laughter.

"Did you say rarely?" asked Mr. Carson.

"I said rarely. I might have said never."

"Nothing you ever write is true?"

"Not true in the sense of correspondence to fact; I represent willful moods of paradox, of fun, nonsense— but not true in the sense of correspondence to the actual facts of life."

Mr. Carson continued in this vein and questioned me about *The Picture of Dorian Gray*. He tried to imply that among Gray's sins was sodomy. I pointed out that the text is ambiguous and that each man sees his own sins in Dorian Gray.

In the afternoon, Mr. Carson read whole passages from *Dorian Gray* but focused particularly on Basil Hallward's confession of love to Dorian. I had another victory when Mr. Carson tried to use Hallward's words against me.

"Have you ever had that feeling of adoring madly a beautiful male person many years younger than yourself?" he asked.

"I have never given adoration to anyone but myself."

The spectators roared with laughter and I had to make a mighty effort to refrain from smirking. If I could keep them laughing, I could perhaps turn Carson's insinuations into a joke.

Mr. Carson continued questioning me about *Dorian Gray* at such length that I began to wish that I had never written the book. Finally, when he had worn out the patience of both the judge and the jury, he turned to the letter that Alfred Wood had used in his blackmail attempt.

"I want to ask you a few questions about this letter that was brought to you. This is a letter, as I understand, which you wrote to Lord Alfred Douglas?"

"Yes," I said.

"It was a letter in answer to something that he sent you?"

"Yes, in answer to a poem which he had sent me."

"Is that an ordinary letter?"

"Ordinary? I should think not," I said. There was laughter in the court.

"'My own dear boy,'" read Carson from the letter. "Was that ordinary?"

"No," I said. "I say it is not ordinary."

"You would think, Mr. Wilde, that a man of your age to address a man nearly twenty years younger as 'My own dear boy' would be an improper thing?"

"No," I said. "Not if I was fond of him. I don't think so."

"Not in the least?" asked Carson with great skepticism in his voice.

"I was fond of Lord Alfred Douglas. I had always been."

"Did you adore him?"

"No. I loved him."

There was no reaction from the court and Carson looked disappointed. He lifted the letter again to read from it.

"'Your sonnet is quite lovely,'" read Carson. "'It is a marvel that those red rose-leaf lips of yours should be made no less for music of song than for the madness of kissing.'"

"Yes," I said loudly with pride in my voice.

Carson glared at me as if addressing a degenerate.

"Do you mean to tell me, sir, that that was a natural and proper way to address a young man?"

"Yes, I think it was a beautiful letter. If you ask me if it was proper, you might as well ask me whether King Lear is proper, or a sonnet of Shakespeare is proper. It was a beautiful letter. It was not concerned with the object of writing propriety; it was written with the object of making a beautiful thing."

Carson looked slightly frustrated at not getting any answers he desired.

"Suppose a man who was not an artist had written the letter to a handsome young man, as I believe Lord Alfred is. A man some twenty years younger than himself—would you say that it was proper and natural kind of letter to write to him?"

"A man who was not an artist could never have written that letter."

The spectators seemed to find this reply amusing although I meant it as a simple statement of fact.

"Supposing a man had an unholy and immoral love towards a boy or a young fellow. I believe that has happened?"

"Yes," I admitted.

"And he addressed him in language that would perhaps be used in a love letter—he might use that language?"

"He certainly could not use such language as I used unless he was a man of letters and an artist. He could not do it."

Mr. Carson paused for a moment to collect his thoughts. I was apparently not as easy prey as he had imagined.

"There is nothing very wonderful in this: 'that those red, rose-leaf lips of yours should be made no less for music of song than for madness of kissing.'" He read the sentence with a lustful leer on his face.

"Literature depends upon how it is read, Mr. Carson. It must be read in a different way."

"Is there anything wonderful in that?"

"Yes, I think it is a beautiful phrase."

Carson looked at the letter again and read: "'Your slim gilt soul walks between passion and poetry.' Is that a beautiful phrase, too?"

"Not when you read it, Mr. Carson."

There was a great and satisfying roar of laughter. I felt the tide of sympathy turning in my direction.

"I don't profess to be an artist, Mr. Wilde." Mr. Carson read the letter again. "'I know Hyacinthus, whom, Apollo loved so madly was you in Greek days. Why are you alone in town? And when do we go to Salisbury?' Is that a beautiful phrase?"

"That is an enquiry—nothing particular about that," I said.

"'Do go there and cool your hands in the grey twilight of Gothic things and come here whenever you like. It is a lovely place and only lacks you. But go to Salisbury first. Always with undying love.' So that is a beautiful phrase?"

"Yes," I said.

"Was that the ordinary way in which you carried on your correspondence with Lord Alfred Douglas?"

"One could not write a letter like that every day. It would be like writing a poem every day. One could not do it."

"Did you ever write any other letter expressing that he was your 'own boy' and your love for him in that way?"

"I have often written to Lord Alfred Douglas as "My own boy." He is much younger than me. I write to him as 'My own boy' and feel undying love for him as I say I do. He is the greatest friend I have."

"Do you think it that is a proper kind of letter to write?"

"I think it was a beautiful letter."

This was growing tiresome. I could sense the jury's growing impatience with Mr. Carson and I struggled to conceal my own irritation.

"Did you write to other persons in the same way?"

"Oh, never."

"To young boys?"

"No."

"To any other young men?"

"No."

Mr. Carson went to his table and took up another piece of paper.

"Now here is another letter I believe you wrote to Lord Alfred Douglas. As I read the last one so badly, would you read it?"

"I decline."

Mr. Carson held up the letter. "'Dearest of all boys, your letter was delightful—red and yellow wine to me: but I am sad and out of sorts. Bosie, you must not make scenes with me: they kill me. They wreck the loveliness of life. I cannot see you, so Greek and gracious, distorted by passion—I cannot listen to your curved lips saying hideous things to me. Don't do it. You break my heart. You are the divine thing I want—the thing of grace and genius, but I don't know how to do it. Shall I go to Salisbury? There are many difficulties. My bill here is forty-nine pounds for the week.'"

This pedestrian detail caused another ripple of laughter through the court, although I didn't believe this bit of humor helped my cause. But neither did it help Carson's.

Carson continued to read.

"'I have a new sitting room over the Thames. But you—why are you not here, my dear, my wonderful boy? I fear I must leave. No money, no credit and a heart of lead. Ever your own, Oscar.'"

Carson stared at me as if the very act of reading that letter had been a minor triumph. He took a step toward me.

"Is that an extraordinary letter?"

"I think everything I write is extraordinary. I think that is an extraordinary letter. I don't pose as being ordinary. Good heavens! I am not ordinary. Ask me any questions you like about that letter."

"I'm afraid I have a great deal to ask you. Isn't that a love letter?"

"It is an expression of love."

"Is it the kind of letter that one man writes towards another man?"

"It is the kind of letter that I have written to Lord Alfred Douglas. What other men write to other men I know nothing, nor do I care."

Mr. Carson seemed to realize he was going to get little satisfaction pursuing this line of inquiry. He took a few steps away and then turned and faced me again.

"Now, let us talk about other letters. You told my learned friend, I think, that a man named Wood first came to you about certain letters that he had got in Lord Alfred's coat. Who made the appointment with this man?"

"The appointment was made through Mr. Alfred Taylor who knew Mr. Wood."

"Where did you first meet Mr. Wood?"

"At the Café Royal. Lord Alfred Douglas asked me to help Wood find a situation. Wood wanted to get a position as clerk and had asked Lord Alfred for help. Lord Alfred asked me to see what I could do, and he then telegraphed Wood and told him I would be at the Café Royal. Alfred Wood came in and knowing me by sight, as many people do, came over to my table and introduced himself."

"Did you become friends with Wood?"

"No. I only saw him three or four times."

"Did you ever ask him to go to Tite Street?"

"Never."

"Was he ever there?"

"Never."

"Do you swear that?"

"Yes."

"Did you ever have immoral practices with Wood?"

The atmosphere in the courtroom instantly changed with this question. Every eye was on me and every ear alert for my answer.

"Never in my life," I said.

"Did you ever open his trousers?" Only a slight tension in his voice betrayed Mr. Carson's reluctance to ask this question.

"No!" I said.

"Put your hand upon his person?"

"Never."

"Did you ever put your own person between his legs?"

"Never."

"I say to you that on several occasions you did that."

"I say that is entirely, absolutely untrue."

I looked Mr. Carson in the eye and did not waver until he looked away.

"When Wood came to talk to you about your letters, did you consider that he was wanting to levy blackmail from you?"

"He disarmed me by handing me the letters."

"You thought he was going to levy blackmail and you faced it by giving him sixteen pounds to go to America."

"That is an inaccurate description of what occurred," I protested.

"You gave him sixteen pounds."

"I thought he was going to produce letters of mine to Lord Alfred Douglas, which might contain private things. He wished to extort money. When I wrote these letters, they were of no importance. I didn't want them. But he told me a long story of people who wanted to get these letters from him. I gave him sixteen pounds. I did it foolishly, but out of pure pity and kindness."

"You were not afraid of anything contained in them?"

"Oh, there were things in them—family matters—that I certainly would not have liked to have had published. No one likes their private correspondence to be published."

"And you thought it worthwhile to give him sixteen pounds?"

"I did not give him sixteen pounds for that."

"Did you give him five pounds the very next day?"

"Yes."

"What did you give him that for?"

"He asked me to see him before he went to America. He said the passage out cost him more than he expected. I gave him five pounds additional. I did it out of kindness."

"Do you really suggest to the jury that you gave him twenty-one pounds out of charity?" Mr. Carson shook his head as if such a suggestion was unthinkable.

"It is not for me to make suggestions to the jury, Mr. Carson."

There was some laughter at my remark. Mr. Carson looked vexed. He continued his questions for most of the afternoon. He seemed to know of every young man that I had ever met and asked me about the details of every friendship. I was forced to repeatedly deny that I kissed these young men or had taken them to bed.

It was nearly the hour of five o'clock when the court adjourned for the day. Unlike a play, the day's proceedings did not draw to a climax but merely ended without a satisfying conclusion. I am content with my performance. I trust the jury sees me as an artist with a democratic taste in friendship, magnanimous and tolerant. If they also think me a trifle unwise in my friendships, that is not to be regretted. It is distasteful to be repeatedly questioned about physical intimacies, of course, but I summoned all my righteous indignation when replying to indelicate queries.

It is curious how one feels outraged at being accused of things one knows to be perfectly true.

SIXTY-ONE

Dear Miss Darling:

I had not seen Sidney Webb for some weeks when he summoned me to a meeting with William Hewins, a lecturer on economics who Mr. Webb hoped could be persuaded to take on the directorship of the London School of Economics. Mr. Webb met me at a cozy restaurant not far from Paddington Station, a location designed to be convenient for Mr. Hewins who does not live in London.

Mr. Webb greeted me with earnest enthusiasm and talked about his work on the London County Council. Since we had last met, he had been elected to that body, a fact that both surprised and impressed me because I had always assumed his interest in politics was more theoretical than practical. It turns out that committee work for the Fabian Society and his career at the Foreign Office has prepared him admirably for Council work and he claims to enjoy the give and thrust of politics.

We were able to chat for only half an hour before Mr. Hewins arrived for our appointment. He turned out to be a clean-shaven man of about thirty with a pleasant face. But the bridge of his nose was broad and this gave his countenance an appearance of strength. After Mr. Webb had introduced me and tea had been poured, Mr. Webb laid out his reasons for being unable to assume the directorship of the London School of Economics and his reasons for believing that Mr. Hewins would be a fine director.

Mr. Hewins listened politely, but then shook his head.

"I am flattered, of course, that you would consider me. But I am at the beginning of my career and a venture such as this would entail a great deal of risk. If the school should not be a success . . . " He trailed off and shook his head in manner that suggested he was contemplating the ruins of a once-promising life.

Mr. Webb began to speak, but in my excitement, I interrupted him.

"Mr. Hewins, it is now, while you are young, that such an opportunity must be seized," I said. "Do you imagine that you will have the energy for such a venture when you are old? I believe that the director must be a young man of great vigor, at least during the early years of school. There will be innumerable obstacles to surmount and it will take the passion and determination of a young man to overcome them."

"That may be true," he conceded. "But I think I would be a better school director in my maturity."

I shook my head.

"You should consider whether it is likely that you will encounter such an opportunity again. Do you think that such opportunities present themselves every year? It may be that when you are old and prosperous and so secure in your career that such an offer would be welcome that no such offer comes. And it may be that a lifetime of keeping to the safe path will prevent you from even being considered for such a position even if one is available."

This argument seemed to make an impression on him, but I was just warming to the topic.

"I believe that when considering what path we should take in life, we must value more than our own self-interest. We must consider what good we can do in the world and how we can change the world for the better. Mr. Webb conceived of the London School of Economics because he saw the need for such an institution, and I believe that such a school would do great service to England and the world. The man who captains such a school will likewise do great service and will share in the glory of its achievements. If I were man with administrative skill, I would seize this opportunity with both hands and fight desperately to hold on to it come what may."

As I talked, my tone became more and more emphatic and I leaned forward and never took my eyes from the eyes of Mr. Hewins. At last, Mr. Webb placed his hand upon mine and I realized that I had been preaching over-zealously.

Mr. Webb smiled at Mr. Hewins. "Miss Potter is passionate on the subject of education."

"Forgive me," I said.

Mr. Hewins smiled. "There is nothing to forgive. You are quite right. This is a rare opportunity. I would be foolish to let it pass by. It was only cowardice that made me hesitate. I would be honored to assume the directorship."

We spent another hour discussing the particulars of the school plan and then Mr. Hewins took his leave.

I looked at Mr. Webb and shook my head.

"I almost scared him away."

"You were magnificent. I could never be so articulate on the spur of the moment. You saved the day."

We congratulated each other for a few minutes, but when I asked Mr. Webb to tell me more about his work on the London County Council, he said that he had another appointment and took his leave.

Mr. Webb's departure left me strangely downcast. Why should that be? We accomplished the task we had set for ourselves. The London School of Economics now has every chance of success. My own manuscript on the cooperative movement is nearly complete and I will soon submit it to the publisher. The events of my life are conspiring to my satisfaction.

I suppose my unease stems from the unsettled nature of my friendship with Mr. Webb. Although he professed to be pleased to see me and gave every appearance of rejoicing in the success of my writing, I sensed a reserve in his manner that has not been there before. Although Mr. Webb's manners were impeccable, he seemed eager to depart and I fear my company may be painful to him. The room seemed strangely empty once he had left it and I realize that weeks without his daily company have put his virtues in perspective. I love my sisters and my father, but no one can talk to me on the subjects most important to me as Mr. Webb can.

It occurs to me that most of the important moments of our lives are constructed of little more than talk. It is therefore of paramount importance to have the best possible conversational partner in one's life.

Returning to my manuscript to toil alone on this gray day seems infinitely tiresome despite the knowledge that my task is nearly done. I've therefore spent an hour writing this letter to you in the hope that my enthusiasm for correspondence will transfer to the writing of my book. As I finish this letter, I realize my hopes are in vain.

But let me slip on the harness once again and pull the wagon of my hopes up the hill of my ambition.

Sincerely,
Beatrice Potter

SIXTY-TWO

From Oscar Wilde's secret journal:

Disaster! Despair! It has all gone wrong. How could I have been so foolish as to pursue this prosecution?

How will I make Constance understand? How will I explain to my boys?

But I cannot think of them now. I will set down the events of the day as best I can remember them and hope that this exercise will calm my mind.

The day was devoted to Mr. Carson's continued cross-examination of me. He seemed to know my movements and appointments better than I knew them myself and he had questions concerning every young man who had crossed my path during the past few years.

In the morning, a great many questions concerned Alfred Taylor. (Why are so many men connected to this case named Alfred?)

No matter. Mr. Carson knew far too much about Alfred Taylor and the comings and goings at his place of residence.

"Wasn't Taylor notorious for introducing young men to older men?" Mr. Carson asked me.

"No, I never heard that in my life. But he did introduce some young men to me," I admitted.

"How many men did he introduce to you?"

"I should think six—seven—eight."

"That you became intimate with?"

"Became friendly with, I think, is the better word. I think about five."

"Such men as you would call by their Christian name?"

"Yes."

"Were these all men of about twenty years of age?"

"I should think twenty or twenty-two. I like the society of young men. I delight in it."

"Did you give money to any of them?"

"Yes, I should say money and presents."

"Did they give you anything?"

"Me? No."

"Now, did he introduce you to Charles Parker?"

"Yes."

"Was he a gentleman's servant out of employment?"

"I have no knowledge of that at all."

"Did you never hear that?"

"I never heard it, nor should I have minded. I don't care two pence about people's social positions."

I knew that saying this was dangerous. Men who care little for class differences may be thought to care little for other proprieties. At least, that is the way the conventional mind works. But I was determined to stick to the truth as much as I was able.

"Even if he was a gentleman's servant out of employment you would become friendly with him?"

"I would become friendly with any human being that I liked."

"What was his age?"

"I should about twenty; he was young. That was one of his attractions, the attraction of youth."

"He was seventeen."

This was vexing. I had not intended to be inaccurate.

"You cannot ask me a question about which I know nothing. I don't know his age. He may be sixteen or he may be forty-five. I have never asked him his age. It is rather vulgar to ask people their ages."

Some laughter from the spectators made me believe that at least some of them agreed with me.

"How much money did you give to Parker?"

"Oh, I should think I have given him four or five pounds."

"For what?"

"Because he was poor, because he had no money and because I liked him. What better reason is there for giving a person money than that?"

"Where did you first meet Parker?"

"I met him at Kettner's Restaurant."

"With whom?"

"With Mr. Alfred Taylor."

"You had never seen Charles Parker before in your life and he immediately became your guest at Kettner's?"

"Yes, it was Mr. Taylor's birthday. I had asked him to dinner, and I said, 'Bring any friends of yours that you like.'"

"Did you call him Charles?"

"Yes, certainly."

"The first evening?"

"Yes."

"I suppose it was an expensive dinner?"

"Well, Kettner's is not so gorgeous in price as other restaurants. The prices are fair."

"You bought them plenty of champagne?"

"They had whatever they wanted."

"After dinner did you say: 'this is the boy for me.'"

"Most certainly not."

"Where did you go after dinner?"

"I went back to the Savoy Hotel."

"Did you bring him with you?"

"No."

"Did you give Charlie Parker at the Savoy that evening two whiskies and sodas?"

"No, he did not come back with me to the Savoy."

"Or two small bottles of iced champagne?"

"He was not there."

"Was that a favorite drink—iced champagne?"

"Yes, strongly against my doctor's orders."

"Never mind your doctor's orders."

"I never do."

The laughter from the spectators went a long way toward redeeming the last hour of testimony. Mr. Carson's relentless questions were wearing on my nerves and I feared my impatience was showing.

And more than that: he was documenting the extent of my folly. Had I truly spent so much money on so many strangers? While I believe that a life lived for pleasure is as honorable as any other, Mr. Carson was reminding me of how often I had neglected the pleasures of home and family for the more dangerous pleasures of the flesh. While I do not regret indulging my appetites, I could see now that I had been recklessly indiscreet. Every fine hotel in London seemed to be the site of some rendezvous. Every restaurant the scene of an assignation.

All the long morning, Mr. Carson questioned me about meetings with young men. All the long morning, I denied improprieties. In the afternoon, the questions continued until in my weariness I made an error.

"Did you know Walter Grainger?" asked Mr. Carson.

"Yes," I answered.

"What was he?"

"A servant at Lord Alfred Douglas's rooms in Oxford."

"How old was he?"

"I should think about sixteen."

"You used to go down to those rooms sometimes?"

"In 1893, yes."

"Were you on familiar terms with Grainger?"

"What do you mean by familiar terms?"

"Did you ever have him dine with you or anything of that kind?"

"Never in my life." My tone expressed my vexation.

"What?"

"It really is very trying to ask me such a question. He waited on me at table. He did not dine with me."

"I thought he might have sat down. You drew no distinction."

"Do you think that in Lord Alfred's rooms, I would dine with a servant?"

"You told me yourself—"

"If it is people's duty to serve, it is their duty to serve; if it is their pleasure to dine, it is their pleasure to dine."

"Did you ever kiss him?"

"Never in my life; he was a peculiarly plain boy."

Even as the words escaped my lips, I could sense the error I had made. I could taste the change in the atmosphere of the courtroom, as if all the wholesome air had been instantly replaced with some poisonous gas. The faces of the spectators altered in some subtle way; in the blink of an eye, curves of sympathy straightened into rigid lines of hostility and revulsion.

"He was what?" asked Mr. Carson.

"I said I thought him—" I stammered. I felt a great rush of blood in my face as if all my shame had been exposed to every inhabitant of London. "Unfortunately, his appearance was so very ugly. I mean, I pitied him for it."

I cannot record the final hours of my humiliation. I know the questions went on and on. I know I stammered out answers like a guilty thing. I know that I felt such hostility toward me that I had to try not to shield my face with my hand like a man expecting a blow.

It was only a few days ago that I sat in the audience of the St. James Theatre and felt the applause fill me like air fills a balloon. Indeed, such was the power of their adoration that I almost believed I could rise above the throng and float like a kite on the gales of their approval. I was London's Lord of Language and I could enchant whole populations with my magical pen.

And now I am cast down! I can see the coming verdict in the faces of the jury. I can see my fate in the downcast countenances of my barristers. I can see triumph on Queensberry's face and disdain in the eyes of the spectators.

The cup of bitterness has been prepared. Soon it will arrive and I will be forced to drink.

SIXTY-THREE

From the memoir of Robert Ross:

Once Oscar lost his case against Queenberry, his arrest and prosecution for gross indecency became an inevitability. Oscar sent me to cash a cheque for him and when I delivered the money to him at his room in the Cadogan Hotel, I found that our friend Reggie Turner had arrived to show his support.

"Where is Bosie?" I asked.

Oscar was seated by the window, a glass of sherry in hand. I had never seen a face that seemed to so sag with defeat. He looked like man crushed utterly by life.

"Bosie has gone to see his cousin George Wyndham," said Reggie. "He's a member of Parliament. Bosie hopes he has enough influence to stop any prosecution of Oscar."

I thought the chances of Wyndham's success were remote. The trial had been followed avidly by the press and now that the facts had turned against Oscar, the government would be under enormous pressure to prosecute lest it seem to sympathize with those regarded by most as sodomites and degenerates.

I went to Oscar and put my hand on his shoulder.

"Oscar, you should catch a train for Dover. You could be in France by tonight."

"I've been saying that," said Reggie. "He won't listen."

"It's too late to flee," said Oscar.

"It is not too late," I said. "You speak French like a native. Go now. It would be more like a holiday than exile. Don't just sit here and wait for the police."

Oscar took my hand. "Robbie, you must do me a great favor."

"What is it?" I asked.

"You must go to Tite Street and tell Constance all that has happened."

This request produced a great dread in my chest. The thought of being the bearer of such terrible tidings to Constance was horrifying. But at the same time, I realized that Constance might be able to spur Oscar into action if she correctly understood the situation.

"I will tell her," I said.

"Thank you, Robbie. You've always been a good friend."

I pulled Reggie Turner aside. "Try to get him to stop drinking. And if you can, get him to flee! Don't wait for my return. Get him on a train at once."

Reggie nodded. "Of course."

The ride from the Cadogan Hotel to Tite Street was the most depressing that I had taken in my young life. The stone-gray sky above London seemed to mirror my mood.

It was too distressing to think about Constance and her sons, so I pondered Oscar and his mistakes instead. Why did he make such a colossal error as to take Queensberry to court? Why did he allow Bosie to substitute his judgment for Oscar's own? Why was he so weak-willed when it came to that blond youth? Was it that Oscar truly judged people on their beauty as he so often claimed and that he therefore valued Bosie above all others? Did the spectacle of a precipitous fall have a perverse appeal? After having tasted all the glories of worldly success, did he now feel the need to become England's great Uranian martyr? Or had he merely relied so much on his personal charm to sail through life that he didn't realize the limits of its appeal?

I decided that I would never know a final truth. Oscar's foolishness—like his genius—was too great and strange to be comprehended whole. I had flirted with scandal myself more than once and perhaps I had escaped Oscar's fate by a mere hair's breadth. Perhaps I who could see the danger in Oscar's actions was blind to the hazards of my own. Perhaps the great folly of his decisions was only apparent to those with the perspective of distance; to Oscar his choices may have seemed reasonable in each of their separate moments as my choices seemed reasonable to me.

The cab ride was over all too soon and I forced myself to knock on Constance's door. It had once been Oscar's door as well, but it was clear to me now that it had ceased to be that some months ago.

Constance answered the door herself and our faces told each the news more quickly than our voices could have. It was clear she had expected bad news and my expression was mere conformation of her worst fears.

"Oh Robbie," she said and hugged me.

She let me into the parlor, but neither of us felt like sitting.

"How bad is it?" she asked.

"We expect that the police will come for him, if he doesn't escape to France."

"Why doesn't he leave?"

"I don't know," I said. "He seems to be stunned. I don't think he fully realized that it could all go against him."

"What happened?"

I had to describe the last two days of the trial to her and much of Oscar's testimony. As I was doing so it occurred to me that this might be the first description of Oscar's secret life that Constance had ever heard, and I felt a great guilt at the back of my soul. Oscar had gambled not only with his own fate, but with that of his wife and sons as well and I had played my part in that gamble. Constance and Cyril and Vyvyan would all be punished for sins they had no part of and for indulgences they had no knowledge of. The poison of scandal would taint all their days no matter how spotless their own souls.

For the first time, I felt anger at Oscar for creating this injustice, but instantly realized that I deserved to be the target of such wrath as well.

"I think you should leave London," I said. "Do you have relatives you can stay with?"

"Yes," said Constance. "We'll go at once."

"Good."

Constance stepped toward me and took my hand. I realized it was strangely like the gesture that Oscar had made less than an hour before.

"Robbie, get him to flee. Tell him I want him to go to France. We can join him there soon. Tell him to go."

"I will."

As I hurried out the front door, it occurred to me that Constance had not asked me if Oscar was guilty or not. But the thought quickly followed that she probably already knew the answer to that question.

Reggie Turner was still with Oscar at the Cadogan Hotel when I returned, but they had been joined by Bosie and George Wyndham, a man of middle age who sported a mustache even broader and more luxurious than Reggie's. Oscar was still seated in the same chair as when I had left and he looked, if possible, even more despondent.

"I can do nothing," Wyndham declared. "The government is terrified of the press. If they decline to prosecute, they fear being labeled as allies of decadents. You must flee to France. That is my advice to you."

"That is apparently everybody's advice to me," said Oscar. "There was once universal delight when I appeared. Now, everyone clamors for me to leave."

I stepped past Wyndham and hunched down before Oscar.

"Oscar, Constance and the boys are going to stay with relatives. They will join you in France shortly. You must be there when they arrive."

"Constance wants to go to France?" said Oscar in a voice that made me realize he had had far too much to drink.

"Constance wants you to go to France. You can be with your family there. You can start again. You wrote *Salome* in French. You can write other plays."

Oscar began to nod as if beginning to see this new life.

"Your friends will come visit you in the Paris cafes," I said. "You can write at a table with a view of the Seine.

Or the Eiffel Tower. Or turn your back on it, if you're like de Maupassant and think it's ugly and vulgar."

I think that if I had had a few more minutes, I might have convinced Oscar to flee. But there was a knock at the hotel room door, and everyone turned toward it with apprehensive looks. For a long moment no one moved. But when the knock came again, I stepped to the door and opened it.

A waiter stood in the hall with two stern men wearing coats standing behind him.

"Sir," said the waiter in a nervous voice. "There are two men from the police here to see Mr. Oscar Wilde."

I nodded solemnly. I looked back at Oscar and he nodded.

"Come in, gentlemen," I said.

And then there were no more decisions to be made.

SIXTY-FOUR

Dear Miss Darling:

What an odd and miraculous day I have had. A day that may change my life forever. And yet the great surprises I have encountered happened not in the world, but within my own heart. How my own feelings remained a mystery to me for so long seems now a great puzzlement.

But let me explain in a more conventional way.

I had submitted my manuscript about the Cooperative Movement in Great Britain several days before and had finally been summoned to the office of my editor, Llewellyn Smith, to hear his suggestions for revisions. Although the sun was shining brightly and the sky was a brilliant blue, my mood was as dark as if I was approaching the place of my execution on a cold midnight in winter.

My fears were no doubt exaggerated, but still understandable. I had never written anything of such length before and if my editor simply handed me back my manuscript and said, "Poor job, begin again," I do not think I would have the confidence to make a new beginning.

Mr. Smith was a man in his fifties with a neatly trimmed beard and an air of dignified politeness. He ushered me into his small office and carefully closed the door. I sat in a chair opposite his desk and I could not but notice my manuscript placed neatly in the center of the desk. It would take but a moment for him to hand the pages back to me.

Mr. Smith seated himself carefully behind his desk and then touched the pages with one finger.

I held my breath.

Mr. Smith cleared his throat.

"Miss Potter, I am very pleased. Both your organization and your prose are cleaner and stronger than I had hoped. Any suggestions for revisions that I may have will be relatively minor. We will be proud to publish this book."

I felt such a wave of relief in my chest that it took a great effort to suppress a sob of joy.

"Thank you very much," I managed to say in a voice that was not unlike that I use every day.

"Your style is very much improved."

"I had help," I said. I smiled as an ordinary person might smile and did not grin like that very odd cat in Lewis Carroll's *Alice's Adventures in Wonderland*. But in my mind a cat was grinning, and it had flagstone teeth the color of cream.

"Everyone has help," said Mr. Smith. "The problem is that most help just makes things worse. I think I just underestimated you, Miss Potter."

This injustice to Mr. Webb was intolerable.

"No, you don't understand. I really had wonderful help. Advice on style and organization and . . . "

Mr. Smith nodded. "Intelligent advice is very useful, yes."

"But he didn't just help me to write. He helped me to think...to see." I struggled to express the depth of my debt to Mr. Webb. "He challenged me to surpass myself. He inspired me to become as dedicated and clear-thinking and as warm-hearted as he is and—"

A great fountain of emotion rose in my soul as if I could see the whole of the previous year in one glance, and everywhere I looked I could see Mr. Webb at my elbow, steering me, guiding me, debating me. He had tolerated my cold friendship with few complaints while I had rewarded his devotion with condescension and a dry companionship that satisfied neither his body nor his heart.

I unexpectedly sobbed out loud and Mr. Smith looked startled to hear such a sound. He may have seen women weep in his office, but doubtless there were few who wept with gratitude.

"Miss Potter," he said, shocked to see tears streaming down my face. He pulled out a pocket handkerchief and offered it to me.

"Thank you," I stammered as I wiped my face.

"Are you all right?"

"I've been very stupid," I said, standing. "I must go."

"But we have to decide—"

"I shall write to you tomorrow. Forgive my foolishness. Good-bye."

I hurried out the door and heard a puzzled "Good-bye" from behind me.

I hailed a hansom cab without knowing where I was going. I realized that I did not know where Mr. Webb lived. But then I remembered Mr. Shaw bragging about the piano duets he played at Fitzroy Square and I realized I had a destination.

"Fitzroy Square," I said as I climbed into the cab.

Once I was settled in the cab, my tears of joy turned into bursts of laughter. How silly I must have looked to

Mr. Smith! I must have seemed the very model of the emotional female author.

And how happy Sidney would be to hear from me! He would perhaps not understand how his absence had worked an alchemy in my soul that all his eloquence could not. I had needed time and distance to see his friendship in all its fullness and glory. What his passion had not accomplished his patience and companionship had.

At Fitzroy Square I descended from the cab and then was the witness to an odd spectacle.

As a letter carrier approached along the sidewalk, Mr. Shaw popped out of his door and descended the steps to confront the public servant.

"Shaw? Any letters for Shaw?" he demanded in a tone that suggested there was a conspiracy to deprive him of his mail.

"Nothing this morning," said the letter carrier and he stepped around Mr. Shaw and continued his way.

"Damnation!" cursed Mr. Shaw and then he turned and saw that I was approaching.

"Waiting for a letter from Miss Payne-Townshend?" I asked. I was aware that I might be stepping on a corn, but in my present mood I was determined to be direct.

"I seem doomed to be sending her letters that are returned as undeliverable. She is as easy to find as a willow o' the wisp and as likely to stay in one place as one."

"Well, I don't know where she'll be next week," I said, "but this week she is staying with Lucy Phillimore in Surrey. She sent me a cheque for the London School of Economics by mail and mentioned that she would be there."

"Lucy Phillimore? Is she the one they call Lion?"

"Yes, I believe that's her nickname."

"Lucy and Robert Phillimore are socialists. I think I know where they live."

"That's wonderful," I said. "Now, I'm sorry to trouble you, but I am looking for Mr. Webb. I don't know where he is."

"What time is it?" asked Mr. Shaw.

"I believe it is nearly one o'clock."

"Then Mr. Webb is likely at Waterloo Station. He is lecturing in the north and is catching the one-thirty train for Liverpool."

"Oh no," I said. "Good-bye!"

I hurried away, looking for a main thoroughfare where I could catch another cab.

Luck was with me and I easily found a cab to take me to Waterloo Station. I paid my driver and was congratulating myself on the speed of my journey as I hurried up the steps to the entrance of the great gray building.

Directly in front of me, Mr. Chamberlain emerged from the main door of the station. He held the door for a pretty young woman who did not look yet twenty years of age.

I stopped in my tracks. My breath seemed to freeze in my lungs.

As Mr. Chamberlain took the arm of the young woman, he looked up and saw me. His expression was one of astonishment.

We stared at each other for a long moment, until the young woman noticed the connection our eyes had made. I finally stepped forward with an out-stretched hand and a smile on my face.

"Mr. Chamberlain, how very good to see you again. I hope your sister and your daughter are in good health."

Mr. Chamberlain stared in surprise at this display of good feeling. It took him a long moment to collect himself.

"Miss Potter, what an unexpected pleasure. Allow me to introduce my wife Mary." Mr. Chamberlain turned to the young woman. "Miss Potter is a friend of both my sister and my daughter."

I turned to Mary Chamberlain who looked taken aback at seeing a loud unaccompanied woman appear before her.

"Mrs. Chamberlain, please accept my heartiest congratulations on your wedding," I said." All of London rejoices that Mr. Chamberlain is happy once again."

To my great surprise, I found that I meant every word that I was saying. I discovered that I sincerely hoped this pretty young woman could make the Great Man happy and perhaps inspire him to do his best work.

Mary Chamberlain smiled awkwardly as I pumped her hand.

"Thank you, Miss Potter," she said in her Yankee accent.

"I find American accents so attractive," I said to them both with a genuine smile.

"Yes. Quite." Mr. Chamberlain did not know how to react to this barrage of good cheer.

"I must be off!" I declared. "Meeting a friend! Good luck to you both!"

I squeezed Mr. Chamberlain's hand one last time before hurrying away.

I strode through Waterloo Station feeling giddy with excitement. I had encountered the Great Man and his new wife and had laughed and smiled. How had I accomplished this miracle? What strange magic had so transformed my soul? If I looked in the mirror would I recognize myself?

I found the platform for the train for Liverpool and saw that the train was waiting, but where was Mr. Webb? Was he already on board? I paced the platform in an agony of indecision.

At last, I saw Mr. Webb walking briskly down the platform, a portmanteau in hand. I hurried to him with indecorous speed.

"Sidney!"

He looked quite startled to see me. He stopped where he stood and let me approach.

"Miss Potter. This is a surprise."

"Yes," I said and then could say no more. Fear grew in my throat and smothered my giddiness.

Mr. Webb smiled awkwardly at me. "I cannot chat, I'm afraid. This is my train."

"Mr. Webb—Sidney—I've been very foolish," I stammered.

"I can't imagine that."

"I've caused you so much pain. And...and . . . "

I tried to pull my scattered thoughts together, but a strange nervousness had banished coherence from my mind.

Mr. Webb smiled a sad smile. "I must go. Good-bye, Miss Potter."

As he stepped away from me, I blurted out: "I love you."

He turned to look at me, a skeptical expression on his face. I believe that for a moment he wondered if I was teasing him.

"Excuse me?"

"I love you, Sidney." I stepped toward him and all skepticism vanished from his face.

"How marvelous."

He stared at my face for the longest time, as if to assure himself that I was both sincere and sane. My smile seemed to convince him and in the next moment he kissed me. It was as awkward as these things usually are, but also delightful.

At last, Sidney took a step backward and said: "I must get aboard."

"We shall get aboard together. I have bought a ticket."

"Really?"

I held it up and showed it to him. He laughed.

A minute or two later, Sidney had stowed away his portmanteau and we shared a seat. I sat near the window.

"For how long will you be in Liverpool?" I asked.

"Just overnight. I am giving a speech to the working man's club and will return to London by tomorrow night."

"You have your speech?"

Sidney reached into a pocket and pulled out several folded sheets of paper. He handed them to me.

I unfolded them and began to read.

Mr. Webb coughed nervously. "When did you decide you loved me? And what prompted this change of heart?"

I put my finger to my lips. "We can discuss that shortly. I'm not sure about this paragraph. The last sentence has force, but the middle sentences are a soggy quagmire."

Sidney found a pencil in his portmanteau and I went to work, pruning his thicket of dense prose.

We had a delightful trip to Liverpool and not all of it was spent editing and lecturing.

What an odd turn my life has taken! How could my own emotions have taken me by surprise?

Sidney and I are strange creatures, but oddly suited to one another. We shall not marry until after my father dies; he would not understand my choice and would find Mr. Webb a great disappointment as a son-in-law. Sidney is willing to wait.

Until then there is a great deal of work to be done. Books to be written, political parties to influence and a public to inspire. Utopia will not be constructed in a day, but I trust that a lifetime of labor may bring us closer.

Have I amused you with this account of the odd romance of Beatrice Potter? I certainly amuse myself. At times, I look back on the past year and I shake my head at my own obtuseness.

Sidney believes hard work can atone for all. We shall be yoked to the plow together and accomplish more than either could alone.

Your happy friend,
Beatrice

SIXTY-FIVE

From the unpublished memoir of Bernard Shaw:

Miss Potter unexpectedly arrived today like a messenger from Providence with the news that Miss Payne-Townshend was staying with the Phillimores in Surry. She was in a strange, excited mood, but the news filled me with such exaltation that I did not take the time to inquire why she was flitting about London like a mad thing.

As soon as Miss Potter hurried off, I wasted no time. I grabbed a flat cap, an apple and my bicycle and set out for Victoria station without consulting a train schedule.

At the station, as I wheeled my bicycle down the platform, I spotted a porter and hurried to him.

"The train for Surry, where is it?"

The large man turned and pointed at the rear of a distant train car disappearing into the distance.

"You just missed it."

I cursed under my breath. But Surrey was far closer to London than Suffolk and I had my bicycle. I set out in a southwesterly direction and made up my mind not to stop peddling until I was in Charlotte's presence or both tires had gone flat.

I had left Greater London behind and had reached picturesque country lanes when it began to rain. I hoped it would turn out to be the usual gentle English shower, but after a few minutes it became a downpour and I struggled down mud-choked roads out of sheer determination. After nearly an hour of torrential rains, it began to let up. Soon, the sun was shining again, and I had the misfortune of being both thoroughly wet and uncomfortably warm.

I had to knock on a few doors and ask directions to be sure that I was headed in the general direction of Woking, but at some time in late afternoon I arrived at the house that fit the description of the Phillimore residence. By this time, I was shaking with fatigue and I stopped across the lane from the house to give myself time to recover.

The Phillimores lived in a brick Georgian house set back from the lane with plenty of open land about it. There was a stable or carriage house behind the main house, but no sign of any inhabitants or servants. Of course, the rain would have driven them all indoors.

When my breathing had slowed to a normal pace, I walked my bicycle across the lane and leaned it against a tree. I strode to the front door, removed my wet cap and attempted to make myself presentable. I fear my efforts were wasted. At last, I knocked.

The door was opened by a formidable-looking woman with a swirl of gray hair and an expression that is usually reserved for discouraging salesmen.

"May I help you?" the woman said without warmth.

"Good afternoon. My name is Bernard Shaw. Do I have the honor of addressing Mrs. Lucy Phillimore?"

At the mention of my name, the woman's face assumed an even more hostile appearance and a man less determined than myself would have retreated from that furrowed brow. But the woman said nothing, apparently convinced that her Medusa face could repel all invaders. I could see why people called her Lion.

"I was led to believe that Miss Charlotte Payne-Townshend was staying here."

At last, the woman spoke: "I don't know who could have told you that."

"That is not a denial. Please tell Miss Payne-Townshend that I am here."

The woman weighed her options and at last decided I was not being unreasonable. "Very well. Wait here."

The woman closed the door and I waited. The wait seemed interminable. At last, the door opened, and the same woman appeared.

"She does not wish to see you."

"She will see me! It took me over fours on bicycle just to get here!"

"Then I suggest you start for home. It will be dark soon."

The woman closed the door.

I collected my bicycle from the tree and went across the lane. A stone wall provided a place to sit. I sat and watched the house and considered how little I could do to obtain an audience with a woman determined to avoid me.

Sometime later, I saw a curtain drawn back and Mrs. Phillimore peered out at me. I waved at her and the curtain instantly dropped back into place.

I waited until the fading light of afternoon became the gray of twilight. I realized that I must soon abandon my post or reconcile myself to sleeping on the muddy ground with only my flat cap as a pillow.

The nickering of a horse drew my thoughts away from this unpleasant decision. I stood up straight and grabbed the handles of my bicycle.

A carriage and pair appeared from behind the Phillimore's house. A coachman leaned forward and flicked the reins as the carriage pulled into the lane.

I hopped onto my bicycle and pedaled after the carriage with all my might.

"Charlotte! Charlotte!" I called.

The coachman looked back at me and spurred his horses to greater effort.

I pedaled like a madman in a race. I stayed to the right of the carriage and began to gain on it.

Mrs. Phillimore opened the door of the carriage and yelled at me: "Sir! Will you go away, please!"

I pedaled even faster as I yelled: "Charlotte, I must speak to you!"

Charlotte's face appeared in the doorway. "Bernard, what are you doing?"

"Charlotte, will you stop this confounded carriage?"

"No."

"I must talk to you," I called. "I must—

But this second sentence was never completed, because my front tire entered a wide puddle that was a deep rut. The handlebars jerked in my hands and I was suddenly flying over the front of my bicycle to land in the tremendous puddle.

I struggled to sit up, various parts of my body aching. Dirty water dripped from my hair and I wiped my eyes with a hand that was none too clean. I could see that the front wheel of my bicycle was bent beyond hope of repair and I knew I had ridden that noble machine for the last time.

"Get out of the puddle."

I turned and saw Charlotte standing in the lane. The carriage was stopped forty feet or so away and Mrs. Phillimore stood by the open door watching with disapproval.

I struggled to ease my body out of the puddle. This was more difficult and painful than I expected.

"Are you trying to kill yourself?" asked Charlotte. Her tone was the loving voice of a mother with a foolish child.

"I was prepared to throw myself under the wheels of your carriage if necessary."

"You are behaving ridiculously."

"On the contrary, I am the quintessence of rationality. It is you who are ridiculous: fleeing the love and happiness I offer as they were their opposites."

"Bernard, don't joke about—"

"Damnation, woman! I didn't bicycle though the equivalent of an Indian monsoon to be accused of joking."

Charlotte nodded. "I'm sorry."

I tried to sit up straight before speaking.

"I came to tell you that I have discovered that life is infinitely more interesting with you than without you. Perhaps we could live long and productive lives without each other, but to attempt to do so now seems to be folly of almost criminal stupidity. You said much the same thing to me not long ago. At the time, my monstrous self-conceit kept me from realizing the truth of what you said. I apologize for the hurt I caused you then and I acknowledge fully your superior wisdom. Will you forgive me?"

It probably took her only a moment to reply, but it seemed to me to take an eternity.

"Bernard—of course I forgive you."

"Good. Will you marry me?"

"Do you mean that?"

"Four short words—how could you possibly find a joke in them?"

My outrage was so extreme that Charlotte had to laugh.

"Don't laugh. Answer me."

Charlotte stepped closer. "Oh, I suppose, Bernard. If it will make you happy."

"It makes me very happy indeed."

I tried to stand and felt such a shooting pain that I collapsed again into the mud.

"Give me your hand," I said.

Charlotte shook her head. "I've already said that I would marry you. Now, please get—"

"Charlotte, give me your hand. I think I've broken my ankle."

With the news that Charlotte and I were to be wed, the Lion became a kitten. With the help of Mrs. Phillimore's coachman, I was deposited in the carriage. A doctor was summoned to the Phillimore house and my ankle was examined and bandaged.

My new occupation as an invalid gave Charlotte a chance to fuss over me. She found clothes that belonged to Robert Phillimore that would fit me and my filthy torn wet clothes were disposed of. We returned to London by train and I returned to Fitzroy Square by carriage. Strange to think that at the ripe old age of forty, I am finally cutting the apron strings and leaving my mother to fend for herself.

My mother has taken the news that I am to be wed with skeptical disdain. She may suspect that I am playing an elaborate joke on Charlotte and she is unlikely to change her mind before my twentieth wedding anniversary.

The wedding will be a simple one at the registrar's office in Covent Garden. I want to invite Sidney, but he seems to have disappeared. He should have returned from Liverpool by now. Where could he have gone?

After the simple ceremony, I want to take Charlotte to the Camden High Road and show her the site where they are building a new women's lavatory. The first of the projects that we have accomplished together, but not, I trust, the last.

AFTERWORD

Oscar Wilde was prosecuted for acts of indecency, found guilty and sentenced to two years imprisonment at hard labor. He never saw his sons again. Upon his release in 1897, he went to Europe and never returned to England. He died penniless in Paris in 1900.

Sidney and Beatrice Webb were active in politics their entire lives. Sidney held Cabinet rank in two Labour governments: in 1924 as President of the Board of Trade and in 1929 as Colonial Secretary. He was appointed to the House of Lords as Baron Passfield. Beatrice died in 1943; Sidney in 1947. They are the only couple to be buried together in Westminster Abbey. They had no children although the London School of Economics continues today.

Bernard Shaw remained a Socialist his whole life, although he is remembered today more for his plays. He was awarded the Nobel Prize for Literature in 1925 and won the Academy Award for Best Screenplay in 1938 for *Pygmalion*. He is the only person to have won both awards. Charlotte died in 1943. Shaw died in 1950 at the age of 94.

THE AUTHOR

Kris Hall earned his playwriting Master of Art's degree at Rutgers University, studying under Roger Cornish, an expert on British theatre.

While living in New York, Kris met his future wife at a reading of his play: The Fabian Waltz. The bold, feminist beliefs of the Victorian characters intrigued Kim and she asked to meet the author. They've been together ever since.

Kris and Kim have two grown girls: Wyatt and Kally. They enjoy a hobby farm in West Virginia, with many animals. Inky the cat is Kris' faithful writing companion.

THE ILLUSTRATOR

Kim Harbour, Kris' wife, created the interior sketches and designed the book. Kim has a Master of Art's degree from Parsons School of Design. She worked in New York children's book publishing and Los Angeles interactive marketing for more than 15 years. Now, she is a project manager for the state of West Virginia. Kim thanks Joe and Jacob McCullough for being models.

Learn more: www.fabianwaltz.com